D0055322

THE VALET WHO LOVED ME

THE FOOTMEN'S CLUB SERIES

VALERIE BOWMAN

JUNE THIRD ENTERPRISES, LLC

This is a work of fiction. Names, characters, places, and incidents are products of the author's imagination or are used fictitiously and are not to be construed as real. Any resemblance to actual events, locales, organizations or persons, living or dead, is entirely coincidental.

The Valet Who Loved Me, copyright ® 2020 by June Third Enterprises, LLC.

All rights reserved. No part of this book may be reproduced in any form or by any electronic or mechanical means, including information storage and retrieval systems, without permission from the author, except for the use of brief quotations in a book review.

Print edition ISBN: 978-0-9893758-8-7

Digital edition ISBN: 978-0-9893758-5-6

Book Cover Design © Lyndsey Llewellen at Llewellen Designs.

For my aunt, Dr. Ramona Shires.
The Footmen's Club wouldn't be here without you.
With love.

He's on a top-secret assignment

All of London knows Beau Bellham as the Marquess of Bellingham, but only a trusted few know he also works for the Home Office. His specialty? Scouting out traitors to the Crown. So, when one of his friends pretends to be a footman at a house party in order to find a wife, Beau decides posing as a valet at the same gathering will be the perfect cover for him to spy on the men he suspects of treason. What Beau *doesn't* count on, however, is butting heads with a far-too-certain-of-herself maid who gives him hell at every turn.

She's about to blow his cover

Miss Marianne Notley is a lady's maid with more secrets than hairpins. When she meets her employer's new valet, she distrusts him immediately. Never mind his dashing good looks and irrepressible charm, he's a bit too sure of himself and asks a few too many questions for her liking. She's on a mission to reveal the mysterious valet's true identity, and she's not above wielding her own considerable charms to do it. But before long, all the pretending Marianne and Beau are doing feels alarmingly real—and a lot like falling in love. When they finally discover the truth about each other, will it spark a face-off for the ages or a love that lasts for all time?

THE PLAYERS

Lucas Drake, the Earl of Kendall
Dark-brown-haired, green-eyed, former navy hero turned earl, who needs to find a lady to make a countess. His friends cook up an insane plot to help him.

Rhys Sheffield, the Duke of Worthington
(aka Worth)
Black-haired, dark-blue-eyed, devil-may-care rake and gambler with a love of horses. He's tall, dark, and handsome and has a past with a certain lady, who may just be bent on revenge when the perfect opportunity presents itself.

Beaumont Bellham, the Marquess of Bellingham
(aka Bell)
Blond-haired, light-blue-eyed, in control of everything in his world. Bell is a spy for the Home Office, and nothing misses his notice, that is until he just might meet his match in the most unexpected of places.

Miss Marianne Notley, lady's maid to Lady Wilhelmina Copperpot
Red-haired, vividly-blue-eyed, Marianne is savvy, intelligent, and entirely used to relying upon herself. When she meets her employer's new valet, she immediately distrusts him. He may be handsome. He may be charming. But he's absolutely hiding a secret. She ought to know—she is too.

Miss Frances Wharton, daughter of Baron Winfield
Brown-haired and eyed, she's determined to fight for the

rights of the poor, has a tiny dowry, reads too much, and is too particular according to her mother. Frances has no interest in marriage until she meets a footman who just might change her mind.

Lady Julianna Montgomery, daughter of the Duke of Montlake

Blond-haired, light-green-eyed Lady Julianna is gorgeous, rich, and comes from an excellent family. Once considered the best catch of the Season, she's happily engaged to the Marquess of Murdock. But when she finds her ex-flame, Worth, pretending to be a groom in the stables at a house party, she decides it's the perfect opportunity to pay him back for jilting her.

Ewan Fairchild, Viscount Clayton

Boon companion to Kendall, Worth, and Bell, and host of the infamous summer house party. Married to his true love, Theodora, whom he met when she broke her leg trying to sneak into his stables.

AUTHOR'S NOTE

The Footmen's Club Series includes the stories of the Earl of Kendall (book 1, *The Footman and I*), The Duke of Worthington (book 2, *Duke Looks Like a Groomsman*), and the Marquess of Bellingham (book 3, *The Valet Who Loved Me*).

The prologue of the first three books is the same scene written from each hero's point of view. Rest assured, with the exception of the prologue, no other content or scene is repeated. If you haven't read the other books, the prologue will help you understand the infamous bet. If you have read the other books, the prologue will give you a bit more insight into the hero of that book.

PROLOGUE

London, July 1814

Beau Bellham, the Marquess of Bellingham, was on alert. He was always on alert when he went out drinking with friends. As the only one *not* imbibing, he took the responsibility of ensuring nothing untoward happened. Beau didn't drink. But he also didn't fault his friends for doing so. He merely wanted to ensure they all made it home safely.

They were sitting at a four-person table in an alcove near a window at The Curious Goat Inn, and Beau was waiting for the perfect opportunity to introduce an idea to his friends that they might just find...ludicrous. He'd been mulling over the various ways one might introduce a ludicrous subject to one's closest friends when Kendall sat down his mug on the rough-hewn tabletop and said, "I think it's time I find a wife."

Beau's head snapped to face him. Apparently, Kendall would be the first to introduce a ludicrous notion tonight.

Worth and Clayton were *also* staring at Kendall as if the

man had lost his mind. Now, *this* stood to be an interesting conversation. An interesting conversation, indeed.

As usual, Rhys Sheffield, the Duke of Worthington, was the first to speak. Despite his late father's influence, Worth was a good man. A bit of rogue when it came to ladies and a dedicated gambler, Worth enjoyed a good competition, and while he did his best to pretend as if he was devil-may-care, Beau knew that Worth would sacrifice his life for his country if it came to it. He nearly had once.

Shaking his head vigorously in response to Kendall's statement, Worth winced and sucked in his breath. "A *wife?* Good God, man! There's no need to rush into anything so…*permanent.*"

"We're not getting any younger," Kendall replied.

"On the contrary," Worth continued, "at nine and twenty, we're pups. My father was over *fifty* when I was born."

Kendall was dedicated to his role as a new earl after the death of his brother from consumption. He took the title and its responsibilities quite seriously. Specifically, he'd taken up the cause of the Employment Bill his brother had been so dedicated to getting passed in Parliament before his death. But with this talk of marriage, Kendall was clearly forgetting what had happened the *last* time he'd been betrothed.

Beau decided it was time to speak. He narrowed his eyes on Kendall. "Are you certain you're ready? It's only been two years since…" He allowed his sentence to trail off. No need to open the scab that had healed over the man's heart. Unlike himself and Worth, who'd both always been far more aloof when it came to dedicating oneself to a member of the opposite sex, Kendall felt things deeply. He'd been devastated when Lady Emily Foswell had tossed him over—just before they were set to marry—for a man with a title.

Worth was dedicated to a bachelor lifestyle, while Beau considered himself married to his position at the Home

Office. He'd even attempted to renounce his bloody title to serve in the Army, but the idea of him traipsing across Europe being shot at hadn't pleased the Crown. Instead, they'd allowed him to use his talents in another way. As a spy for the Home Office, his specialty was scouting out traitors, and there was honestly nothing he enjoyed more.

"Thank heavens," Clayton exclaimed, jolting Beau from his thoughts. "I cannot wait until I'm no longer the only one of us with the parson's noose around his neck."

Ewan Fairchild, Viscount Clayton, had recently married and was just back from his honeymoon. The viscount loved his wife, politics, and science (in that order). Wealthy, friendly, and loyal, Clayton clearly adored his wife Theodora, and married life appeared to agree with him.

Beau pushed his mug full of questionable-looking water around the tabletop as he contemplated each of his friends. The four of them had met as lads at Eton and remained dedicated to each other through the years. Each of them played a unique role in their group.

Kendall was preoccupied with duty. A loyal Navy man, he'd promised his brother on his death bed that he would ensure the Employment Bill was passed by Parliament, and he'd promised his mother the same day that he would see to the business of begetting an heir. The man carried heavy burdens. But Kendall didn't relish the idea of having to find a wife, not after the Lady Emily debacle.

Worth served as the comic of the group, making astute comments with the type of sarcastic humor he was known for. He liked to think he was a ne'er-do-well, but with his title and fortune, he wasn't a particularly convincing one. Still, the man was loyal to a fault. He would never forgive Lady Emily, for instance, for tossing over his good friend, Kendall.

Beau himself was always preoccupied with his latest

mission, and he was currently obsessed with his hunt for the Bidassoa traitor. Someone in Parliament who was privy to the plans of Wellington's force in Spain last autumn had betrayed the British army at Bidassoa by writing a letter to the enemy, revealing the strategy.

The plan had been foiled, thank Christ, and the British had won at Bidassoa, but it didn't make the act of the traitor any less dastardly. There was nothing more important to Beau than finding the culprit and turning him over to the authorities for justice. Hence the ludicrous notion that was currently bobbing in his brain while they discussed Kendall's want of a wife.

"I'm entirely serious," Kendall continued. "I must look to secure the earldom. I fear I've been too preoccupied with the Employment Bill. I've been remiss waiting this long to find a bride."

"I certainly won't disagree with you that you've been too preoccupied with the Employment Bill," Worth replied. "Obsessed is more like it."

Kendall shrugged. "Well, now that the Lords have tabled the vote until the autumn session, I have more time to rally the votes I need. I might as well get about the business of looking for a wife in earnest."

Beau narrowed his eyes. A thought had just occurred to him. Another *ludicrous* thought.

"I never bother to vote in Parliament," Worth said. "Don't happen to care for the hours. And all the arguing is downright exhausting."

Beau gave Worth a long-suffering look and shook his head. "God forbid you take an interest in your seat or any of the issues the country is dealing with."

Worth responded by providing them all with his most charming grin. No doubt that self-possessed smile had been the downfall of quite a fair number of ladies. "I'm entirely confident you chaps can handle it," Worth replied, clapping Beau on the back.

"When the time comes for the vote for my brother's law," Kendall continued, addressing his remarks to Worth, "I'll drive to your town house and drag you out of bed myself."

Beau laughed loud and long along with Clayton.

"Let's not talk of such unpleasantness," Worth replied with a sigh. "You mentioned finding a bride, Kendall. That's much more interesting. Now, how old are you again?" The duke shoved back in his chair and crossed his arms over his chest, narrowing his eyes at Kendall.

Kendall arched a brow. "The same age you are, old man."

Worth was only teasing Kendall. They were all the same age, save for a matter of months.

"Well, then," Worth declared. "You've plenty of time to find a wife as far as I'm concerned."

"That's easy to say, coming from a man who's never given a toss about securing his *own* title," Kendall shot back with a grin.

Worth returned the smile. "I cannot argue with you there." He gave the barmaid a wide smile and ordered another round of drinks for the table.

"Yes, well, if you're seriously looking for a wife, Kendall, the Season has just ended," Clayton interjected. "It seems you've missed your chance. The entire *ton* is about to retire to the country as soon as Parliament closes next week."

"I'm well aware," Kendall replied with a curt nod. "The Season makes my skin crawl. Full of simpering maids and purse-eyeing mamas eager to show off their best behavior in the hopes of snaring a rich husband. I don't want to find a wife that way."

"How else do you intend to find one?" Beau asked. Yes, his ludicrous idea just might work if this conversation took the turn he thought it might.

"I don't know how exactly." Kendall took another drink. "But this time I intend to find a lady who loves me for myself."

There it was. Kendall's only allowance to Lady Emily Foswell.

"Yes!" Worth pounded his fist against the table. The duke's normally jovial voice had filled with anger. "I think we can all agree that Lady Emily is the lowest of the low. There's no excuse for what she did, tossing over one man for another with a better title. As far as I'm concerned, she no longer exists."

Leave it to Worth to name the lady. Though it was true that Worth had been the angriest of all of them over Lady Emily's behavior. And the most interested in ensuring Lady Emily knew that she'd inadvertently tossed over a future earl for a baron.

"Can we *not* discuss Lady Emily, please?" Kendall groaned and covered his face with a hand.

Worth's good humor returned with the arrival of the barmaid who'd appeared with their drinks. "Keep 'em coming, love," he said to her, before turning back to Kendall and adding, "I'm merely pointing out that if you want a lady who loves you for yourself, the Season and its ridiculousness are the last place you should go."

"Yes," Kendall replied with a sigh, lifting his mug into the air in salute of Worth. "Didn't I already say that? The Season and its *fetes are* the last place I should go, which is why I've avoided it like the pox for the last two Seasons."

"Oh, is *that* why you haven't attended the boring balls at Almack's?" Worth replied, his voice dripping with sarcasm. "I thought it was the tepid tea and small talk. That's why I steer clear of them."

"You avoid them because they don't serve brandy and we

all know it," Beau said, staring fixedly at Worth, his arms crossed tightly over his chest.

Worth winked at him. "That and they won't give me the bank that Hollister's will."

Beau rolled his eyes. Hollister's was the duke's favorite gambling hell. Hollister's had given Worth *carte blanche* and he won and lost small fortunes there regularly.

Kendall scratched his chin and stared blindly at his mug. "If only the ladies of the *ton* didn't know I am an earl, I'd have a much better chance of finding a match."

Worth's laughter filled the air. "I'd pay to see *that*. An earl dressed up like a common man to find *true love*. Has a certain poetic ring to it, don't it?"

Clayton laughed too and shook his head, but Beau merely narrowed his eyes further and said, "It's not a *completely* outlandish idea." He tilted his head to the side. Yes. The conversation was turning in the *precise* direction he'd wanted it to.

"What's not?" Kendall had nearly forgotten what he'd said.

"The idea of pretending you're a commoner to find a wife," Beau replied.

Worth slapped Beau on the back again. "Are you mad, man? You're not even *drinking*."

Beau leaned forward to address his remarks directly to Kendall. "Given the right circumstances, it could work, you know?"

"Pretending I'm common?" Kendall replied, blinking. "I don't see how."

"Everyone in the *ton* knows him," Clayton pointed out. "How would he ever manage it?"

"Are you suggesting he wear a mask or alter his appearance?" Worth asked. The duke stroked his chin. His eyes began to narrow, too, as if he were also taking the idea seriously.

Kendall glanced back and forth between Worth and Beau. "You cannot be serious, either of you. Clayton's right. How would it ever work?"

"No, not a costume." Beau addressed his remarks to Worth. "I was thinking something more like the right…situation."

Worth leaned forward. "Such as?" he replied, drawing out both words.

"You two are frightening me, you know?" Kendall said. "You seem as if you're actually trying to plot out a way this ludicrous idea might work."

Ludicrous indeed. Beau forced himself not to smile. "Like a …house party," Beau replied to Worth, stroking his chin and completely ignoring Kendall's comment.

Worth inclined his head, his eyes still narrowed. "A house party, yes. I see what you mean."

"But it couldn't be just *any* house party, of course," Beau continued. "It would have to be one given by someone who was in on the experiment."

"Experiment?" Clayton sat up straight. "There are few things I enjoy more than an experiment, and I just so happen to be about to send the invitations to my annual country house party."

Excellent. For his idea to work, Beau desperately needed Clayton's help.

"Experiment?" Kendall repeated, blinking.

Beau snapped his fingers. "Your house party would be perfect, Clayton."

"Wait. Wait. Wait. Wait. Wait." Kendall sat between Beau and Worth and he pushed against their shoulders with both hands. "A house party isn't going to change my identity. Ladies of the *ton* will still know who I am at a house party."

"He makes a good point," Clayton replied, taking another draught of ale.

"Not if you invite only the debutantes from this Season," Beau replied with a confident smile. "And not if you create the right circumstances."

Kendall sucked in a deep breath and pushed his mug out of reach. "The ladies may not know me, but some of their mothers do. More than one of them has already been to court with an older daughter making her debut."

"That's where the right *circumstances* come in," Beau replied, crossing his arms over his chest.

Worth scratched at his chin and smiled an even wider smile. "By God, I think you're onto something."

Excellent. If Worth saw the merit of his plan, Beau stood a greater chance of convincing the other two.

"I refuse to wear a mask if that's what you're thinking. That's positively medieval," Kendall said, shaking his head.

"Not a mask," Beau replied, settling back in his chair and plucking at his lower lip. Ah, plotting something was such fun.

"Or a costume, either," Kendall continued, pushing his mug farther away.

"Not a costume...precisely." Beau exchanged a wolfish grin with Worth.

"By God, I'm going to have the *best* time watching this." Worth nodded.

"Watching what?" Clayton's nose was scrunched. The viscount obviously hadn't caught on yet. "I don't know what in the devil either of you is talking about any longer."

"I'm talking about Kendall here pretending to be a servant," Beau replied, the grin still on his face.

Kendall blinked. "A servant?"

"Yes. It's perfect," Worth added, nodding.

Kendall turned and stared at the duke as if he'd lost his mind. "Perfect? Me? Being a servant? How is that perfect?"

"That still doesn't fix the problem of the ladies' mothers recognizing him. Even if he's dressed as a servant," Clayton pointed out.

"Ah, but it does," Beau replied. He'd been waiting for this particular argument and was already prepared with his defense. "That's the beauty of it. Most people don't look at servants. They don't pay attention to the majority of things beyond what they need and want. My training as a spy has taught me much about the human failure to notice details. I'd be willing to bet that not one of those ladies of the *ton* will look twice at Kendall if he's dressed as a servant and performing servants' duties. He'll be wearing livery, knee breeches, and a powdered wig, after all."

"And it has the added advantage that a servant will be in a particularly excellent position to discover how a lady truly behaves." Worth brushed his long dark hair off his forehead with his fingers. "I'd wager she's at her best when addressing a potential bridegroom and at her worst when addressing a servant. God knows, I've seen it time and again from my mother."

"You're both truly mad, you know that?" Kendall replied.

"I dunno." Clayton tugged at his cravat. "But it sounds like quite a lark to me. I'm perfectly willing to offer my upcoming house party as a venue for such an experiment."

Excellent. This was one of the advantages of his friends drinking. Ideas that might normally sound ludicrous were much easier to convince them of.

"You've gone mad too, then," Kendall replied to Clayton.

"Think about it," Beau said, turning his attention to Kendall, who still obviously required a bit more convincing. "It has the potential to give you precisely what you want. An unencumbered look at the latest crop of debutantes behaving precisely how they would when they don't know you are watching."

Kendall narrowed his eyes on Beau. "It's positively alarming that you don't see the problem with this plan."

Beau shrugged. The more nonchalant he appeared, the better. "What problem? The risk is not too great. If anyone recognizes you, we'll simply ask that person to play along. No doubt they'll enjoy the game too."

"What if I find a lady I fancy?" Kendall replied. "Am I supposed to simply rip off my livery and declare myself an earl and expect she'll fall madly in love with me?"

"Not at all," Beau said. "I'm merely suggesting that you get to *know* these young ladies on the basis of how they treat servants. I've no doubt the best-natured ones will be kind and pleasant. Once you have a few candidates, you will know who to court next Season."

Kendall shook his head slowly. He pulled his mug back toward his chest. Perhaps he'd decided to drink a bit more after all. "You're suggesting that I choose a future bride on the basis of how she treats a footman?"

Beau's brow shot up. Enunciating each word slowly for emphasis, he asked, "How did Lady Emily treat servants?"

"I see by the look on your face that you recognize my point," Beau drawled as Kendall clenched his jaw.

Beau could tell he was winning the argument. Kendall's face took on a thoughtful look and he bit his lip as if weighing the possibilities. It was time to introduce the most ludicrous of notions.

"I'm willing to do it with you," Beau tossed out as casually as possible with another shrug.

"What?" A frown appeared on Worth's face. "Why would *you* do it?"

Beau straightened his shoulders and settled back into his

chair. "Because I've narrowed down my hunt for the Bidassoa traitor to one of three possibilities."

"The man you've been hunting for the Home Office?" Thank Christ Worth lowered his voice as he said it.

"Precisely the one," Beau replied. "And if Clayton here will invite those three men to the house party, I will also pretend to be a servant to watch them."

Worth tossed back his head and laughed. "I should have known you had another motive all along, Bell. His Majesty's work is never far from your mind. Even when we're drinking."

Beau allowed his grin to widen. He could never fool Worth, but then again, he wasn't trying to fool his friends. He merely wanted their assistance. "Why shouldn't we use the opportunity for two useful pursuits instead of one? I'll admit, I was already thinking about this plan before Kendall informed us of his search for a wife, but if it helps both of us, all the better, I say. We will truly have to behave as servants, however. We'll have to wait on the guests and do all the tasks servants must do."

"Hmm. I do quite like the idea of spying going on under my roof." Clayton took another draught of ale. "Gives the whole affair a bit of intrigue. And since I haven't been a soldier or served His Majesty otherwise, I feel it's my duty to say yes to this ruse. Not to mention my love of an experiment. Will you do it, Kendall?"

Kendall drained his mug and wiped the back of his hand across his mouth. "Now that Bell's doing it with me, how can I refuse?"

Beau pressed his lips together to keep from displaying a victorious smile. He still needed to ensure they were all willing to play along with this plan. Not just tonight, but in the harsh light of sobriety tomorrow morning and beyond.

The barmaid returned with another mug of ale for

Worth. The duke tossed her a coin and gave her a flirtatious grin before turning back to his friends. "I, for one, am so interested in seeing such a situation play out, not only will I attend to watch the spectacle, I will also settle a large sum on the outcome as to whether you two can pull this off. Care to bet me?"

Beau rolled his eyes. "Everything's a bet with you, Worth."

"Perhaps, but you must admit, this is a particularly tempting bet." Worth lifted his chin. "Five hundred pounds say you are both outed by a keen-eyed mama within a sennight."

"I'll take that bet!" Clayton declared, pointing a finger in the air. "You'll be attending as a guest, I presume, Worthington."

Kendall's snort of laughter interrupted Worth's reply. "Of course he's attending as a guest. Our mate Worth here could *never* pass for a footman." Kendall shook his head sympathetically toward the duke. "You couldn't last one night serving others, I'm afraid."

Worth flared his nostrils and straightened his shoulders. "I take offense to that. If you two sops can do it, surely I can."

Clayton puffed up his cheeks and shook his head. He didn't meet Worth's gaze. "Hmm. I'm not exactly certain I agree with that, old chap."

Worth crossed his arms over his chest and eyed the viscount. "You truly don't think I could do it?"

"No," Clayton admitted, looking slightly shamefaced. "Not if you actually have to fill the role of a servant and do real chores. No."

Worth's gaze swung to Beau. "You don't think I can do it either?"

Beau shook his head. If he actually thought his friend would be hurt by the notion, he might have pulled his punch, but Worth's self-confidence was legendary. Besides, the duke had to know that pretending to be a servant wouldn't be a particularly strong skill of his. "Not a chance. Apologies, Your Grace, but you're far too used to being waited upon to wait on anyone else."

"But that's how I know how to do it properly," Worth replied, obviously annoyed by his friends' lack of support.

Kendall snorted. "I'm afraid seeing one serve and actually *serving* are two entirely different things."

Worth's eyes went wide. "You're a bloody earl for Christ's sake. Why do you think *you* can serve?"

"I may be an earl but I'm no stranger to hard work. I spent years in the Navy doing chores like picking oakum and deworming hardtack. And those two tasks were pleasant compared to some of my other tasks," Kendall said.

Worth smacked the table with his open palm, causing the mugs to bounce. "Fine. One *thousand* pounds says I can make it through the entire fortnight as a servant too. Or at least I can last longer than either of you."

"Now who is being mad?" Clayton waggled his eyebrows at Worth.

"I'm quite serious." Worth's jaw was clenched. He clearly wasn't about to back down. "One thousand pounds, gentlemen. Who will take the bet?"

"I will," all three called in unison.

CHAPTER ONE

Getting rid of a valet was a far simpler task than Beau had anticipated. In fact, all it had taken was a few discreet inquiries around the village where Lord Copperpot lived, a well-timed visit to a pub that milord's valet was known to regularly frequent, and an offer of forty pounds sterling.

The sum was undoubtedly more than the valet made in a year's time, and the man was only too happy to declare himself extremely ill directly before he was to attend Clayton's house party with his master.

Beau's cohorts at the Home Office were no strangers to feigning employment at a popular work agency in London and in the span of twenty-four short hours, Beau arrived on Copperpot's doorstep ready to fulfill the recently vacated role of valet to his lordship.

Beau had chosen Copperpot for several reasons. First—and most importantly—he was one of three men whom the Crown suspected of being the Bidassoa traitor. Second, Beau had never officially *met* Copperpot before, and that was a hefty requirement given the fact that valet or not, the man might recognize him had they been introduced. Third, and not insignificant, Copperpot was known to have a valet who liked to drink and was often short of coin. Those three reasons combined nicely to make Copperpot the perfect nobleman for Beau to serve for the next fortnight at Clayton's house party.

Kendall had even named their experiment: The Footmen's Club. Though Beau had explained to his friends that *he* needed to pretend to be a valet instead of a footman. Kendall had decided to keep the name, however, even after Worth had also begged off being a footman for a spot as a groomsman in the stables at Clayton's estates.

After taking a great deal of valuable instruction at Clayton's London home from Mrs. Cotswold, the housekeeper, Beau had spent the next week studiously following his own valet, watching everything the man did and asking scores of questions.

Under Malcolm's tutelage Beau learned to tend to clothing, coats, and boots, to ensure the washbasin was filled, to verify that the dressing room was cleaned and aired properly, and to sharpen and strop the razors.

He'd even learned how to cut hair, should that task be required of him during his brief "employment" with Copperpot. Though he secretly hoped (for Lord Copperpot's sake) that the request was never made.

Beau and Malcolm spent an entire two days on how to tie the perfect cravat in a variety of styles. Beau became such a nuisance trailing his own valet around that he was half-worried Malcolm would resign his position.

Beau was soon called to Copperpot's country estate and given the job of valet based on the recommendation of the Duke of Worthington himself. The duke provided Beau with a reference indicating that one Mr. Nicholas Baxter was a very fine valet who would make any household proud. The marquess-turned-servant was nothing but glad that he'd taken the time to prepare so thoroughly

Less than two days after he'd paid off Copperpot's current valet, Beau was set to travel with his lordship's entourage directly to Clayton's country estate.

THE COPPERPOT ENTOURAGE set out to Devon with three carriages: one containing the lord and lady and their eighteen-year-old daughter Lady Wilhelmina, one containing the female servants, and the third containing Beau, two footmen, and a steward.

The ride was long and bumpy, but Beau decided to use the time wisely to subtly probe one of Copperpot's footmen for information. He waited until the other men were half-asleep, lulled by the rocking of the carriage and the warm afternoon sun beating down on the conveyance.

"How long have you been in his lordship's employ?" Beau asked as nonchalantly as he could to the footman who sat directly across from him. He'd even disguised his voice by affecting a less proper tone. In addition to following Malcolm around to learn his duties, he'd also spent a considerable amount of time mimicking his speech and mannerisms.

The footman, whose name was Charles, pushed back against the seat, his legs spread wide in front of him as the coach bounced its way along the road. The other footman, whose name was Harry, was fast asleep on the seat next to his friend and snoring to wake the dead.

Charles sat up and scratched his head. "Near on two years now, I reckon."

Beau nodded. Bidassoa had happened last autumn. That meant Charles had been in Copperpot's employ at the time.

Beau pulled out a pack of betel nuts and offered some to Charles. According to Malcolm, betel nuts went a long way toward establishing, if not trust, at least goodwill among servants. Beau had brought several bags full of the small brown nuts that caused a warming sensation and increased alertness.

"Thank ye, Mr. Baxter," Charles said, tipping his hat toward Beau and taking a handful of the nuts.

Beau continued their conversation, careful not to ask too many prying questions. He needed to gain the man's trust before he appeared too interested in the workings of the household.

Of course Copperpot might be innocent. There were two other noblemen suspected of treason. Having been privy in a special council of Parliament to Wellington's intentions to cross the river Bidassoa in Spain last autumn, one of the men had written a letter to the French, warning them of the British plan.

The letter had been intercepted by a solider, who had been shot soon after intercepting it. But the heroic chap had managed to make it back to the British camp and provide the missive to Wellington. The earl had the honor of bestowing a medal on the unfortunate soldier just before the man died from his wound.

The British, along with their allies, the Spanish and the Portuguese, had won the battle at Bidassoa, but the outcome might have been much different had the private not given his life to stop that letter from reaching the French commander, Soult.

The treasonous letter had been promptly sent back to the Home Office where a score of spies and experts spent weeks attempting to discern the handwriting of a traitor. Only a handful of men in Great Britain had known about the British plans to cross the river. Two were ruled out for their loyalty and their lack of opportunity. Three were left: Lord Copperpot, Lord Hightower, and Lord Cunningham.

After weeks of study, the Home Office had declared that the letter hadn't been written by any of the three lords. They were not, however, cleared of suspicion. It was believed that someone in their employ wrote the letter for them, for the express purpose of concealing the man's identity. This line of thinking opened up the possibility that someone in one of the three lords' employ knew about the treason and had actively participated.

It stood to reason that one of the servants had been paid well to write the letter. And if Beau knew one thing about a man who could be paid well to betray his country, it was that the same man could be paid just as well to betray the culprit behind the treason. That is precisely what he hoped to accomplish by pretending to be Lord Copperpot's valet for a fortnight.

As it happened, Clayton was friendly with all three of the suspected lords. Clayton was friendly with everyone. That's what had made his house party the perfect spot for this particular intrigue. As it also turned out, quite conveniently, all three of the suspected lords had daughters who had just made their debuts and had received no offers, which made a house party for debutantes a particularly alluring draw for all three of them.

Beau ensured that Clayton invited all three men. Beau further ensured their attendance by intentionally spreading the rumor within the special council that Clayton's house party would be attended by the Prince Regent himself. Which was one of the reasons that Sir Reginald Francis, that blowhard, had to be invited. Sir Reginald was harmless, and he tended to get the Regent out of Carleton House for the odd house party. If there was one thing that Copperpot, Hightower, and Cunningham had in common, it was their never-ending desire to impress the Prince Regent and spend time in his company whenever possible.

Clayton had reported last week via letter that all three men had accepted and were expected to be at the house party in addition to Sir Reginald and hopefully, the Prince Regent. Everything was falling into place. This wouldn't be the type of mission that could get one shot and killed. Beau had been on plenty of those types of missions in France over the last few years.

No, this was a subtler mission, one that involved a good deal of acting, and if his friend Kendall happened to find a wife in the process, all the better. Meanwhile, there was no possibility Worthington would survive playing a servant for longer than forty-eight hours, even if he were in the stables pretending to be a groomsman. So, in addition to doing his job and possibly helping Kendall find a wife, Beau also stood to win a considerable amount of money if he was the last servant standing.

As the carriage rattled toward Clayton's estate, Beau leaned back in his seat, pulled his hat down over his eyes, and pretended to sleep. By the time the fortnight was over, he fully intended to have uncovered the Bidassoa traitor and turned the filthy blackguard over to the authorities to be tried for disloyalty to the Crown.

It was only a bit of playacting at a summer house party, after all. How difficult could it possibly be?

CHAPTER TWO

Viscount Clayton's Country Estate,
Devon, August 1814

M iss Marianne Notley stared at the costly gowns, gloves, and other assorted *accoutrements* strewn about the bedchamber floor and sighed.

Her mistress, Lady Wilhelmina Copperpot, was nothing if not consistent. They'd only been at Lord Clayton's house party for the better part of one day, yet her young mistress had already made a mess of her room.

The debutante tended to try on multiple articles of clothing and discard them like so much rubbish on the floor, waiting for Marianne, her lady's maid, to pick them up and restore them to their rightful locations.

Marianne grabbed up the first gorgeous gown from the floor. It was ice-blue satin with delicate lace trimming around it. How she would have loved to wear something this beautiful even once in her life, let alone every day like Lady Wilhelmina did.

For a few fleeting moments, Marianne held the gown to her chest and looked down the length of it. She and her beloved Mama—God rest her soul—had pretended so many times. Marianne would fetch one of Mama's old gowns from her wardrobe and dance around the room with it in front of her. Now, she glanced at herself in the *cheval* mirror across the bedchamber. She smiled and curtsied to an imaginary suitor. "Why yes, thank you, my lord. I should love to dance the waltz with you."

She couldn't help her laugh, but she quickly let the gown drop away from her neck, and folded it over her arm. There was no time for such silliness. She needed to return the gown to the wardrobe with all the other lovely gowns she would never wear. There was no use wanting what you could not have. And pretending that she was a debutante was certainly that.

Marianne had only been in the Copperpots' employ since the start of the year. She'd been recommended to Lady Copperpot by Lady Courtney from Brighton. Marianne had grown up in Brighton and had known Lady Courtney her entire life. She was fortunate to count such a fine lady as her friend. Lady Courtney had known her Papa—God rest his soul. After Mama's death, Lady Courtney had employed Marianne as a companion for the last five years until her own niece was of age and able to come from Surrey.

That left Marianne looking for work, and she'd scoured the papers from London until she found an advertisement for a lady's maid for one Lady Wilhelmina Copperpot, who had just come of age.

Taking a position as a lady's maid with one of the finest families in London was not something Marianne had ever imagined, but after asking Lady Courtney for a reference, Marianne found herself traveling to London less than a fortnight later to meet Lady Copperpot and her daughter Wilhelmina.

Marianne was only five years older than Lady Wilhelmina, but they could not have been more different. Lady Wilhelmina was tall and blond and frightened of things like bugs and horses. Marianne was short and red-haired and hadn't found much that frightened her yet.

Marianne had been to London numerous times as Lady Courtney's companion, but she'd never been privy to the comings and goings of a debutante until her acquaintance with Lady Wilhelmina.

It was certainly a social whirl. During the Season, the young lady had attended parties, balls, and dinners seemingly every night, and Marianne had been ready to ensure that Lady Wilhelmina's clothing was properly set out and cared for, and that the debutante was dressed and ready for each and every occasion.

Marianne helped milady with her hair and toilette before each event, and she stayed up into the wee hours of the morning, sometimes nodding off in a chair in Wilhelmina's bedchamber, waiting for her charge to return so Marianne might help her undress and prepare for bed.

After the Season had ended, Marianne had enjoyed a respite from the social whirl—that is until Lady Copperpot had announced last week that the family would be packing up and traveling to Devon to attend Lord Clayton's house party.

Despite Lady Wilhelmina's beauty and family connections, the young lady had not secured a match during her first Season. It was the source of much discussion and angst between mother and daughter. In fact, the Copperpots seemed obsessed with seeing to it that Lady Wilhelmina secured an engagement as soon as possible.

So, when Lord Copperpot had received an invitation to Lord Clayton's summer house party, there had been considerable joy in the household on Hertford Street in London. Apparently, Lord Clayton had a number of friends who were bachelors, each of them highly eligible.

Marianne had just picked up the last article of clothing that had been left on the floor—a delicate pink satin reticule —when the door opened and Lady Copperpot and Wilhelmina came traipsing into the bedchamber.

"I'm not pleased, I'll tell you that," Lady Copperpot said, dropping her golden shawl from her shoulders onto an emerald-green velvet tufted chair near the door. Her voice took on a nasally quality when she was irritated, and she was most certainly irritated at present.

"They might still arrive, Mama," Wilhelmina replied, kicking off both of her silver slippers and dropping her own silver shawl onto the center of the floor. Marianne scrambled to pick up all three of the items before making her way back to the wardrobe where she neatly arranged both the slippers and Wilhelmina's shawl.

Marianne had learned in this position that she should be fast and efficient, stay out of the way, and say very little. It was quite unlike her position with Lady Courtney, who often asked her opinion on things and dined with her and spoke to her and never dropped clothing in the middle of the floor.

"I doubt it," Lady Copperpot replied to her daughter. "I specifically asked Lady Clayton if either Lord Kendall or Lord Bellingham intended to join the party, and she was quite vague. If they were coming, surely she would have said so."

"One of the young ladies said that the Prince Regent might attend," Wilhelmina told her mother. The poor girl was always trying to please her mama, who never seemed pleased with much.

"Think, Wilhelmina," Lady Copperpot snapped, "what good will a visit from the prince do for you? The man is already married. We need *eligible* gentlemen here, and there are no two more eligible gentlemen than Kendall and Bellingham."

Marianne made it her business to look busy arranging the articles of clothing in the wardrobe, but they were all already perfectly arranged. She was nothing if not orderly and efficient, but she did like to overhear Lady Copperpot and Wilhelmina's schemes. It usually gave Marianne an idea of how well things were going and how long they intended to stay. Apparently, they hadn't got off to a good start at this particular house party. That did not bode well.

Lords Kendall and Bellingham. Marianne had heard those names before. Mostly because she'd also made it her business to remember all of the names of the eligible bachelors who Lady Copperpot and Wilhelmina discussed. There were scores of bachelors, and all of them were ranked by the ladies in order of eligibility.

The only names that had been higher on the list than Kendall's and Bellingham's last Season were those of the Duke of Worthington, who was apparently a drunken lout—although a young, handsome one—and the Marquess of Murdock, who was no longer a part of their discussions because he had become engaged to the fortunate Lady Julianna Montgomery during the Season, thereby crushing the hopes of many a mother/daughter pair.

Kendall and Bellingham, however, hadn't been present at any of the events of the Season. At least as far as Marianne could discern, and apparently, the two gentlemen remained eligible, as evidenced by Lady Copperpot's desire for them to attend the house party.

"Surely, there will be others here, Mama," Wilhelmina offered in a gentle voice, clearly trying to appease her mother again. "Lord Kendall and Lord Bellingham aren't the only two eligibles after all. And didn't you say Lord Clayton is known to associate with the Duke of Worthington?"

Lady Copperpot rolled her eyes. "Yes. They are said to be fast friends, but *Worthington* is a bit of a lofty goal for you, Wilhelmina dear, don't you think?"

Her face still hidden in the wardrobe, Marianne winced. Lady Copperpot tended to say such things to her daughter. Things that were hurtful and a bit mean as far as Marianne was concerned.

Marianne thought back to her own childhood. Her parents' home hadn't been stately or grand, but it was filled with love and the laughter of her parents and her two older brothers. There may not have been things like fine clothing and jewels and balls, but there had been joy. Marianne couldn't imagine either one of her parents saying anything as cruel to any of their children as Lady Copperpot said to Wilhelmina on a daily basis.

Marianne shook her head. She had lingered long enough. It was time to retreat from the room as unobtrusively as possible. She shut the wardrobe with a soft click and padded toward the door that connected Wilhelmina's room to that of her parents.

She was about to leave when Lady Copperpot's voice stopped her. "Oh, Marianne, dear, there you are."

Marianne couldn't help her wry smile, one that thankfully Lady Copperpot couldn't see. She'd been in the room the entire time, and Lady Copperpot acted as if she'd just noticed her. That happened quite regularly.

"Will you please take my shawl into my room by way of the corridor, so that you may ask one of the housemaids to bring us tea?" Lady Copperpot continued.

Marianne swiveled around and curtsied. "O' course, milady," she responded. "I'd be happy ta." She hurried over to where Lady Copperpot sat and pulled her shawl from the back of the chair. Just before she left the room she asked, "The usual fer tea today, milady?"

"Yes, please," Lady Copperpot replied curtly.

"Thank you, Marianne," Wilhelmina said with a soft smile. She might be untidy, but Wilhelmina was kind. She always made it her business to thank Marianne. Not that Marianne expected thanks.

She'd been briefed by Lady Courtney to ensure that she remained quiet, useful, and efficient, and to never expect special treatment. The most one could hope for in some positions in London households was a lack of abuse, regular meals, access to some medical care when one was ill, reasonable accommodations, and wages paid on time. The Copperpots certainly weren't abusive, and they treated her with respect, but they rarely thanked her or showed her much notice, unless Wilhelmina was around.

Marianne returned Wilhelmina's smile as she slipped from the room. She'd intended to go down the servants' staircase at the back of the manor to find a housemaid and request tea, but as it happened, a maid was passing by when she exited the room.

After sending the order along with the maid, Marianne hefted the shawl in her hands, turned, and made her way to the entrance of Lord and Lady Copperpot's bedchamber.

The room would be empty. Lord Copperpot was out riding with the men this morning. Milord's valet, a man named Broughton, drank to excess and rarely did any work when his master wasn't watching him. And Lady Copperpot's maid, Mrs. Wimbley, was aged and didn't walk up and down stairs more than she had to. As a result, Marianne had taken over a great many of Mrs. Wimbley's duties in order to help the older woman.

Marianne turned the knob, opened the door, and stepped

inside. She hadn't taken more than two steps into the room when she stopped and caught her breath. There was indeed a valet in the Copperpots' bedchamber, but he certainly wasn't Lord Copperpot's valet.

CHAPTER THREE

Beau had only been in Lord Copperpot's bedchamber a few minutes when the door handle turned and in walked a diminutive, red-haired maid, who stopped short when she saw him.

The brightest blue eyes he'd ever seen blinked at him. He thought she was going to smile and introduce herself when instead she plunked her hands on her hips and said, "What are ye doin' in milord's chambers?"

Beau turned to face the woman with his most charming smile. She had to be one of the Copperpots' female servants, and he wanted to make friends with all of them, as it would only help his mission. "Good morning, Miss. What is your name?"

The redhead narrowed her eyes on him. She was wearing a bright blue dress with a bright white apron, black slippers, and her hair was caught up in a tight bun on the back of her head. She looked neat as a pin and angry as a hornet. "Ye didn't answer me question."

Her accent was working-class with a hint of Irish to it.

Beau cleared his throat. He was clearly getting off to a bad start with this young woman. "My apologies." He bowed. "I am Lord Copperpot's valet."

If it were possible, her blue eyes narrowed even further until they were brightly lit slits in her otherwise adorable face. "Yer no such thing. Mr. *Broughton* is milord's valet."

Beau straightened to his full height and folded his arms behind his back. He wanted to seem as non-threatening as possible in order to restore some peace between himself and the spirited maid. "You're perfectly right, of course. I am merely serving as Lord Copperpot's valet for the fortnight."

She crossed her arms over her chest and arched a pale eyebrow. "And where is Mr. Broughton?"

Beau cleared his throat. "Taken ill from what I understand—quite unfortunate, poor chap." His arms still folded behind his back, he rocked back and forth on his heels, feigning total innocence as to the affliction that temporarily had taken the dear Mr. Broughton from them.

"Ill from the bottle more like," the redhead replied.

Beau had to bite the inside of his cheek to keep from laughing aloud at that astute observation. The reaction surprised him. He normally wouldn't have to resort to such tactics to control himself.

"Perhaps," he replied, once again trying to sound nonchalant. "I was not informed as to the nature of his complaint." Lies, all of it, but this was the first time in weeks he'd enjoyed himself, verbally sparring with someone.

The maid still clearly didn't trust him. Instead, she glared at him and tapped one slippered foot on the wood floor. He got the distinct impression that she might tackle him if he tried to leave the room. And he just might enjoy that, too.

She was clearly interested in protecting the Copperpots' welfare. Good for her. He *had* been peering about the room.

She had every reason not to trust him. Obviously, no one had seen fit to inform the female servants that Mr. Broughton had taken ill.

"Wot is yer name, please?" she finally asked, still tapping her slipper in a distrustful rhythm.

"What is yours?" he countered, still taking pleasure in the exchange.

She did not look amused. "Ye didn't answer me question."

Very well. There was no sense antagonizing her further. He might not be able to charm his way back into her good graces. "My name is Nicholas, Nicholas Baxter."

She lifted her chin slightly, but her eyes remained filled with suspicion. "Baxter, eh?"

"Yes, and I'd be ever so grateful if you would tell me your name, please." He smoothed one hand down his shirtfront and blinked at her expectantly.

"Why?" she asked, taking a step back, and continuing to eye him warily.

He watched her carefully. He was expert at sizing up people quickly. Everything about her told him she didn't trust anything about him. He'd never met a more distrusting soul, and he'd been around spies for the better part of the last few years, for Christ's sake.

He smiled and took a step back himself, wanting her to feel as comfortable as possible. "I told you my name, Miss. I think it's only fair you return the favor."

She kept eyeing him as if she expected to find his pockets sagging with the family silver, but she finally dropped her hands to her sides and said, "Me name is Marianne. Marianne Notley."

"Nice to meet you." He gave her a bright smile.

"That remains ta be seen," she countered, eyes still narrowed.

Beau sighed. "I was attempting to be pleasant. Apparently, that's a foreign concept to you." He couldn't help making the jab. Her blatant mistrust was beginning to bother him. He was used to charming and being charmed. Even by people who knew he was lying. It was how the game was played. This young lady obviously knew nothing about such intrigues.

Her arms remained tightly crossed over her chest. "His lordship doesn't take kindly ta folks peeping about his bedchamber when he's not here."

"I wasn't peeping," Beau replied evenly. Yes. He was. But he wasn't about to admit it to Miss Disapproval here.

"Ye looked ta be peeping ta me," she shot back.

Her accent deepened when she was riled. Interesting. But it was time to turn the tables on her inquiry. "If Lord Copperpot dislikes servants in his bedchamber when he's not about, what were *you* doing coming in?" Beau countered, crossing his arms over his chest and giving her another false smile.

She pulled up her shoulders and lifted her chin, clearly affronted. "I am Lady Wilhelmina's maid. I was sent here by Lady Copperpot, who asked me ta put away her shawl." Miss Notley lifted the shawl as evidence before brushing past him to put it in the wardrobe.

Beau turned toward her and inclined his head. "Well, if you must know, I wanted to take a look at his lordship's clothing to see if I could be of service to any of it." He did his best to sound affronted as well. It often helped in such situations.

Her mistrustful stance softened a bit at this logic. When she turned back to look at him, some of the skepticism had left her eyes. Beau seized the opportunity to straighten his shoulders and take a deep breath. He was going to have to completely start over with this one. She'd clearly set her cap against him.

Perhaps he should attempt to charm her again. Obviously arguing with her wasn't getting him anywhere. He usually preferred to leave the charming bit to Worth, but Beau certainly could display charm upon occasion when he was inspired to.

He cocked his head to the side, bit his lip, and smiled at her. "I may be temporary, but I do try to do my very best work no matter when and where the occasion takes me."

That stopped her short and she looked him up and down. It was really too bad she was such a mistrustful sort because she was quite pretty. The freckles along the bridge of her nose were downright intriguing… Where the hell had *that* thought come from? What was he, lusting over angry lady's maids now?

She arched a pale brow again. "There's no harm in wantin' ta do a proper job, Mr. Baxter, but somethin' tells me ye weren't looking at the clothing before I came in."

"Why, pray tell, would you think that?" he countered, the fake smile still plastered to his face, while simultaneously thinking that Miss Notley was astute, quite astute indeed. Blast it.

"Fer one thing, ye weren't anywhere near the wardrobe." She crossed her arms over her chest again, blinked at him, and gave him a tight, fake smile too.

Damn it. The usual falsehoods weren't working on her. They both eyed each other carefully. She was going to be trouble. Geniality hadn't worked. Charm hadn't worked. And effrontery only seemed to beget more effrontery. Very well. Perhaps they were to be enemies. Either way, he wasn't about to allow a mistrustful lady's maid to ruin his carefully laid plans.

"I had just come in and was on my way toward the wardrobe," he replied.

How the hell had he got into this tit-for-tat with a female servant? It was entirely ridiculous, and a waste of valuable time. Even if he was still enjoying it…a bit.

Marianne shut the wardrobe door with a loud thump and turned from him. "Fine. Whatever ye say, Mr. Baxter." But her tone clearly implied she didn't believe a word of it. "I'm willin' ta give ye the benefit o' the doubt, but I'm warnin' ye, if I see ye so much as pokin' yer nose in the water closet if it don't belong, I'll bring it directly to milady's attention, and don't think I won't."

Blast. She'd clearly set her cap against him. More charm was in order. "I wouldn't dream of, as you say, poking my nose 'where it don't belong.'" He certainly wasn't about to poke it in the water closet, of all places.

He'd anticipated a variety of issues during this particular mission: being recognized, or failing to be a convincing valet when it came to his duties, but he hadn't counted on—hadn't even considered, really—being taken to task by another servant.

He narrowed his eyes on her this time. He didn't like it when he encountered anyone who was as certain of themselves as he was. He certainly wasn't used to it.

She brushed past him again and made her way toward the door. "See that ye don't."

Beau's nostrils flared. The woman's egregious self-assurance made him want to grind his teeth. And he *never* wanted to grind his teeth. In fact, he prided himself on keeping his cool at all times.

Regardless, he refused to allow her the last word. He would leave first. Besides, he had an appointment to meet his friends in the library to see how their first day as servants had gone.

He took large steps to catch up with her. "I've found in life that those who are the most distrustful of others are the ones with the most to hide themselves, Miss Notley," he said in an even, calm voice.

And with that he strode past the redhead and left the room with a wide smile on his face that she couldn't see.

CHAPTER FOUR

Marianne watched Nicholas Baxter go. She hadn't believed a word he'd said. The man had been standing near Lord Copperpot's bedside table when she entered the room. Milord usually kept his pocket watches and jewelry there. Had Mr. Baxter been looking over the goods?

Mr. Broughton, the regular valet, drank too much and was lazy, but at least he wasn't a thief. She'd never known of anything going missing on his watch.

She'd been rude to Mr. Baxter, especially if he had been innocently browsing around as he said—but she didn't trust new people quickly, and there was something about the man that made her suspicious.

He didn't have the look of a valet about him. He was tall and straight-backed with broad shoulders. He was blond and almost ridiculously good-looking, with crystal blue eyes and a perfectly straight nose. But there was something about him. Something she couldn't quite identify, that… his teeth. It was his teeth. They were white and straight and flawless. She'd never seen a valet with teeth like that before.

Over the years, she'd learned to size up people quickly. She'd learned to look for details and question them. She spent a good deal of time listening to what her gut told her. Her gut was never wrong.

In addition to his highly suspicious teeth, the man looked too fit to be a valet. Most valets she'd known were in constant service to their masters. They didn't have noticeable muscles hugged by their shirtfronts. Mr. Baxter's shirtfront had been entirely too snug for her liking. The man looked more like an Adonis carved from stone than a flesh and blood man who spent his days tending to clothing.

She had good reason not to trust—both good-looking men and people who looked out of place. And Mr. Baxter fit both of those conditions.

A memory of William flashed through her mind. Tall, handsome, charming. He'd been the love of her life, the man of her dreams, or so she'd thought. She'd quickly turned into a lovesick fool within days of meeting him. There was no possible way she would make that same mistake again.

But she'd been barely eighteen years old when she'd met William. She'd been *naïve* and trusting and all the things she no longer was. William was the type of man who thought a handsome face and a charming smile would disarm anyone of the opposite sex. Mr. Baxter was of the same ilk. She could tell. Little did he know, she'd learned years ago how dangerous such men could be.

Yes, Mr. Baxter was a bit too handsome for his own good. Suspiciously good-looking. She would have to keep an eye on him *and* keep him at arm's distance.

But she'd got off on the wrong foot with Mr. Baxter. She'd been far too obviously suspicious of him. Her immediate mistrust of him had made her careless. If she truly wanted to know what he was up to, she needed to beat him at his own game. In order to deal with a man like Nicholas

Baxter and find out if he was really up to no good, she would need to charm the charmer.

A smile slowly spread across her face. She could do that. Oh, yes, she could.

CHAPTER FIVE

Beau didn't see Miss Notley again until after dinner that evening. He'd been in the antechamber with Lord Copperpot while she'd helped Lady Copperpot in the main bedchamber. In their own home, lord and lady each had their own bedchambers and antechambers where they dressed and slept. But because they were guests and the other bedchamber assigned to them was being used by their daughter, Lord and Lady Copperpot were sharing a room at Clayton's estate, which made for tight quarters between the lady's maid and the valet.

Given that, Beau again regretted getting off to such a bad start with the young woman. He'd temporarily lost his even-keeled temper and that was unlike him. And they were certain to have to deal with each other quite a bit during the next fortnight.

He'd resolved to be kinder the next time he saw her, to try to be friendly. His work here would involve him attempting to overhear a great many conversations, and Miss Notley could make that more difficult for him if she set herself against him.

Beau was just coming out of the antechamber when she was leaving the main bedchamber. He hurried down the corridor after her, intent on making amends with the woman.

"Miss Notley," he called in his most agreeable voice.

She quickly pivoted with a bright smile on her face. "Mr. Baxter." Her demeanor was completely unlike how it had been earlier. Instead of being cold and standoffish, it was almost cheery—and it made him wonder. But he might as well say what he'd intended to say.

He cleared his throat and wiped his countenance of all humor in an effort to appear humble. "I wanted to apologize for my rudeness earlier. You were just trying to protect your mistress and her husband, and I should have respected that."

He followed this little speech by giving her his most disarming smile. The same smile that had once charmed a princess, a duchess, and one of the most highly paid actresses in Covent Garden. Surely a lady's maid couldn't be *entirely* immune to his allure, when he chose to be alluring.

"On the contrary, Mr. Baxter," Miss Notley replied, still smiling at him in a way that brought out the brightness of her eyes. "I shouldn'ta been so quick ta judge."

What was this? The lady was admitting to being too disapproving. It was so different from her earlier stance that he briefly narrowed his eyes at her. But he certainly wasn't about to look the gift horse in the mouth. This was what he'd wanted, after all. Friendship. Or at least cordiality. He returned her smile.

"I'd like it very much if we could be friends," he continued.

She clasped her hands in front of her and nodded. "Friends. Yes, I'd like that, too."

"You would?" The words flew from his lips before he'd had a chance to examine them. Frankly, he hadn't expected to be so successful so soon. He'd been convinced it would take much more than a few more assurances to convince Miss Notley to drop her suspicions about him.

"Why not?" Miss Notley replied, fluttering her eyelashes at him. "We both be here wit a job ta do and I, fer one, intend ta do it correctly. As long as ye do, too, there's no reason we shouldn't be friends." She turned and continued to walk down the corridor toward the servants' staircase at the back of the house.

Beau jogged to keep up with her, still wanting to ensure he hadn't misheard her. "I absolutely intend to do my job to the best of my abilities," he heard himself say inanely. "And I'm glad we can do so and still be friendly with each other." Well, that was perhaps one of the dullest lines he'd ever delivered. Where had his impeccable charm gone? Where was his polished, debonair manner?

She didn't slow down, but she did look at him out of the corners of her eyes and he could have sworn the hint of a smile touched her lips.

She didn't say anything for several seconds, prompting him to add, "That is, there's no need to be unfriendly, is there?" Christ. That was neither charming, nor debonair. Awkward and ill-advised, more like. Not to mention repetitive. And the entire time he'd been blathering this nonsense, she remained steadfast in her march toward the door, which meant he was chasing after her like a friendless puppy.

Miss Notley made it all the way to the door to the staircase before opening it and turning to face him. She gave him another bright smile. "I couldn't agree wit ye more, Mr. Baxter. There's no need ta be unpleasant, is there?"

"Excellent." He inclined his head toward her. There. He'd accomplished what he'd set out to do. Make friends with Miss Notley. So why did it feel so...unsatisfying?

"Truce?" He held out his hand.

"Truce," she allowed, shaking his hand with a surprisingly firm grip that sent an unexpected tingle up his arm, before slipping through the door to the staircase and disappearing from sight.

Beau let her go, shaking his head. He listened as she made her way up the staircase to the high servants' quarters on the fourth floor. He didn't want her to think he was following her up, so he waited until he heard two doors shut upstairs before he slowly climbed the stairs up to his room. He rubbed his chin, considering the situation.

Ostensibly, he'd accomplished his goal of making friends with her. But something about the entire exchange had bothered him. There was more to Miss Marianne Notley than met the eye. He knew it, and he was rarely wrong about people. He needed to find out more about her, and quickly.

CHAPTER SIX

Marianne had just served her charge breakfast in her chamber the next morning and was laying out Lady Wilhelmina's clothing for the day when Lady Copperpot came sailing into the room.

"Willie, there you are," Lady Copperpot said. "You won't believe what I just heard down at breakfast."

Lady Wilhelmina pushed herself up in her chair and sipped her tea while blinking at her mother with great interest. "What, Mama?"

Lady Copperpot came over and sat on the edge of Wilhelmina's bed. She had a bright, happy smile on her face. The woman looked like a cat who'd just found the cream bowl. "According to Lady Clayton, Lord Kendall is looking for a wife!"

Wilhelmina's eyes went wide. "Lord Kendall? Is he here?"

Lady Copperpot's face fell and she pursed her lips. "Well, no, not yet, but Lady Clayton says he may arrive soon, and that he intends to find a bride before spring if he can."

"Oh, Mama that *is* good news...but there are so many

lovely young women here." Wilhelmina stared into her teacup and blinked, dejected.

"Willie, you must have more confidence," Lady Copperpot declared, patting her daughter's leg through the blankets. "How do you intend to win Lord Kendall's hand if you assume he'll want another young woman?"

"I don't know, Mama, I—"

"Well, stop it this moment. When Lord Kendall arrives, you'll have to ensure that you talk to him, laugh at his jokes, ask him about his pursuits, and what he enjoys. According to your father, Kendall is dead set on ensuring the Employment Bill passes. Ask him about that, for heaven's sake."

A cloud of worry passed over Wilhelmina's face. "Mama, I don't know anything about the bills in Parliament."

Lady Copperpot rolled her eyes. "Of course you don't, you silly girl. You don't need to. He'll be the one talking; you just smile and nod and agree with everything he says."

Staring into the wardrobe, Marianne rolled her eyes. What sort of nonsense was Lady Copperpot spouting? As if a woman should just nod and smile at a man and take everything he said for granted. That was ridiculous. Dangerous, even. Trusting a man could lead to regret.

Marianne almost felt sorry for Wilhelmina. The poor girl didn't know what awaited her. Of course, she would marry well and live a life of privilege, so Marianne couldn't feel *too* sorry for her—but Wilhelmina was still young and *naïve* and didn't realize that a man would say anything a young woman wanted to hear, for his own advantage.

Lord Kendall might be of the Quality, but that hardly made a difference. There even more reason to be distrustful of such men. William had been a knight, after all, and he'd been nothing but a scoundrel.

Scoundrels. A vision of Nicholas Baxter flashed across Marianne's mind. Mr. Baxter had obviously made it his business to get her to trust him. Why? Oh, she was *pretending* to trust him now. Or at least to have declared a truce, but his insistence on their friendliness made her distrust him all the more. She simply had no intention of letting *him* know that.

"I heard something else that was interesting while I was downstairs," Lady Copperpot continued, pulling Marianne from her thoughts once more.

"What, Mama?" Wilhelmina asked, still sipping her tea.

Lady Copperpot smoothed her skirts across her lap and leaned forward. "Apparently, Sir Reginald Francis has his sights set on Miss Frances Wharton."

"Oh, dear," Wilhelmina replied, blinking. "Poor Frances." Wilhelmina shook her head.

Lady Copperpot sat up straight and glared at her daughter. "What do you mean, 'poor Frances'? That girl could do much worse than Sir Reginald. She and her sister have no dowries to speak of, and everyone knows it. Why, she should be grateful Sir Reginald has taken an interest in her. He's rich as Croesus."

Wilhelmina scrunched up her nose. "But he's so…old, and he has a smell about him, and…they're both named Francis."

Marianne had to bite the inside of her cheek to keep from laughing aloud at that. She wasn't certain who Sir Reginald was, but Wilhelmina's description of him certainly made her feel a bit sorry for Miss Wharton, whoever she was.

"Nonsense," Lady Copperpot continued. "That girl would do well to marry him and her mother is quite aware of it. Mark my words, they'll be announcing their engagement before the end of the house party."

Wilhelmina sighed. "Well, if Frances *wants* to marry him—"

Lady Copperpot tossed her hands in the air. "Who cares if *Frances* wants to marry *him*? Her mother is no fool. She'll ensure the match is made. Now, as to your introduction to Lord Kendall…"

Marianne barely heard another word. It was utterly disheartening, really, when one stopped to consider how the young ladies of the *ton* were sold off to the highest bidder on the marriage mart.

Marianne closed her eyes. If she thought very, very long and very, very hard, she could remember a time when she'd dreamed of marriage. Not just marriage, but *love* and marriage actually. It had been nothing more than a dream, but she'd been foolish enough to believe in it. Foolish enough to believe William when he'd told her he intended to marry her.

Was Wilhelmina's situation much different? The only difference Marianne could think of was that Wilhelmina's mother would ensure she received an actual offer, and that a wedding took place. In that way, perhaps the ladies of the *ton* were wiser than she had been. Marianne, of course, had made the ultimate mistake.

CHAPTER SEVEN

L ater that afternoon, Beau stood with his ear to the door of Clayton's study. Copperpot, Hightower, and Cunningham had convened in the room not ten minutes earlier, and those three having a conversation was something Beau needed to hear.

That the three noblemen were having any type of meeting was interesting. They were all on the special council, but they weren't particularly close outside of Parliament. Beau had done months' worth of research on each of them and knew such things. What could they possibly have to say to one another?

Clayton, thrilled with the prospect of being an unofficial spy, had tipped him off to this particular conference. Beau had been down in the servants' hall in the basement, where he spent most of his time when he wasn't attending to Lord Copperpot's needs. Clayton himself had come looking for him to tell him he was needed in the corridor outside of the study, posthaste.

But Beau's time in the servants' hall hadn't been wasted. The servants, he had found, were a treasure trove of information, just as he'd hoped. In addition to Harry and Charles, the Copperpots' footmen, Beau had also learned a bit about Lord Copperpot's comings and goings from the coachman, who often visited the servants' hall from the stables in order to procure a snack or two. Beau had taken to sitting next to the coachman and offering him betel nuts in order to probe him for information. Of course, just as he had with the footmen, Beau began with seemingly innocuous questions. Establishing trust was the most important element in his work.

Trust. That was the problem with Miss Notley. The woman had started off not trusting him and it was damned difficult to earn trust after it had been lost. She was pretending to accept their truce. He could tell. But why was she so suspicious in the first place? She must have seen her fair share of questionable activities below stairs. Perhaps she'd been too trusting a time or two.

It always helped to know more about a person if one wanted to understand why they behaved the way they did. Beau had seen enough of human behavior—studied it—to realize that. Being a spy was nothing if not a trade that involved people. Convincing people of the things you wanted them to believe, and learning to trust—and not trust —the right people.

In Beau's profession, one's life wasn't worth much if one didn't learn to read people quickly and effectively. Miss Notley had a past, perhaps even secrets, and if he wanted to truly earn her trust, he needed to learn her secrets.

He'd written a letter to his cohorts at the Home Office yesterday asking for every bit of information they could find on one Miss Marianne Notley, lady's maid to Lady Wilhelmina Copperpot. He hoped to receive a reply soon. In the meantime, he had a conversation upon which to eavesdrop.

Beau stuck his ear to the study door, while carefully listening with his other ear to any noise in the hallway that might alert him to someone coming down the corridor. It wouldn't do to be found eavesdropping, no matter who walked past.

It took a moment for Beau to orient himself to what he was hearing on the other side of the door. The first words were definitely those of Copperpot. "Is it all set then?"

"Yes," replied Hightower. "Confirmed."

"What is the date again?" Cunningham asked.

"The fourteenth of October," Hightower replied.

"Ah, perfect, we'll all have time to get home from this party and settle into the new session of Parliament," Copperpot replied.

"Yes, I thought we could use the rest." Hightower said.

"Do you have the money?" Copperpot asked next.

"Yes, here," Cunningham replied.

"Here's mine," Hightower said.

There was silence and some shuffling as two of the men clearly gave Copperpot some sort of payment. What was that about? Were all three of them up to something together? It seemed unlikely, but he couldn't discount what he was hearing. They had something planned for the fourteenth of October, and whatever it was involved the exchange of funds.

"I can only hope we're not discovered," Copperpot replied.

Hightower laughed nervously. "Our lives won't be worth a farthing if that happens."

"Agreed, gentlemen," Cunningham added with a slight laugh. "Here's to success. For all three of us!"

A volley of hear-hears ensued. Beau steeled his jaw. Damn it. He had he missed the first part of this conversation in which they had most likely spoken more specifically about whatever they were planning. It may have been his only chance to discover what they were up to. The fourteenth of October was more than a month away. He would have time to question the servants more closely.

Beau kept his ear pressed tightly to the door, hoping one of them might say a bit more before they emerged from the study.

"Well, gentlemen, good luck to all of us, I suppose," Copperpot said.

"We're going to need it," Cunningham replied.

The sound of someone padding down the corridor caused Beau to move away from the door and straighten up. He pressed his back to the wall and crossed his arms over his chest, fully intending to act as if he just happened to be taking a small respite in the hallway.

The interrupter soon came into view, a flurry of bright blue skirts and a perfectly starched white apron. Beau expelled his breath and hung his head. *Of course* it was Miss Notley. He wasn't lucky enough for it to be someone else.

The moment she saw him she stopped short, and Beau had the fleeting impression that she'd actually mentally wrestled with the idea of turning and walking in the opposite direction, to pretend as if she hadn't seen him.

Pasting a patient smile to his face, he cocked his head to the side and waited. Hoping against hope the three men wouldn't choose now to exit the study. Copperpot would recognize him as his errant valet, but Hightower and Cunningham, if they looked closely, just might recognize him as the Marquess of Bellingham, and not only would his ruse be up, it would be exposed in front of Miss Notley—and for some reason, he particularly disliked that idea.

Apparently, Miss Notley thought twice about turning around, because she continued walking toward him, pasted her own patient smile on her face, and said, "Good afternoon, Mr. Baxter."

Beau bowed. "Miss Notley."

Far from ignoring him, she surprised him by coming to a stop beside him. Apparently, she'd chosen this most inopportune time to want to chat.

"Wot are ye doin' here?" she asked next.

Oh, wait. Did she want to chat, or did she merely want to know why he was standing around in the corridor for no apparent reason? The woman was as curious as he was.

Beau shrugged one shoulder as nonchalantly as he could. In a tone dripping with irony, he replied, "Why, I was listening through the keyhole, of course."

"I wouldn't put it past ye," she replied, giving him a saucy wink, before she brushed past him and continued down the hallway.

Beau took only a moment to look after her, admiring the way her hips sashayed from side to side, before mentally breathing a sigh of relief and turning to go. He might just be able to get out of the corridor before the three noblemen came out. But he still couldn't help himself. "Miss Notley," he called, not even knowing why he was stopping her.

She halted and turned her face slightly the side to acknowledge him. "Yes?"

If she was going to be contrary, so was he. "May I ask what you *believe* I'm doing in the corridor?"

Miss Notley turned away so he couldn't see her demeanor when she said, "I've no earthly idea, Mr. Baxter. But I do know that Lord Copperpot and his friends went inta that particular room some time ago, and I admit that you bein' there makes me wonder about men with a penchant fer always seemin' ta be in the wrong place at the right time. Especially when they look like ye do." She didn't pause, instead she lifted her skirts and marched from his view.

Frowning, Beau pushed his back away from the wall and

made his way in the opposite direction. He plucked at his lip. What the devil had she meant by being in 'the wrong place at the right time'? And what *precisely* did she mean by, 'Especially when they look like you do?'

But most intriguing of all was the fact that she'd apparently been paying attention to the room's occupants, as well. What exactly was *she* doing walking down the corridor herself?

Beau only knew one thing for certain: his friends in the Home Office couldn't get him information on Miss Marianne Notley quickly enough.

CHAPTER EIGHT

The next day, Marianne made her way down the staircase into the servants' hall with tentative steps. She didn't like it down here for one reason—Mr. Baxter tended to be here. In fact, the man spent most of his day down here when he wasn't tending to Lord Copperpot. She might have a pretend truce with him, but Marianne had vowed to spend as little time as possible around Nicholas Baxter. He was too good-looking by half, and she still suspected he was up to something.

She'd been forced to come down to the servants' hall this afternoon, however. Lady Wilhelmina had torn the hem of one of her gowns last night at dinner and Marianne needed to mend it. At present, Lady Wilhelmina and Lady Copperpot were taking naps in their respective bedchambers, so Marianne had decided it was time to go down to the servants' hall to see if Mrs. Cotswold, the housekeeper, had any silver thread.

The hall was quiet and mostly empty this time of day. Marianne marched past the open servants' dining room on her way to Mrs. Cotswold's small office. There were a few odd workers in the dining room sitting on the benches behind the long table, but Mr. Baxter was not one of them, thank heavens. Marianne breathed a sigh of relief before knocking on Mrs. Cotswold's door.

A quick conversation with the efficient, matronly housekeeper ensued, and a few minutes later, Marianne found herself walking down the corridor to look in the storage room at the end of the passageway for the spool of thread Mrs. Cotswold had promised.

The door to the storage room was slightly ajar. She pushed it opened only to see Mr. Baxter, of all people, sitting atop a keg in the corner. His booted feet were dangling along the side of the keg. His buckskin breeches were indecently tight, and his white lawn shirt was open at the throat, showing a sinful glimpse of his muscled chest. No cravat. No coat. No hat. His blond hair was ruffled as if he'd recently run a hand through it, and he was staring at his lap, in which he appeared to be writing a letter. A small inkpot sat on a crate next to him and he held a quill in his left hand.

"Ye can write?" The words flew from her lips before she had a chance to choose them.

He looked up and a wry smile immediately spread across his handsome lips. She gulped, wishing very much that she hadn't said a word. Instead, she wished she'd backed up quietly and left before he'd looked up.

"I can," he replied in a tone that was a mixture of amused and sarcastic. "Can you?"

He'd added that just to be contrary. She knew it.

"I can," she replied, her back stiffening.

"Excellent. That makes two of us." He dropped his gaze back to the letter.

What was he writing? She couldn't help but wonder. No doubt one of many love letters to women who believed they were the only one. The way this man looked, he probably had a lady in every town. She shook her head. She shouldn't be thinking such things about Mr. Baxter. She shouldn't be thinking *any* things about Mr. Baxter. She'd come here to fetch thread, and that's all she needed.

She glanced around the small room. There were scores of supplies of every type. Bags of flour and sugar, kegs of ale, bottles of wine, tins of beans, and all sorts of dried herbs in small pots. But she didn't see any thread.

"Looking for something?" he asked.

She cleared her throat. "I came ta get some thread fer milady's gown. Mrs. Cotswold told me there be thread in here."

Mr. Baxter lifted his head again and glanced around. "I'm happy to help you look for it."

"That won't be necessary." She gave him a tight smile. She didn't need Nicholas Baxter doing her a favor. He seemed like the kind of man who would expect one in return.

Nonetheless, he set down his letter, jumped from the keg, and began opening cupboard drawers and doors. So did Marianne. As they continued to search in silence, she could feel the unspoken competition between them. He went faster and faster and so did she. She'd rather be struck with the plague than allow him to find the thread first.

As she worked, she made her way around to the far side of the room where his letter sat atop the keg. As she opened a nearby drawer to look for the thread, she couldn't help but glance at the letter. Confound it. The man had laid it down face first. Would it be far too obvious if she flipped it over?

"Found it!" he called out, startling her from her thoughts.

She whirled around. "Where?" Her voice was much harsher and more accusatory than she'd meant it to be. She closed the drawer she'd been looking in and glanced back to see him pointing to a cupboard door that was quite a bit higher than she could have reached.

"Up here," he replied, a smug smile on his face.

She waited a few moments for him to hand it to her, and when he didn't seem inclined to do any such thing, she finally extended her hand and said, "Well?" while tapping her foot on the ground.

"Well, what?" His smile was downright merry.

"Well, aren't ye goin' ta hand it ta me?"

"Oh, would you like me to, Miss Notley?" His smile went tight.

She could feel the glower on her face. "Yes, Mr. Baxter, I would."

"There is a word, Miss Notley, that people often use in such situations, a word that is said to have great power."

She narrowed her eyes on him. She wanted to slap his ridiculously handsome face. "And that word is?"

"*Please*, Miss Notley. The word is *please*."

The man enjoyed torturing her. She could see it in his ice-blue eyes. She refused to make it any more enjoyable for him. She needed to get this over with and be on her way. Him staring at her that way unnerved her. She refused to look at him. Instead, she picked a point on the wall beside his head to focus her gaze. "Will you *please* hand me the thread, Mr. Baxter?" she asked in her most sickeningly sweet voice, while batting her eyelashes in a ridiculous fashion.

He scooped the thread from the shelf and handed it to her gently.

"Thank ye," she replied, performing an exaggerated curtsy.

"My pleasure." His smile was beatific now.

"I doubt it." She swiveled toward the door, intent upon leaving immediately.

"May I ask you something, Miss Notley?"

He was still enjoying himself. Trying to rattle her more. She stopped and sighed. "I suppose so, Mr. Baxter."

"What sort of a child were you?"

Marianne couldn't help the strange sound that flew from her throat. It was a mixture of a laugh, a snort, and some sort of an exclamation. The man had surprised her. He might have asked her a score of things, but she never would have guessed he'd ask *that*. She turned to face him once again.

"You know, your laugh is beautiful," he replied quietly. "But I'm curious, what was funny about my question?"

She immediately squelched her smile. Her laugh was beautiful? That noise she'd emitted? Hardly. And he'd said it just like a charmer. A man who used women and tossed them aside like so many used handkerchiefs. His words might fool some of the young maids, but he wasn't about to fool her. "Why in heaven's name would ye want ta know about me childhood?"

"I'm not asking you to recount the entire thing," he replied with a grin. "I was merely wondering if you were the type of child who told on others when they broke the rules."

"Ah, is that wot ye think o' me?" She turned the small spool of thread over and over in her hands. This conversation was making her nervous. She needed to get back upstairs and mend Wilhelmina's gown.

Mr. Baxter came to stand near her. He leaned one shoulder against the wall near the door. "You do seem to be a mistrustful sort."

"Wot, me?" she said, squelching her smile.

"Yes, you," he replied with a nod.

She crossed her arms over her chest and arched a brow. "Have ye given me anythin' ta be trustin' ye fer?"

He scratched his chin and cocked his head to the side. "I suppose not."

"Well, then, there ye are." She gathered her skirts in one hand and made to step around him through the still-open door.

"In such a hurry?" He was so close his words brushed her ear.

She froze, still looking straight ahead. "I have work ta do."

"Do you never take a moment to enjoy yourself?" The words were like silk. The siren song of a skilled seducer?

She turned her head ever so slightly to the side to look at him. It was a mistake. He was far too close and far too handsome. She forced herself to speak slowly so her voice would remain steady and sure. "Is that wot this is? Enjoyable?"

"It could be, if you'd like."

A rush of heat spread through Marianne's limbs. Oh, he was good. A bit too good. "The truth is, I'm wonderin' why ye're so interested in findin' out about me, Mr. Baxter."

He bit his lip. Dear lord, the man had to know how good he looked when he bit his lip. "Perhaps because you're a mystery, and I enjoy solving mysteries."

She met his gaze with her own steady one. "I'm no more a mystery than ye are."

"Fair enough." He nodded slightly. "Before you go, may I ask you one more question, Miss Notley?"

"Very well."

"Why did your accent change when you asked me to hand you the thread?"

CHAPTER NINE

Miss Notley was hiding something. Beau was certain of it. Yesterday in the storage room, she'd quickly brushed off his question about her accent changing. She told him she'd no idea what he was talking about. But he was in the business of noticing details, and he had not been mistaken; the young woman's intonation had changed. Slightly, perhaps, and temporarily, but he heard it. She'd spoken one complete sentence without the hint of either an Irish or a lower-class accent.

He had to tread carefully. She clearly didn't trust anyone, and she'd already put up her guard around him. If he pushed her too far, she might refuse to speak to him at all, and then he'd get nowhere. He'd backed off of the question once he'd seen the look on her face, a mixture of shock and the stubborn refusal to admit the truth. He'd sensed that if he pressed her for an answer, he would not like the results.

Last night, for the first night since he'd come here, he'd had trouble sleeping. He'd tossed and turned on his cot in the little room on the fourth floor where he slept. Miss Notley's room wasn't far away. It was on the other end of the hallway where the upper female servants slept. He'd watched her disappear into her room last night after she'd seen to Lady Copperpot for Mrs. Wimbley, who'd taken ill with gout and was confined to her own bedchamber.

While he'd tossed and turned, he'd come to the conclusion that he was spending far too much time wondering about Miss Notley. She might be hiding something, but he highly doubted she had anything do with the traitor of Bidassoa. Even if Lord Copperpot was the traitor, it was unlikely that he'd asked a female servant in his daughter's employ to help him write the letter.

Beau would do much better to focus his attention on the male servants of Copperpot, Hightower, and Cunningham. The odds were much higher that one of them—specifically, one of their valets—was involved. That was the assumption the Home Office was working under, at least. Aside from speaking to Copperpot's groomsman, Beau had been attempting to spend more time chatting up Hightower's valet, Mr. Broomsley, and a Mr. Wilson, Cunningham's man.

The two men couldn't have been more different. Broomsley was a talker who left nothing unsaid, while Wilson barely uttered more than a word or two no matter how many questions Beau asked him or how friendly he attempted to be. He was beginning to wonder if Wilson was somehow distantly related to Miss Notley.

Of course, Beau had already discarded the notion that Mr. Broughton, Copperpot's regular valet, had been the one involved. According to all reports from the other Copperpot servants, if the man wasn't working, he was drinking and was otherwise indolent and unreliable. Beau doubted that Copperpot would have called on a man like that to help him write such an important letter. No. Whoever had written the Bidassoa letter had been quite close to and trusted by his master indeed.

A slight knock on the door to his small but private bedchamber made Beau glance up. He'd been writing another letter to the Home Office. This time asking for their help in gathering information about the two other valets.

Beau had been writing a different letter yesterday when Miss Notley had found him in the cupboard in the servants' hall. That letter had been his report of the conversation he'd overheard between the three men in the study. He'd seen Miss Notley standing beside the letter near the keg. She'd wanted to flip it over and see who he was writing. He could tell. She'd kept moving closer and closer to the letter, circling like a carrion bird. It must have driven her mad to wonder to whom he was writing. Good. He smiled to himself.

"Come in," he called, putting aside his latest letter, and standing to face his visitor.

Clayton pushed open the door and entered. He glanced around the room. "It's a bit small, but I do hope it's comfortable, Bell," he said with a grin.

Beau spread his arms wide. "Trust me. I've slept in worse. Much worse."

"I don't doubt it," Clayton replied before slipping his hand into his inside coat pocket and pulling out a letter. "You received this in the morning post. I came all the way up here to deliver it to you. I thought it might be important."

Beau took the letter from his friend and glanced at the address. Definitely a private letter from the Home Office. He was no stranger to receiving them. They usually looked precisely like this, plain and innocuous.

"More about your covert operations?" Clayton prodded, his gaze darting back and forth between Beau and the missive.

"Perhaps," Beau replied. Clayton obviously wanted to know what was in the letter. He'd been thrilled to have his house used for a covert operation such as one of His

Majesty's spies trying to root out a traitor. Clayton had never been to war. He'd never participated in any missions for the Crown. Using his house party as the locale of a cat-and-mouse game was as close to a patriotic act as the viscount was likely to get.

Beau had no intention of humoring him, however. Such things were top secret. He took the letter and tossed it onto his bedside table. "Thank you for the delivery, Clayton."

Clayton's face fell but he quickly recovered. "You never did tell me. What did you overhear at the study door the day before yesterday?"

Beau shook his head and put his hands on his hips. "They seem to be planning something."

"Do they?" Clayton arched a brow. "What could it be?"

"I'm not certain, but I suspect that money changed hands. And whatever it is, it's planned for the fourteenth of October."

"Hmm." Clayton narrowed his eyes. "They didn't say what?"

"I didn't hear much more, because Miss Notley walked past. I swear that woman is like a night watchman."

"Miss Notley, the lady's maid?" Clayton's blue eyes twinkled. "Getting under your skin is she, Bell?"

Beau shook his head again. "I wouldn't say that."

"You've mentioned her twice now. The other morning when we met in the library, and again just now." Clayton immediately swiveled and opened the door to leave. "No need to deny it, Bell. I'll just go and leave you to your letter."

Beau wanted to argue with the man. He wanted to insist that Miss Notley was *not* getting under his skin. No one got under his skin. But more than winning an argument with Clayton, he wanted to read his letter immediately and in private.

Clayton left and Beau shut the door and returned to the

bedside table where he scooped up the letter and carried it to the small, dark wooden desk and chair that sat in front of the window. He took a seat and broke the seal on the envelope. His eyes scanned the words written inside.

Baxter,

At present we've found no record of a Miss Marianne Notley other than as a recent lady's maid to Lady Courtney of Brighton. However, we haven't exhausted all options. We'll continue to research and provide you more information as soon as it's available.

'Baxter.' The Home Office always used his assumed name when he was on a mission, no matter how safe the mission appeared. But the letter didn't offer much. So, Miss Notley had worked for another high-born lady in Brighton. It didn't exactly indicate the maid had something to hide.

Beau ripped the letter into long pieces and burned them in the flame from the candle that sat on the desk. Habit from years of secrecy. This particular letter didn't contain much of interest, but one couldn't be too careful. Besides, if Copperpot, Hightower, or Cunningham suspected he was watching them, there was no telling what any of them were capable of.

Then there was the lady's maid.

Frankly, he didn't trust Miss Notley not to poke around his bedchamber, either. If there was one thing he'd learned as a spy, it was precisely what he'd told her that first day. A person with no past is usually hiding something. That made Miss Notley a prime suspect.

CHAPTER TEN

Nicholas Baxter was hiding something. Marianne was certain of it. It was far too great a coincidence that he had appeared the night after Mr. Broughton took ill. Marianne didn't believe in coincidences, especially when they came in the form of an Adonis.

As far as the Copperpots knew, she was a quiet little church mouse of a maid who'd rarely left Brighton and had been in Lady Courtney's employ since she came of age.

That was partially true, but Marianne had lived a great deal of life outside of her employment with Lady Courtney. She had seen and done things that Lady Wilhelmina and her mother would be shocked to learn, and Marianne had absolutely no intention of allowing either lady to ever find out. Something told her that Mr. Baxter was up to no good, and she intended to find out what that was.

She waited for him to leave his bedchamber the next morning before glancing about to ensure she was alone in the corridor of the upper servant's quarters—and then sneaked inside his room.

It smelled like him. And much to her chagrin, it wasn't

unpleasant. Those were her first two thoughts when she shut the door behind her, her heart hammering in her chest. In fact, the scent was a combination of spice and wood and something indefinably male that she didn't want to think about for long. Strangely, it also smelled as if something had been recently burning.

She forced herself to put those unsettling thoughts aside and get to business. A quick glance around the room told her there wasn't much to see. A bed, impeccably made. A wooden desk, bare save for a single candle. A matching wooden chair.

There was a small pile of ashes in the candleholder on the desk. Hmm. That was interesting. Had Mr. Baxter wanted to destroy something? And why? She leaned over to examine the ashes, but she couldn't make out anything. The front page of the letter was still there and intact. She picked it up and turned it over. The letter had been addressed to Mr. Nicholas Baxter. At least he didn't appear to be lying about his name. An innocent man didn't burn letters, however.

The only other object in the room was a small wooden wardrobe. She moved over to it and opened the doors wide with both arms. The scent of starch and soap hit her nostrils. Two shirts, two pairs of breeches. One other pair of boots. She briefly went through the drawers on the bottom of the wardrobe. Two handkerchiefs, two neck cloths, one pair of suspenders, one pair of stockings. A variety of items for the care of men's clothing. No doubt used in his position as valet. Hmm. There was nothing else here. It was as if the man owned nothing else. His small rucksack lay in the bottom of the wardrobe. It was empty, its contents having been hung up and put in the drawers.

The man was tidy. She'd give him that. But there was absolutely nothing personal here. Not one thing. Even she had a small cross her younger brother had given her before he'd left for the army, and a book of poems her mother had given her for her sixteenth birthday. But this man, it was as if he didn't exist.

There was absolutely nothing in this room that could give her a hint about him. She stood staring blindly into the wardrobe. She opened the first drawer again. A bit of marking on the edge of one of the handkerchiefs caught her eye. His initials! Perhaps he was lying about his name after all. She grabbed it up. *NLB*. Blast. Perhaps not. What did the L stand for? She couldn't help but wonder. But it was odd for a valet to have monogrammed handkerchiefs… unless they were a gift from a former employer.

Feeling a bit desperate, she leaned down and looked under the bed. It was completely barren. There wasn't even a dust ball. Confound it. She'd no idea what she'd hoped to find coming in here, but she hadn't found anything at all. Well, nothing more than a suspiciously burnt letter.

Standing up again, she turned in a circle, her hands on her hips. That was it. There was no other place to hide anything. She was just about to admit defeat and leave the room when the door slowly swung open and Mr. Baxter himself stood leaning one shoulder negligently against the frame.

"Ah, Miss Notley. So good to see you. May I help you with something?"

CHAPTER ELEVEN

Beau stood with his arms crossed over his chest blinking at Miss Notley with a smug smile pinned to his lips. Two thoughts raced through his mind simultaneously. First, he'd been right to burn that letter. Second, this couldn't have gone better if he'd planned it himself.

He finally had Miss Notley precisely where he wanted her. At the moment, given her stammering and flushed cheeks, that place was at a distinct loss for words.

"Mr.... Mr. Baxter," she finally managed to choke out.

"Yes?" he asked agreeably, still smiling at her. The woman had some explaining to do and he couldn't wait to make her do it.

"I... I..."

"Umm hmm," he prompted, grabbing his opposite wrist behind him, and rocking back and forth on his heels.

"I was lookin' fer..." Her eyes darted back and forth. The poor woman was clearly floundering for an excuse.

"Yes?" he asked, frankly on tenterhooks to see what she

would come up with. Just how good of a liar was Miss Notley? He was about to find out.

"I was lookin' fer my room, and must have got lost."

He shook his head. Obviously a very, very poor one. "Oh, come now, Miss Notley, surely you can do better than that."

She turned a shade of pink that was most becoming, and her freckles stood out in stark relief against her pale skin.

"I didn't mean ta…" Her lips pursed and her eyes darted back and forth. She looked as if she might attempt to grab her skirts and run past him.

"What?" he asked, ensuring that his form filled the doorway. He wasn't about to let her run away from this. "You didn't mean to poke through my things? I see you opened my wardrobe. What were you hoping to find?"

She looked as if she wanted to sink through the floor, poor woman. He might feel sorry for her if he wasn't having such a grand time watching her squirm. After all of her high-handedness, accusing him of being untrustworthy, she had just been caught poking around *his* private room. Comeuppance was delightful. He'd always thought so.

"No need for further excuses," he said. "I see you're as meddlesome as you are condemnatory, and honestly, I like it."

"What?" Her eyes became round blue orbs and her jaw fell open.

He nodded once. "You heard me." He wasn't about to point out that her accent had disappeared yet again.

Her brow furrowed. "Ye like it?"

Oh, apparently her accent was back. He stood to the side and rested one shoulder on the doorframe again. "Yes, because now you won't be so self-righteous around me. You've no excuse to be."

She opened her mouth, no doubt to issue some sort of

scathing retort, but quickly snapped it shut and blinked at him instead.

"Well, that's a first. I've left you speechless, have I?" He chuckled.

She smoothed her hands down the front of her bright white apron and nodded slowly. "I suppose ye're right. I've no excuse. I shouldn't be here."

Beau looked her up and down. By God, he didn't hear a hint of sarcasm in her tone. She'd been caught *in flagrante delicto*, and she was *admitting* to being wrong. Now *that* was something he could admire. In his line of work, he'd generally met people who would lie till their dying breath, in the face of overwhelming proof to the contrary.

He gave her a lascivious grin. "May I ask, then, *why* you're in my bedchamber, as I seriously doubt it's for the reason I might hope?"

Her blush deepened. She'd obviously caught his meaning. She placed a hand on her throat, her fingertips leaving white impressions along the pinkened skin. "I thought ye might be hidin' somethin'."

He arched a brow. "Like what?"

"Like proof that ye're not who ye say ye are." Her hand dropped back to her side and she smoothed her skirts again, a move he'd come to recognize as her nervous habit.

"And?" He crossed his arms over his chest. "Did you find anything to prove your suspicion?" He fluttered his eyelashes at her, knowing full well that there was nothing in his room that would disprove his assumed identity. He was no rank amateur. He'd even had his false initials monogrammed onto handkerchiefs, for Christ's sake. This wasn't his first mission.

She shook her head. "No. I didn't find anythin'," she replied.

"Now do you trust me?" he asked, enjoying every moment of the conversation.

She dropped her chin to her chest. "I've been self-right-eous, haven't I?"

He couldn't help his smile. This was the moment he'd been waiting for. "You have been. But *I'm* willing to let bygones be bygones, if you are."

Relief washed over her features and she smiled at him. A bit of the pink drained from her complexion. "I would like that." She sounded positively relieved. He actually believed she wanted to start anew.

He inclined his head toward her. "So would I."

She stepped past him out into the corridor.

He glanced up and down the hall. Thankfully, no one was there.

She paused and turned to him, lowering her voice to a whisper. "Ye won't tell anyone…"

"I don't think Lord or Lady Copperpot need to know anything about this," he assured her in an equally quiet tone. "Or anyone else for that matter."

She expelled her breath and nodded. "Thank ye, Mr. Baxter." She began to walk slowly down the hall toward her room.

Watching her go, Beau had an idea. Now that he'd found her in his room, she could hardly continue to treat him as if *he* were untrustworthy. And, if he *was* untrustworthy, at least they both knew he wasn't the only one. Tonight had been a start, but he needed to find a way to get her to lower her guard even further. He already had a plan for step two.

It involved a game of cards.

But not tonight. No, tonight he'd let her go. But not before sending her off with one last thing to think about. He jogged a few feet to catch up with her and cleared his throat. "I'm willing to forget this entire incident ever happened. Although…"

She stopped, turned her head to the side, and frowned. "Although wot?"

The side of his mouth quirked up in a half-smile. He had to admit there was a devilish part of him that wanted to see her blush one more time. "Next time you come to my bedchamber; I do hope it's for a different reason altogether."

CHAPTER TWELVE

This time Marianne went *looking* for Mr. Baxter in the servants' hall. Well, if not actually *looking* for him, at least she wouldn't mind if she found him. He'd been funny and forgiving yesterday after the incident in his room. He'd had every reason to tell Lord Copperpot what she'd done, and he hadn't. She had to be grateful to Mr. Baxter for that.

No doubt she would have been tossed out on her ear if Lady Copperpot found out she'd been poking about in another servant's room, let alone a *male* servant's room. There was absolutely no excuse for it, and she and Mr. Baxter both knew it.

It still didn't mean that she believed Nicholas Baxter was entirely trustworthy, but she could no longer act as if she had the moral high ground when it came to dealing with him. She'd been every bit as guilty and suspicious-acting as he had.

When she'd been searching for the silver thread, he'd mentioned that her accent had slipped. That had nearly sent her into a panic. It had taken every ounce of self-control she had to act as if she had no idea what he was talking about. The man made her tense. She found it difficult to maintain her *façade* around him.

There was no use denying any longer that she was powerfully attracted to him. Why, he looked like a statue come to life. Heat had coursed through her body when he'd looked at her with those ice-blue eyes of his and said, "Next time you come to my bedchamber; I do hope it's for a different reason altogether."

His tone had been positively indecent, let alone the words. They had been entirely inappropriate of course, but the truth was…she wanted to take the man up on the offer.

She would not. Of course not. Never. But she'd certainly had a difficult time falling to sleep last night while thinking about what it might be like going to his room for a different reason altogether.

She wiped the back of her hand across her forehead. Confound it. She was sweating just thinking about it.

After the embarrassment of being caught in his room, she'd decided to change tactics with him. Instead of being openly suspicious or haltingly charming, she'd decided to be…coquettish. Or at least as coquettish as a girl who'd been raised with two brothers could be.

She knew from the way that some of the other male servants looked at her that she wasn't entirely unfetching. She'd been called pretty a time or two. She doubted someone as good-looking as Mr. Baxter would be overwhelmed by her beauty, but he seemed to enjoy ribbing her and flirting with her. She'd decided to try to beat him at his own game.

She'd barely entered the servants' hall when she saw him. He was standing next to the doorway that led to the servants' dining room, leaning one shoulder against the doorframe. She'd noticed that about him. He always seemed to be standing in strategic spots, seemingly resting or loafing, but she had the distinct impression that he was…watching.

But no matter, today she had been looking for him, and she'd found him.

"Ah, Miss Notley, good afternoon." He bowed to her.

She took the opportunity to eye him up and down. He looked as good as usual in his snug breeches, black boots and white shirt. At least today he wore a neckcloth and looked halfway decent. But when his shirt pressed against his muscled abdomen, Marianne couldn't look away.

She swallowed hard and curtsied in kind. "Good afternoon, Mr. Baxter."

His smile nearly melted her middle. Why did the man have to be so very handsome? It was entirely unfair.

He pushed himself away from the doorframe and stood at his full height. "The Copperpots have gone to a picnic by the lake. I was just about to play cards in the storage room. I was planning to play Patience, but I could be persuaded to play *Vingt-un* instead."

She blinked at him. "Are ye…invitin' inviting me ta play cards wit ye?"

He blinked. "Was it unclear? I'm terribly sorry. Miss Notley, would you care to play cards with me in the storage room?"

She glanced around. The nearest other servants were sitting at the dining table on benches having a rowdy discussion about politics. Mrs. Cotswold's door was closed.

Marianne glanced back at Mr. Baxter and bit her lip. Normally, when she had free time, she did things such as mend clothing and ensure the bedchambers were spotless. She rarely took time to do anything for sport. But why not? Perhaps she should enjoy herself for once. And perhaps this would be the perfect opportunity to find out a bit more about the mysterious Mr. Baxter. "I…I suppose so."

His lips curved in a smile. "You overwhelm me with your enthusiasm."

She laughed at that. "My apologies. It's just that I'm not used ta takin' time fer meself."

He inclined his head toward her. "Yes, well, perhaps you should. And I already told you that you should laugh more. I assure you it's quite a lovely sound."

She pressed her lips together and blinked at him, slightly embarrassed that he'd noticed her laugh again, but determined to do her best to flirt. She blinked her eyelashes in her most dogged impression of Lady Wilhelmina when she was practicing speaking to gentlemen in the looking glass. "I thought ye were just sayin' that ta be charming."

His brows shot up. "Am I charming?"

"Yes, ye are, and I'm certain ye know it," she said, laughing again as she followed him down the corridor to the little storage room.

He sighed. "I suppose I'll take that as a compliment." He held open the door for her and let her precede him.

She walked past him into the small room that smelled like spices and sugar. She took a seat at one of the two chairs standing on either side of the small table in the center of the room.

Mr. Baxter produced a deck of cards from his inside coat pocket. Funny. She hadn't noticed the deck when she'd been rifling through his room last night. He must carry them with him.

When he began shuffling the cards, the deck came to life in his hands.

Marianne's brows shot up. "Ye've played before, an' often."

Still shuffling the cards like an expert, he inclined his head toward her. "Astute of you to notice, Miss Notley."

"Where did ye learn ta do that?" she asked.

"Ah, ah, ah. Not so fast. Here's how we'll play. For each hand, the winner gets to ask the other a question."

Marianne watched him closely, her eyes narrowing as she considered this proposition. On one hand, this could end up being a dangerous game. Especially if Mr. Baxter was as good at cards as his skill at shuffling would have her believe. On the other hand, she was much better at playing cards than he knew, or most likely suspected.

In the end, her curiosity won out. She had some questions for him, and she fully intended to win and ask them.

"Very well, Mr. Baxter. I accept the challenge," she told him with a resolute nod.

He continued to shuffle the cards as he said, "Please call me Nicholas. You've been in my bedchamber after all." His words were accompanied by a wink and an unrepentant grin that actually made his seemingly indecent request seem perfectly normal.

A rush of heat shot through her core. But she forced herself to reply in her most unflappable tone. "I suppose ye may call me Marianne…" She gave him an impish grin. "Since I *have* been in yer bedchamber. But please don't call me that in front of the other servants," she added for good measure.

"I wouldn't dream of it, Marianne," he replied with another disarming wink.

Nicholas quickly dispensed the cards into two piles: one for her and one for him. Then he put his hand atop his pile and flipped over the first card. Marianne flipped hers. Two more from each of them. "I win!" he declared after his next card was a king.

Marianne shifted in her seat. Confound it. He was better than she'd guessed. She was obviously sitting opposite a worthy opponent. She steeled her resolve to answer his question. Hopefully she could answer it truthfully.

"Very well, Nicholas," she said, liking the way his name sounded on her tongue. "Ask yer question."

He gathered the cards back into his hands to shuffle again. "Why were you in my bedchamber? What were you hoping to find?"

She cocked her head to the side and gave him a slight smile. "That's two questions, and ye only get one per hand. That was the rule, if I'm not mistaken."

His mouth quirked up in the semblance of a grin. "Very well." The cards flew into an arc between his hands again. "Allow me to rephrase. What were you hoping to find in my bedchamber yesterday?"

She lifted her chin and met his gaze. "Oh, I don't know," she said, picking up the cards as he dealt them to her. "Something suspicious perhaps...like a burnt letter."

His half-smile bloomed into a full one. "What? You don't burn your letters?"

"Not usually," she replied, laying down her first card.

He won again.

She took a deep breath. "Ask away."

"How did you leave Lady Courtney's employ and make it to the Copperpots'?"

Her eyes went wide just before she narrowed them. "How did ye—?"

He pushed the deck toward her. "Now, now, questions are for the winner."

She scooped up the deck intent on winning this time. He flipped one over from the deck. Then another. This time she handily won.

He whistled. "Seems you're not bad at cards yourself, Marianne."

She gathered the cards this time, trying not to think about what it did to her middle to hear him call her by her

Christian name. "My brother taught me. He was excellent at it."

Nicholas's eyes narrowed immediately. "You spoke of him in the past tense. Is your brother deceased?"

She shook her head, forcing herself to push away the painful memory. "I believe it's me turn ta ask the questions, Nicholas."

"You're right." He inclined his head. "What's your question for me?"

"How do ye know I worked for Lady Courtney in Brighton?"

He shrugged. "Never underestimate servants' gossip." He took the cards back and shuffled once more before he dealt and won the next hand.

Marianne sighed, resigned to answering another question.

"You mentioned a brother. Do you have any other family?" he asked.

"I did have. Me mother and me father are dead. The only family I have left is me eldest brother, David."

"I'm sorry to hear that," Nicholas said, looking genuinely concerned before smiling again and asking. "Does David play cards too?"

She settled back into her chair. "That's another question, and we haven't played our next hand yet."

The confounded man won the next hand too, but he surprised her by not repeating his question about David's skill at cards. "You never did tell me the other day. What sort of little girl were you?"

She rolled her eyes but couldn't keep the smile from her face. "I've no idea why ye'd want ta know such a thing, but if ye must...I was a curious one, an adventurous one. I followed me brothers everywhere and did everythin' they did. They taught me how ta be a lad, essentially. I know how ta climb a tree, tie a rope, and shoot a gun."

"Do you?" Nicholas whistled. "Why does that not surprise me about you? And I've already seen your skill at cards."

No sooner were the words out of his mouth than she'd deftly won the next hand. "Yes, they taught me how to play cards, too," she said with another laugh.

"No sisters, then?" he asked next.

"No, it was just the three of us, and don't think I didn't notice ye slipped in another question there."

"Seems I owe you two answers then," he replied.

She let the cards drop and stared at him. "Why do ye want ta know about me childhood?"

Nicholas plucked at the cards in front of him. "People's childhoods are usually the keys to unlocking their secrets. I was hoping to learn from yours why you are so mistrustful."

She drummed her fingertips along the tabletop. "If childhoods are the keys ta unlockin' secrets, then that's me next question fer ye. Wot was *yer* childhood like?"

His face went blank and his smile disappeared. "My childhood was over quickly," he bit out.

She sensed he had no intention of telling her more, and the joviality had been sucked from the room. Hoping to restore their camaraderie, she gathered the cards and shuffled them. They quickly sprang to life in her hands.

His smile returned and he whistled again. "Seems your brother taught you how to shuffle as well."

"Of course," she replied, dealing the cards quickly to each of them.

He won the next hand.

"Very well," she said with a sigh, "what's yer next question for me?"

"What is your dream?"

Her eyes widened. "Dream? Who says I have a dream?" She tried to laugh but no sound came out.

"Oh, come now, Marianne, everyone has a dream."

She shifted in her seat. For some reason she was tempted to tell him the truth. She thought about it for a few more seconds. Very well. The truth it was. "I used ta dream about marriage and family," she said, a wistful tone in her voice.

"Did you?" He studied her face with a furrowed brow.

"Yes." She met his gaze. "But everythin' changed when my brother was murdered."

CHAPTER THIRTEEN

Late that night, Beau lay on his cot with one arm folded beneath his head, staring at the ceiling. The light from the single candle on the desk next to him formed shadows on the wall. A slight breeze drifted through the window, and the sound of crickets out in the meadow provided a steady drone that accompanied his thoughts.

His card game with Marianne had been interrupted by a pair of footmen who'd come into the storage room to fetch some bags of flour for the cook. Beau hadn't had much of a chance to ask Marianne anything more about the startling revelation that her brother had been murdered. But it certainly explained some things about her.

A murder could very well make someone mistrustful. But what had happened to her brother? When she'd first mentioned that he was dead, Beau had simply assumed that he'd been a soldier, or had contracted consumption or some equally dreadful illness. He, himself, may never have been on one of the battlefields on the Peninsula, but he'd seen enough death in his business to last a lifetime. War or disease were the usual causes of death for young men in his experience.

Beau hadn't had a chance today to ask her what precisely had happened, but even though he'd got a bit closer to knowing the truth about her, Marianne was still a mystery to him. She may have let down her guard around him enough to be friendly, but there was no question that she still harbored secrets. He suspected whatever had happened to her brother might be the least of them. He'd listened to her speech closely this afternoon and was convinced that her dialect was affected. Why would she pretend to be less articulate than she truly was?

Despite his misgivings about her, he was attracted to her. Very well— he was ridiculously attracted to her. There was no denying it. There was something about the mixture of how she was so certain of herself and astute, yet vulnerable at the same time, that he'd never encountered in a woman before.

However, his attraction to her didn't change the fact that he was in the middle of a mission, and he needed to keep his mind on his work. It was inconvenient to be attracted to her, but it didn't change anything. He needed to focus on getting closer to the other valets and asking them questions. Ever since Copperpot, Hightower, and Cunningham's talk in the study, there'd been no other inkling of contact between them. He doubted he'd learn much from the men themselves.

A knock at his door startled Beau from his thoughts. He pushed himself off the bed to stand and answer it.

"Good to see you, Bell. Still playacting at being a valet?" It was Clayton. The man asked the question from the corridor in what seemed to Beau to be a booming voice.

"Get in here, Clayton," Beau replied in a much quieter tone, quickly ushering his friend into his room. "And keep your bloody voice down. Clearly, you're not cut out to be a spy."

As he stood aside to let Clayton enter, Beau tried to

ignore the disappointment blooming in his chest. For some reason he'd hoped it would be Marianne at the door. Of course, she wouldn't knock on his bedchamber door, bold-as-you-please, at this hour of the night—but he couldn't keep himself from wishing it.

Clayton tiptoed into the room as if that action would make up for his loud pronouncement moments earlier. "Apologies, old boy," Clayton said. "I clearly had a bit too much wine at dinner."

Beau shut the door behind him and turned to face him. "Why are you here?"

"I've come with another letter." Clayton patted his jacket and spoke in a much quieter tone this time. "It arrived just before dinner. I assumed you wouldn't want to wait till morning to read it."

Clayton pulled the letter from his inside coat pocket and Beau grabbed it and ripped it open. He wasn't about to wait this time. Just like the last one, this letter was from the Home Office. He could only hope they'd uncovered something useful at last. His eyes quickly scanned the single page.

BAXTER,

We've uncovered two bits of information you may find useful. First, Mr. August Wilson has been under suspicion for being part of a club that is known to discuss treasonous plots; and second, we have found no record of a Miss Marianne Notley of Brighton. Before the record of employment with Lady Courtney, no such person exists.

We continue to research Mr. Thomas Broomsley, and hope to have more information for you soon.

"WELL?" Clayton prompted, waggling his eyebrows.

Beau took two steps over toward the candle that still flickered on the desk and began burning the letter. "You know I can't tell you anything."

Clayton sighed and shrugged. "That's what I expected you to say, but I still had to ask." The viscount grinned at him.

"Thank you for bringing this to me right away." Beau gestured to the letter that continued to burn, the little black ashes floating into the brass candleholder.

"My pleasure," Clayton replied. "Don't worry, I'll see myself out." He turned, opened the door, and slipped outside, at least leaving much more quietly than he'd arrived, thank Christ.

Beau finished burning the letter. He stared into the flame, contemplating the contents of the missive. The news about Wilson didn't surprise him at all. He'd already suspected the valet. But no such person as Marianne Notley? Was the Home Office mistaken?

He quickly discarded the notion. The Home Office rarely made mistakes when it came to such things. It had to be true. Whomever the young woman he'd been spending time with was, her name wasn't Marianne Notley. Was anything about her what it appeared to be?

He was just about to blow out the candle and climb back into his cot when another knock sounded at the door. He reached the door in two strides and ripped it open. "Look, Clayton, I'm trying to—"

Beau stopped short. Standing in front of him was none other than Marianne (or whatever her name was). She was wearing her blue gown, but the apron was gone and a few tendrils of red hair had fallen from her usually tidy bun. He poked his head into the corridor and looked both ways. No one was there, and all the doors appeared closed. Decision made. He pulled her directly into his room and shut the door.

He caught her in his arms, steadied her, and stepped back. Her eyes were wide with surprise.

"What are you doing here?" he asked in a voice that was more curt than he'd meant it to be.

She smoothed her hands down her skirts and lifted her chin. "I... I...wanted ta talk ta ye."

"About what?" His arms were crossed in front of him and his bare foot tapped on the wooden floorboards.

"Are ye...angry?" she began, carefully searching his features.

"Perhaps I am. What did you want to speak to me about, *Marianne?*" He emphasized her name as if to mock it.

She turned toward the door. "I think I'll jest go. It was a mistake ta come here."

He clenched his jaw. "I'm in no mood for games tonight."

"Games?" She turned back toward him and furrowed her brow. "What are ye talkin' about?"

"Don't pretend you don't know. And you can stop with that accent, at least in front of me."

She swiveled and yanked open the door. His hand slammed against it, closing it again. "Tell the truth for once," he growled in her ear.

Still facing the door, her chest rose and fell as she took a deep breath. "What do you want from me, Nicholas?"

There. At least she'd spoken in her true accent at last. Her words were carefully cultured. If he didn't know better, he might even believe she was of the Quality. "You came to my room," he barked. "The question is, what do you want from *me?*"

"You're speaking in riddles." She turned her face to the side, away from him.

"Fine then." He leaned forward and whispered in her ear again. "Let me be clear. What if I told you that I've learned there is no such person as a 'Miss Marianne Notley' from Brighton?"

He felt her body freeze. Then she took a deep breath, turned, and met his gaze. There was a steely resolve in her bright blue eyes and a determination that matched his own. "If you told me that," she replied simply, her eyes flashing blue fire, "then I'd have to ask you, who is *'Bell,'* and why are you *'playacting'* at being a valet in Lord Clayton's home?"

CHAPTER FOURTEEN

Marianne hadn't come to Nicholas's door to threaten him, but the minute he'd brought up her assumed name, she'd known she had no other choice. She'd been in the hallway earlier when Lord Clayton came up. She had pressed her back to the wall and refused to breathe for the few moments it took for him to knock on Nicholas's door and gain entry. She'd been astonished when she heard Clayton call him 'Bell' and ask him if he was still 'playacting.'

She'd quickly returned to her room and peeked out her door, waiting until Lord Clayton left the floor. Then she'd quietly made her way down here. She hadn't been entirely certain what she'd say to Nicholas. But after clearly being angry with her for some unknown reason, he'd given her the perfect opening.

The anger immediately drained from his handsome face. "You overheard?" He dropped his gaze to the floor, cursing under his breath.

She pressed her back against the door and crossed her

arms over her chest. It was her turn to be angry. "Yes, and I must say that was quite a convincing job of being the aggrieved party instead of a hypocrite."

"Hypocrite?" he echoed.

"Aren't you accusing me of lying about my identity when you're clearly lying about yours?"

A slight smile spread across his lips. He braced his right hand against the door at the side of her neck and stepped forward. He used his left forefinger to trace the soft skin along the side of her eye, her cheekbone, the side of her lips. "Who are you?" he whispered, in a voice that Marianne was convinced had been the downfall of a number of unsuspecting women.

She shuddered and let her eyes close for a moment. Oh, God. If he was going to try to seduce her, he just might succeed. She had to keep reminding herself that she didn't know this man. He could be anyone. He could be dangerous. She already knew he could be dangerous to her heart.

When she opened her eyes again, she forced herself to meet his heavy-lidded gaze. He towered over her. Leaning down, he moved his right arm to brace against the door above her head. His index finger had made its way to her jaw, and then her neck, and was presently making tiny circles against her skin directly above the neckline of her gown.

"You tell me who you are first," she demanded in a hot whisper.

His smile broadened and he slowly shook his head back and forth, his gaze never leaving hers. "Not. A. Chance."

"Very well," she breathed, wanting desperately for him to kiss her. "Then it seems our identities are to remain a mystery."

Her breasts rose and fell with her deep breathing as she stared up into the icy blue pools of his eyes. His left hand continued to caress her neck and she leaned her head to the side to allow him to touch more.

He dipped his head. "Can I taste you?"

She couldn't answer, could only nod. Her lips formed the word 'yes,' but she couldn't get the sound to leave her throat. When his mouth lowered to the pulse in her neck, she nearly jumped from her skin. His hot tongue dipped against her collarbone and then traced its way up to the sensitive spot just behind her ear. Then he dipped it into the tender crevice of her lobe, and she shuddered.

"Shh," he whispered.

Marianne tried to control her breathing, but it was too far gone. She was nearly panting with desire by the time his mouth traveled along the skin of her cheek and found her lips. The moment his lips met hers, she groaned. He pushed her up against the door and ground himself into her. His tongue dove into her mouth and she wrapped her arms around his neck and kissed him back with all the pent-up passion she felt. She'd wanted this from the moment she'd seen him in Lord Copperpot's bedchamber. Right now, nothing else mattered. Not their true identities, and not the lies they'd told each other. She simply wanted him the way a woman wants a man who has overwhelmed her with desire.

His kiss didn't stop. Instead it went deeper, and his left hand slid down to her waist, riding her hip unmercifully through her gown. He leaned down and caught the bottom of her dress, letting his hand trace its way up along her ankle, up her leg, and along her bare thigh. She shuddered and wrapped her arms around his neck even tighter.

He picked her up and pressed her back hard against the door. Her thighs parted and she hugged his hips with her knees. He held her by her waist and quickly turned her to the desk. With one swipe of his arm, he sent the few articles atop the surface flying to the floor as he sat her atop it and settled his hips between her legs. He grabbed her back and pulled her against him, hard. She moaned and her head fell back. Due to his height, the level of the desk was perfect. No longer supporting her with his arms, his hands moved up under her skirts and caressed her knees, and then stroked the outside of her thighs.

Marianne was lost in a blissful world of desire. Her nipples hardened and beneath her skirts she was wet and ready for him. Oh, God. If he pulled out his member and made her his right now, she'd want it. She wouldn't say no. She couldn't say no at the moment. Didn't want to, at any rate.

His left hand moved down to tug her gown away from one breast. His mouth soon followed. She glanced down. Seeing his head sucking at her breast was so erotic that Marianne wanted to cry out. His tongue flicked her nipple back and forth mercilessly, and when he sucked the hard little nub into his mouth and bit it softly, she clenched her jaw and arched her back.

When his left hand moved under her shift, between her thighs, and he parted her intimately, her head fell forward. His kiss never left her lips. He was ravenous for her and when his finger found the nub of pleasure between her legs and began rubbing her in perfect little circles, she cried out again, but his mouth swallowed the noise.

"Shh," he whispered. "You're beautiful. Let me touch you."

All she could do was weakly nod. His mouth found hers again, his tongue stroking deeper each time. Her hips became restless. She wanted to feel him inside her, but he'd made no move to take her to the bed.

Should she ask him to? No. First, she wanted to find out what else he could do to her body. The man was a virtuoso, and she was his instrument. His finger kept up its gentle assault at her core and when another of his fingers slipped inside of her, she lifted her hips from the desk and wrapped her legs tightly around his hips. Gently, he settled her back atop the wooden surface while his thumb continued to rub her in circles and his dexterous finger continued to slide in and out of her wet heat.

His mouth moved to her ear. "I want you to come," he whispered. They were beyond names now. Beyond caring what either had done or said. All that mattered was the insistent throb between her legs and the ache that was about to explode within her.

Another moment and...explode it did. She shattered into a thousand pieces, her cry hitching in her throat. His mouth returned to swallow it and his tongue ravaged her mouth again. "God, yes," he whispered against her lips. "You're every bit as passionate as I knew you would be."

Her breathing came in hot, heavy pants. She couldn't talk, could barely think as she settled back to Earth from the place she'd shot to among the stars.

He pulled his hands away and trailed kisses along her cheek.

She looked at him, her chest still heaving, nearly bereft. What had he just done to her? And why had he stopped there?

"I'm not...innocent," she said, her breathing coming in hard pants. She hadn't meant it to sound like a confession, but she feared that it had.

He pressed his forehead against hers and his sly smile returned. "That may be, sweetheart," he said. "But I don't bed women whose names I don't know."

He stepped away from her, leaving her stunned, and she barely had time to tug her bodice back into place over her chest before he opened the door to his room and glanced outside.

"All clear," he announced, before scooping her up off the

desk and setting her gently into the hallway. He dropped a kiss atop her head before saying. "If you want more, you're going to have to tell me your real name."

And then that dastardly blackguard had the unmitigated gall to shut his bedchamber door in her face.

CHAPTER FIFTEEN

B eau hadn't been listening to a word his friends said. At present they were in Clayton's study and Beau was staring out the window across the rainy meadow, thinking about how badly he had wanted to make love to Marianne last night.

He could think about little else but their unexpected encounter. Actually, *unexpected* didn't cover it by half, but he could conjure no better word at the moment. The events of the entire evening had been unexpected, from his reading the letter from the Home Office, to her overhearing Clayton—and what had happened after that had been *beyond* unexpected. He couldn't think about it without getting hard. Damn. He was hard right now. He had to get himself together.

He still didn't know why the hell he had done what he'd done last night. Clearly the woman had been ready and willing to go to bed with him, and God knew it had been an age since he'd taken a woman to bed, let alone someone he wanted as much as he'd wanted Marianne last night. But something about the entire thing felt...wrong.

He'd woken up this morning and realized what it was. Guilt. He felt guilt. Actual, true, guilt. And for someone who lied for a living, guilt wasn't an emotion with which he was terribly familiar.

Marianne was right. He had been a damn hypocrite last night. He'd been angry and accusatory toward her when he'd been guilty of the exact same things he'd accused her of: lying about one's identity and having secrets. She'd pointed it out to him, and he'd been confronted with his own inconsistency, and behavior reminiscent of a horse's arse. He should have kept his hands off her entirely last night. He hadn't been able to.

It had been a damn miracle that he'd stopped when he had. But he'd opened his eyes at one point to see her freckles and her gorgeous face and had been struck with that damned guilt. He had no right to take advantage of her. She might be lying to him, but he was lying to her, too.

He'd never made love to a woman under false pretenses, and he wasn't about to begin now. True, he'd seduced them, kissed them, got them to make promises, and pleasured them. But he could honestly say he'd never taken a woman to his bed who didn't know who he truly was. Something about doing so felt absolutely wrong to him.

He wasn't about to make that mistake with Marianne. She wasn't some lonely politician's wife he was attempting to charm in order to probe her for information. He might not know her real name, but he knew he had real feelings for the feisty redhead. Different from any he'd felt during a game like this. He was attracted to her. He was intrigued by her. But most importantly, he *liked* her, and he truly believed she was beginning to like him. It wouldn't be fair to either of them to take advantage of that.

The look on her face when he'd set her into the hall had been priceless. A smile curled his lips. He would never forget that look. But then he winced. Would she ever forgive him?

"You're still in, Bell?" Worthington's question finally pulled Beau from his thoughts.

He turned from the window with a start to face his friends. "What was that?"

"Good God, man. You aren't paying attention at all. I asked if you're still in. No one's discovered you're not a real valet, correct?" Worth repeated.

How to answer that. Blast it. Should he tell his friends that one Marianne Notley (or whoever she really was) had discovered he wasn't who he said he was? Although that alone didn't necessarily disqualify him from the game. The debutantes were the ones who mustn't learn they weren't servants—and even then, there was a bit of uncertainty when it came to that. Worth's former flame had found him in the stables, and for some reason (which Worth had declined to reveal) she was keeping quiet as to his identity.

Beau was entitled to a similar arrangement if he could secure Marianne's silence on the matter. And there was the rub. He hadn't seen her since last night, and at the time they had parted, she'd been far from happy with him. For all he knew, she'd spent the rest of the evening and this morning telling everyone who'd listen that he wasn't who he said he was. He'd have no way of knowing if she'd kept his secret until he had a chance to speak to her again, which he intended to do at his earliest opportunity.

He decided to give his friends the most honest answer he could at the moment. "I believe that is correct."

Kendall arched a brow. "You *believe* it's correct?"

"That's right," Beau replied, clasping his wrist behind his back and rocking on his heels.

"Sounds like someone recognized you," Worth said next, a positively leering grin on his face.

"Excellent," Clayton said, "I'd thought you'd be the last man standing, Bell. I have a much better chance of winning this thing if you're out first."

"I am not out first, to my knowledge," Beau clarified, "and if I am, I have you to blame for it."

Clayton blinked and took a step back. "What do you mean?"

Beau shook his head. "I mean, thanks to you coming to my door last night and practically shouting about my identity for the entire floor to hear, one of the maids asked me about it."

"Oh, no. Remind me what I said," Clayton said, wincing.

Beau arched a brow. "You said, 'There you are, Bell. Still playacting at being a valet?'"

"No!" Clayton gasped. "Damn it. I knew I shouldn't have had that last glass of wine."

"Too late now," Beau replied, crossing his arms over his chest.

"Who overheard me?" Clayton wanted to know next.

"A Miss Marianne Notley," Beau replied. Until he knew her true identity there was no use telling his friends that she wasn't who she said she was. Besides, if he wanted her to keep his secret, he needed to keep hers too.

Kendall frowned. "The maid who's been driving you to distraction?"

The earl didn't know the half of it. "The very same," Beau replied with a tight smile.

"Oh, that's excellent." Worth's crack of laughter bounced off the wooden bookshelves behind Clayton's desk.

"I fail to see the excellence in it," Beau replied, giving his friend a disgruntled stare.

Worth slid into one of the club chairs in front of the desk. "The woman who's been mistrustful and doubting is the one who's learned you're not who you say you are. I'd say that's about as perfect as it could be."

"I'm glad you're finding humor in this, at least." Beau shook his head.

"Is she going to tell anyone?" Kendall asked, pacing in front of the fireplace.

"I'm not certain," Beau replied. "That's why I said I *believe* I'm still in the game."

"Hmm." Clayton smoothed his hands down his sapphire vest. "This does complicate things. I'm sorry to have been so loud, Bell."

"I must find her and ask her if she intends to tell anyone," Bell replied with a sigh.

"How do you know she knows, if you haven't spoken to her?" Worth asked, his forehead crinkled into a frown.

"Let's just say, she made it clear she knows, but we haven't, ahem, discussed the finer points of the matter," Beau replied.

All three men arched their brows at him.

"Very well," Kendall replied. "We'll wait to hear from you. What else have you learned, Bell? About the traitors?"

"Very little I'm afraid," Beau replied, shaking his head. "But I've set up a dinner tonight on the fourth floor. Only upper servants will attend. Mr. Wilson will be there. I have some important questions for him."

CHAPTER SIXTEEN

Marianne could tell that Nicholas had been trying to get her alone all day. But the weather had been particularly uncooperative, so the Copperpots had spent most of the day indoors needing nearly constant attention from their servants.

Marianne and Nicholas passed each only while bringing breakfasts and seeing to the sitting rooms, but they'd never had an opportunity to speak. And, truth be told, Marianne was somewhat enjoying the man's obvious angst. After what he'd done to her last night, setting her out in the corridor like yesterday's milk bottle, he deserved a bit of stewing himself.

Now they were at an upper servants' dinner on the fourth floor in a large sitting room attached to Mrs. Cotswold's bedchamber. The lower servants were busily hustling food and wine up and down the servants' staircase from the basement.

Marianne had made the mistake of sitting next to Mr. Wilson, Lord Cunningham's valet. He was nearly as much fun to talk to as a lamppost. She'd exhausted her set of questions asking him everything from how often he traveled with his lordship to whether they'd been to the Continent any time recently.

"There is a war on the Peninsula, Miss Notley," the old curmudgeon replied. "In case you were unaware."

She bit her cheek to keep from saying the rude words that were on the tip of her tongue; instead, she said, "I'm quite aware, Mr. Wilson, thank ye. My eldest brother be there at present."

"Your brother is in the military?" Nicholas, who sat across from Mr. Wilson and had been doing his part to ask the man questions, directed this question to her.

Until that moment, they'd barely glanced each other's way all evening. She wondered if he'd been doing his best to keep from looking at her just as she'd been doing her best to keep from looking at him. She'd already had one glass of wine too many, which was dangerous. She shouldn't drink to excess, but nerves had got the better of her. Sitting across from Nicholas had her on edge. Memories of what he'd done to her body last night kept flashing across her mind at the *most* inopportune time. If that wasn't enough, sitting next to Mr. Lamppost had put the nail in the coffin of her intention to remain sober.

She lifted her wine glass and cleared her throat, forcing herself to meet Nicholas's gaze. "Yes, my eldest brother be an officer in the army."

"An officer?" Nicholas lifted his brows, obviously impressed.

"Yes—he *earned* his commission, though," she clarified.

"Of course," Nicholas replied, nodding.

The other servants nodded too. Their class knew that the son of a nobleman often paid his way into the upper ranks of the military, while a poor man with no connections had to earn it.

"Hats off to him for his service," Nicholas continued.

Mr. Wilson grumbled under his breath.

Marianne allowed the footman serving the table to fill her wine glass once more. She glanced over at Nicholas. He certainly looked uncomfortable. Good. He deserved it. No doubt he was wondering if she intended to inform the entire table that he was also called 'Bell' and was 'playacting' at being a valet. She had every intention of allowing him to continue to squirm. But she had noticed something about him—something she *could* ask in front of everyone.

"You're not drinking tonight, Mr. Baxter?" She took a sip from her own wine glass as she waited for his reply.

"I don't drink." The reply was simple, yet curt, and she could sense underlying control in his tone. It was obviously a subject he didn't want to discuss further.

He turned his attention immediately to Mr. Wilson. "Wilson, you said you and Lord Cunningham don't normally travel often. Does he ever ask you to do other tasks, such as, say write his letters?"

Mr. Wilson glowered at Nicholas from beneath bushy brows. "At times." That was apparently all the man intended to say on the subject.

"I once worked for a man who could barely write his name. How is Lord Cunningham when it comes to his letters?" Nicholas continued.

Marianne watched him closely. This was clearly more than a simple inquiry as to Lord Cunningham's habit. Nicholas was interested for a reason. She could tell.

"Lord Copperpot writes his own letters from wot I understand," she interjected.

Nicholas inclined his head toward her, but looked slightly bothered that she'd kept Wilson from answering. "He's yet to ask me to write anything for him, but I can't speak to his behavior with Mr. Broughton."

"I doubt Mr. Broughton was asked ta write anythin', either," she replied with a tight smile.

Nicholas ignored her comment and returned his attention to Wilson. "Does Lord Cunningham pay you extra to write his letters?"

"Why ye so interested in what I write for me master?" Wilson said in a gruff voice, eyeing Nicholas with a scowl on his face.

"Just interested in what sort of work we're each asked to do," Nicholas said. He turned his attention to Mr. Broomsley, Lord Hightower's valet, who sat at the far end of the table. "What about you, Mr. Broomsley, do you write letters for Hightower?"

"No," Mr. Broomsley replied jovially. "His lordship prefers to write himself. Can't say I've ever written a letter for him, now that I think upon it."

"Well, I say the more they do for themselves, the better," Mrs. Wimbley interjected. The woman had rallied herself from her bed to attend the dinner.

"Come now," Mrs. Cotswold scolded. "That's hardly any way ta talk. If they did things fer themselves, we'd be out o' jobs, now wouldn't we?"

Marianne didn't miss the glance the older woman exchanged with Nicholas. Did Mrs. Cotswold know that Nicholas was only 'playacting' at being a valet? That was interesting.

The dinner soon ended, and the servants trailed back to their rooms. Due to the copious amount of wine she'd consumed, Marianne fell asleep nearly immediately upon hitting the mattress. She awoke in what felt like the middle of the night to a soft knocking on her door.

She sat up and put her hand to her forehead. She was no longer bottle-nipped but she certainly shouldn't have had so much wine. Ugh.

She pushed off her blanket, stood, padded over to the door, and opened it.

Nicholas stood there in his form-fitting breeches, bare feet, and a white shirt opened to the waist.

She peered out in the hall to ensure no one else was looking, then waved her hand rapidly to beckon him inside immediately. "Come in."

Nicholas stepped inside and she shut the door behind him quickly.

"Thank you for letting me in," he said as soon as the door was closed.

She hurried over to the desk and lit the candle. She was wearing her night rail and hadn't even bothered to put on a dressing gown. Not to mention her hair was streaming past her shoulders and no doubt looked a mess.

"Did I have a choice? I couldn't let anyone see you knocking on my door at this hour." She'd already decided to give up the pretense of the lower-class accent in his presence. He'd already discovered it was false and it felt silly to continue to pretend.

"Everyone is asleep. They all drank too much at dinner," Nicholas continued.

"Except you."

"I told you. I don't drink."

The candle sprang to life and illuminated the small room. "Yes. Why is that?" She turned toward him and crossed her arms over her chest.

"I didn't come here to discuss my distaste for alcohol," he bit out.

She crossed her arms over her chest and eyed him warily. "Then why did you come here?"

He arched a brow. "You don't think we need to talk?"

"About?" She let the word trail off as if she didn't remember what had transpired between them last night.

He gave her a long-suffering stare. "Really?"

She rolled her eyes. "Fine. Go ahead."

Nicholas cleared his throat. "It seems we both know something about each other that we'd rather no one else find out about. Would you agree?"

She tilted her head to the side as she contemplated the matter. "Yes. Agreed."

He nodded and continued. "Then it's in both of our best interests if neither of us says anything about the other. Agreed?"

She nodded too. "Yes. Agreed."

"Very well. I'll leave you to your evening." He turned back toward the door.

"Wait a minute. That's all you have to say?" The outrage in her voice was noticeable.

He turned back around and scowled. "What else is there?"

She put her hands on her hips. "You're not going to ask me my real name? You're not going to tell me yours?"

A grin spread across his face. "I assumed you didn't want to tell me your real name, but if you'd like to, I'm more than willing to listen."

She blinked at him. "Are you going to tell me *your* real name?"

"No."

She nearly stamped her foot. "That's not fair."

"I'm perfectly willing to continue calling you 'Marianne.'"

She shook her head. "Well, then…why are you 'playacting' at being a valet?"

"Why are you using a false name?" he countered.

They stared at each other. *Détente.* Clearly neither of them wanted to be the first to reveal anything to the other.

Marianne crossed her arms over her chest again. "So that's it? We're simply going to pretend as if we don't know anything else about each other?"

Nicholas shrugged. "I don't see any alternative."

"What about last night?" she finally ground out.

His grin was unrepentant. "What about it?"

She leaned back against the small desk and forced her voice to remain calm. "It meant nothing to you, did it?"

Nicholas leaned back against the door and crossed his arms over his chest. "I never said that. I simply don't see what the two have to do with each other."

"You're mad," she blurted.

His brows shot up. "Am I?"

"You're not the least bit curious what my real name is?"

His lips hitched up in a half-grin. "Of course I am, but at this point, I'm not in the least bit certain that if I asked it, you'd tell me the truth."

She rubbed her bare foot against the floor. "What if I promised to tell you the truth?" she offered.

"Why would you do that?" His eyes narrowed and his voice dripped with suspicion.

She lifted her chin. Why was he making this so difficult? "First name only? If I tell you mine, will you tell me yours?"

His smile returned again. "Hmm. That's an interesting proposition. But it also could be dangerous."

"How so?" First names were simple. She didn't understand his objection.

"We'd be halfway to knowing each other's full names," he pointed out with a chuckle.

She flipped a long curl over her shoulder. "I'm willing to tell you mine if you'll tell me yours, but you must go first."

His lips pursed. "That, my love, takes trust."

The words 'my love' made her heart beat faster. "And you don't trust me?"

"Not as far as I could throw you."

Clenching her fists and steeling her resolve, she sauntered over to him and put a hand on his shoulder, then let it move down to his bare chest. She traced a finger along the line of hair that made its way beneath his breeches. Oh, how she longed to follow it. His muscles jumped in reflex. She trailed her hand to his hip and then moved it around the back to cup the top curve of his buttocks.

The entire time, Nicholas had a look on his face like he seriously couldn't believe she'd walked over and begun touching him this way.

"Come closer," she whispered, quirking her forefinger on the opposite hand so that he would lean down to her.

He did lean down and his lips were a scant inch from hers. "What is it?" he breathed.

She took the opportunity to pull open the door behind him. "I don't entertain men whose names I don't know." She pushed him into the hallway and closed the door.

CHAPTER SEVENTEEN

Beau didn't have much time. He was busily rifling through the writing desk in Lord Copperpot's bedchamber, trying to find some sort of handwriting sample. He'd studied the handwriting from the Bidassoa letter so long and carefully that it was burned in his memory. He'd even outlined it and rewritten it time and again in order to remember exactly how the letters were formed. He already knew that Lord Copperpot's own handwriting wouldn't match, but perhaps the man had some other correspondence from the letter's writer in his care.

His concentration was not on his task, however. Instead, it was on the memory of Marianne last night, standing in front of him in her night rail, her gorgeous silken hair falling in luscious locks past her shoulders like molten red lava. The thin outline of the material had revealed her nipples, and he'd wanted to taste them again. It had taken every ounce of strength he possessed to keep from pulling her into his arms and taking her to bed.

She got a bit of her own back last night when she pushed him from the room, and he couldn't blame her for it. Apparently, they were even again. Even if it felt like a losing battle because all he really wanted to do was make love to her. But neither one of them was trusting enough to tell each other the truth, so it appeared they were destined for a mutually secretive relationship that would involve no more touching. Damn it.

Beau shook his head and forced himself to refocus on his search of the desk. He had just pulled open one of the top drawers when the door behind him opened and Mrs. Wimbley, of all people, stepped in.

She drew up her shoulders. "Sir, what are you doing?" she asked in a high-pitched, condemning voice, while peering down her nose at him.

Beau spun around and stared at her. Then he realized that not only had Mrs. Wimbley apparently emerged from her sick bed to come all the way down to the second floor, but Lady Copperpot was on her heels.

"What's this?" Lady Copperpot entered the room and stared at Beau with a questioning look on her face.

"I stepped inside to find this man going through his lordship's desk," Mrs. Wimbley reported, her shoulders still tight.

"That's not his lordship's desk," Lady Copperpot replied. "It's mine. Or at least, I have been using it while we're here, but I am curious, Mr...."

"Baxter," Beau helpfully supplied.

"Mr. Baxter," Lady Copperpot continued. "I, too, am curious as to why you were going through the desk."

Beau took a deep breath, weighting the merits of each of the lies that were hovering behind his lips. He was about to take his chances with the best of the lot when Marianne stepped into the room behind Lady Copperpot.

"There ye be, Mr. Baxter. Did ye find the button I asked ye to fetch?"

Beau cleared his throat and straightened his back. "No,

Miss Notley," he replied. "It wasn't in her ladyship's desk drawer as you'd guessed."

"That be odd," Marianne continued. "I coulda sworn that be where I left it. Well, no doubt the button be in the wardrobe in Lady Wilhelmina's room. I do hope we haven't disturbed ye, milady," she added for Lady Copperpot's sake, as the woman gaped at both of them.

"Oh, so you asked Mr. Baxter here to look in the desk drawer, did you, Miss Notley?" Lady Copperpot asked as if completely satisfied with that answer.

"Yes, milady. I was certain I'd put the button there, but I must be mistaken."

Beau nodded and bowed to all three of the ladies. "Well, if there won't be anything else, my lady?"

Lady Copperpot dismissed him, and Beau was out in the corridor in a flash. *That* had been a near calamity. And he had Marianne to thank for saving him. None of the lies he'd thought of had been nearly as believable as her assistance.

He'd nearly made it all the way to the servants' staircase by the time Marianne caught up with him. They stepped inside the staircase door and allowed it to close behind them.

"Well," she said quietly, a smug smile on her face.

"Thank you," he replied readily, though in a hushed tone. "For that." He gestured back toward the hallway with his chin.

"And?" she prompted.

"And what? Are you expecting payment of some sort?"

"Some sort," she replied, her hands on her hips. "I don't want money, though. I want something else."

Beau arched a brow. "What else?"

"Don't you think my helping you just now should prove to you that I'm trustworthy?"

"Not necessarily."

"Very well," she replied, in a low voice. "You found me sneaking about in your room. I found you sneaking about back there. Now we're even. But I want to know your real name."

CHAPTER EIGHTEEN

Around midnight, a knock sounded on Marianne's bedchamber door. It woke her from another one of her nightmares. The one where her brother, Frederick, was reaching for her, asking for her help. It always made her perspire. She bolted upright and caught her breath, remembering where she was.

A few moments later, the knock sounded again. Quiet but firm. She tossed back the blanket on her cot, stood, and pulled on her dressing gown before making her way to the door.

She cracked the door and peered out. Nicholas stood there. As usual, he was wearing breeches and a white shirt. Only this time his shirt was buttoned, thank heavens. His hands were behind his back, and he looked slightly guilty. "May I come in?" he whispered.

"That depends," she whispered back, blinking at him through the crack.

"On what?" He afforded her a charming smile that served to melt her insides.

She narrowed her eyes on him. "On what you plan to say

when you enter." He'd again declined to tell her his real name earlier. She'd trotted off, leaving him to think about how much trouble he'd have been in had she failed to assist him with Mrs. Wimbley and Lady Copperpot. It *had* to be worth something to him.

"I've come to apologize," he said.

It was the tone of his voice that made her open the door wider. He sounded humble and sincere.

She popped her head out of the door and glanced both ways down the corridor to ensure no one else was in the hallway, then she stepped back and made room for him to step inside, saying with a smile, "In that case, you may enter."

He took two long strides into the room while she closed the door. The moment she turned to face him again, she realized that he'd been carrying a long-stemmed red rose behind his back. "From Lord Clayton's garden," he said by way of explanation. "I removed the thorns."

He still sounded humble and sincere. Humble and sincere and bearing gifts? She was enjoying this side of him. Quite a bit.

She took the rose and held it to her nose. She'd never received a flower from a man before. William had never brought her flowers. He talked about things like bringing her flowers, but he hadn't actually produced any.

"My apologies if roses aren't your favorite," Nicholas continued. "I thought you might find it suspicious if I asked."

Marianne couldn't help her smile. "Yes. I probably would have found it quite suspicious. But thank you. Roses are lovely."

"For the record, what *is* your favorite flower?" he asked next, rubbing the back of his neck as if he was a bit nervous now that his hands were divested of the only thing they'd held. She'd never seen him nervous before. That was appealing, too.

"My favorite...?" She blinked. Did she have a favorite flower? It was certainly not something she'd considered before. Lady Wilhelmina's favorite flower was the lily—she mentioned it often, and usually had vases full of them in her bedchamber back home.

But Marianne had never had an occasion to decide what her favorite flower was. When she was a child, she'd liked to run through the meadow filled with larkspur near the cottage where she'd grown up. That was the only flower she could think of at the moment.

"Larkspur," she blurted.

"Larkspur?" He frowned.

She felt her face flush. The tone of his voice made her think that larkspur wasn't exactly the type of flower one presented to a lady at her door. "I mean roses. Roses are perfect." She clutched the rose even tighter to her chest.

"My apologies. I didn't mean to—"

"You've nothing to apologize for, Mr. Baxter. This rose is lovely. Thank you for it. Is that all you came to say?" Her voice sounded more curt than she'd meant it to, as awkwardness coursed through her veins.

He cleared his throat. "Well, actually, I came to say thank you again for what you did today. In Lord Copperpot's bedchamber, I mean." Humble, sincere, bearing gifts, and now apologetic. She could get used to this side of him. Quite used to it.

She twirled the thorn-less rose between her fingers. "Do you care to tell me what you were looking for?"

"No," he replied simply, shaking his head and smiling at her.

"Very well, but I do think you owe me something more than a rose for my assistance."

A slow smile spread across his face and he arched a brow. "Like what?"

She brought the rose up to her nose again and breathed in its sweet scent. "I already told you. Your name. Your real Christian name."

He expelled his breath and shook his head. "Are you certain I can't go find you some more roses? Or some larkspur?"

"Positive," she replied with another smile, her nose still buried in the dark-red petals.

"Fine. I'll tell you, but only if you tell me what *your* real Christian name is, too."

She nodded promptly. "Very well. I promise."

"And you'll tell the truth?" he countered, his brow arched again.

She lowered the flower from her nose. "If you will," she replied with a sweet smile.

He shook his head again, but the look in his eye told her he was serious. Quite serious.

"I will," she promised, in a much more solemn tone this time.

He turned and took a step toward the window, scrubbing the back of his neck as he looked out into the night. "Damn it. I truly hope I don't come to regret this," he breathed, then hung his head. "But my name is Beau."

"Beau?" She said it slowly and reverently. She never would have guessed it, but it seemed perfectly right. "It suits you."

Turning to face her once again, he waved away her comment. "Very well, it's your turn. What's *your* real name?"

She twirled the rose between her fingers again. "I hope you won't be too disappointed, but my real Christian name is Marianne."

His face fell. "Seriously?"

"Seriously. I told you I'd tell you the truth, and I have. I swear it."

He eyed her carefully. "But your surname isn't Notley, is it?"

"No." She shook her head. "It isn't."

"I don't suppose you want to tell me your real surname then?" he prodded.

"I don't suppose I do," she replied, setting the rose on the small desk near the door.

The hint of a smile still played at the corner of his firm lips. "Clever of you to keep your real Christian name, I suppose. Makes for less confusion."

"Have you been confused by being called 'Nicholas'?" she asked.

He chuckled. "Perhaps. At times."

He gave her a quick nod. "Well, I suppose I should go." But he made no move toward the door behind her.

Marianne took a deep breath. "I suppose you should, but…" A tingle brushed up her spine.

"But what?" he breathed.

"I was just thinking that, last night, I told you I don't entertain men whose names I don't know."

"Yes?" His heavy-lidded gaze made her heart thump faster.

"Well…now I know your name."

She didn't have to say another word. In two long strides, Beau had pulled her into his arms and his mouth descended to hers. His tongue didn't hesitate. It pushed past her lips, claiming her mouth.

Marianne leaned up on her tiptoes and wrapped her arms around his neck, matching his tongue's movement, thrust for thrust.

Beau leaned down and wrapped his forearms beneath her buttocks. Lifting her gently, he carried her the few small steps to the cot, laid her upon it and followed her down.

Again, he didn't hesitate. His lips moved to her cheek, her

neck, her *décolletage*, and he quickly pulled down her dressing gown and night rail to expose one pink nipple to his probing lips.

His mouth sucked her nipple into his wet warmth and Marianne cried out softly, arching her back against the onslaught of sensation his tongue had conjured.

In a flurry of movement, he helped her remove her dressing gown completely, tossing the garment onto the floor before moving back to pull down the other side of her night rail, then lavishing attention on her other breast.

His tongue was velvety smooth against her nipple and she bit her lip to keep from crying out too loudly. Her fingers slid through his hair on either side of his head and she held his mouth to her breast, wanting him never to stop.

Her hips undulated beneath his and she cried out softly again as momentarily he lifted himself away from her to pull his shirt over his head with both hands.

He was only wearing his breeches. She had her night rail pulled down to her waist. They sat there on the cot, panting and staring at each other in awe.

"Are you certain you want this?" he asked in a voice that was strained but still deep and seductive.

"Yes," she breathed.

Apparently, that was all she needed to say, because he pushed himself atop her again and braced his arms on either side of her head on the mattress, grinding his hips against hers, making her head toss fitfully back and forth.

"Beau," she called, loving the way his real name sounded on her lips. She reached down and traced the outline of his manhood beneath his breeches. She squeezed him.

His breath came in hard pants. "As good as that feels, Love, you'll unman me if you continue."

She stroked him once more for good measure before helping him to sit up and pull off his breeches. She pulled her night rail down over her hips at the same time and soon they were completely naked and staring at each other's bodies as if in a trance.

"You're gorgeous," he breathed.

"I thought you looked like Adonis when you were clothed," she replied, her eyes traveling over every inch of his bare skin. "Now I *know* you aren't human."

He laughed softly and shook his head before deftly pulling her atop him on the cot. "Feel free to touch me wherever you'd like…to prove that I'm human."

Marianne froze momentarily. In the few times she'd been with William, she'd never lain atop him, but her indecision only lasted a few moments before she realized the amount of power she'd just been given. She could touch him *anywhere*? With pleasure!

Beau settled onto the cot, folding both arms beneath his head and spreading his legs slightly. Marianne's eyes flared. The man was perfection, sheer perfection, and she intended to touch and kiss every single inch of him.

She began by running her fingers down his chest just as she had last night, but this time she watched in fascination as his muscles jerked beneath her touch. She continued her hands' path past his waist and down to his manhood, which stood out hard and strong against the patch of hair between his thighs.

She wrapped her fingers against his hard length and squeezed him. His breathing hitched so she did it again. His breath began coming in short little pants that filled her with power. She stroked him up and down and he groaned.

"Marianne," he breathed. Oh, God, how she liked the sound of her name on his lips.

Still squeezing him, she leaned down and kissed his lips. His tongue tangled with hers and he made to pull his hands from behind his head, but she stopped him with a finger to his forearm. "No," she commanded.

He nodded but leaned up, trying to prologue their kiss before she pulled her lips away to run them down his rough cheek to his neck. She suckled at the warm, salty skin of his throat and then used her tongue to trace the same path her finger had, down his abdomen.

His hips lurched off the cot and his hands pulled away to grab at the sheets next to his hips. "Marianne, please," he begged as her mouth descended past his waist. "I can't."

"You can't what?" she asked, her breath a hot pant against his manhood.

"I can't stand it if you..." His words were labored. His manhood twitched.

"If I what?" she teased, not entirely certain what she intended to do next. She hoped he'd give her a clue as to what he wanted.

"If you suck me," he breathed.

"An excellent idea," she said with a sly smile, just before her lips descended upon the tip of his member. She took him into her mouth and sucked him, listening with raw pleasure as he gasped.

"What else don't you want me to do?" she asked, teasing him by licking his tip while she asked the loaded question.

"Don't..." His breathing caught. "Please don't drag your mouth up and down me."

Another excellent idea. She did just that. Pushing her entire mouth down the length of him while his hands ripped at the sheets and sweat beaded on his brow. She dragged her mouth back up his hard length and descended again four or five times before his hands grabbed her ribcage and he flipped her over.

"Jesus, I can't take any more," he whispered in her ear, just before his mouth descended down her body.

When he was settled between her legs, she stared down at him in awe. Was he about to—

The first lick of his slick tongue between the folds of her most intimate spot made her back arch off the cot. A deep moan tore from her throat. He did it again and again as her knees fell apart and her fingers tangled in his silken hair.

She was on the verge of the experience he'd given her two nights ago, poised on the precipice of having the entire world collapse beneath her. "Beau, I can't—"

He pulled himself up to match her body with his and kissed her deeply. She tasted herself in his mouth, just before he pushed her knees apart even further with his own heavy knee. She felt him probing between her legs, just before he slid into her in one solid, slick movement that made her cry out.

He stopped. "Did I hurt you, Love?" he asked, still inside her to the hilt.

"No." She shook her head forcefully, her eyes closed, feeling the exquisiteness of him filling her so completely.

He braced his arms on either side of her head and began to move. The experience was wholly unlike her prior experiences with William. Whereas William had plowed at her quickly like a jackrabbit, Beau moved in long, languid strokes, pulling out and sliding back in while her body writhed beneath him wanting more and more.

When he moved one hand to the nub of pleasure between her legs and began rubbing her in tight little circles, she cried out again, exquisite pleasure pulsing through her whole body.

He kept up his strokes, groaning as he pumped into her slowly and his finger never left her most intimate spot, making her hips move in rhythm with it. She stayed with him until dark spots replaced his handsome face above her and shards of pure pleasure radiated from her core, out of her hips, and along her entire body.

She cried out and Beau's mouth was there to capture the sound. He pulled his hand away while her body was racked with shudders. He stroked into her again and again and again before he pulled himself from inside her and spilled his seed on her belly, his own body racked with shudders this time.

His breathing was hot and uneven in her ear for a few moments before he fell to his side and pulled her against him, kissing her disheveled hair. "God, Marianne," he breathed. "That was...amazing."

Amazing was an understatement, she thought as she struggled to right her own breathing. She placed her hand on his chest and felt his pounding heart. "I agree," was all she could manage, little zings of pleasure still zipping through her body. Nothing she'd done with William compared to the ecstasy she'd just experienced with Beau.

She turned to her side, her back to him, and he pulled her against his chest. His arms were around her, his big strong muscles enveloping her. She expelled a breath. The few times she'd laid with William, he had quickly dressed and left. This was different. Why was Nicholas—no, *Beau*—interested in staying, in holding her close? It felt...strange. But she also had to admit, it felt good. She closed her eyes and allowed herself to pretend for one moment that they were in love, that they were betrothed. That he wasn't who he was, and she wasn't who she was.

She allowed him to hold her...until the sweat on her body cooled, until she heard the crickets chirping in the meadow. She allowed him to run his fingers through her hair and kiss her ear.

They stayed that way for what felt like hours but was probably only half of one.

"Marianne?" Beau's whisper finally filtered through the darkness.

"Yes?" she replied, hoping he wasn't about to say something to ruin the bubble of intimacy that surrounded them.

"Will you tell me about your brother's murder?"

She closed her eyes and exhaled her pent-up breath. Too late. The magic was gone. "No, Beau. I can't."

CHAPTER NINETEEN

Beau could have kicked himself for bringing up Marianne's brother in the afterglow of their lovemaking. He'd assumed, obviously incorrectly, that she might have been more willing to share some information after they'd been so close. Instead, all it had served to do was to close her up tighter than a wine drum.

She'd quickly slipped from his arms and the cot and pulled on both her night rail and her dressing gown. Beau had sighed and taken the hint. He dressed and left her bedchamber soon after, doing nothing more than giving her an awkward kiss on the top of the head before taking his leave.

It was probably a good thing he'd left when he had, however, because Kendall, of all bloody people, had come knocking on Beau's door not an hour after he'd made it back to his own cot.

Beau had had to give the chap a talk that mainly involved advice regarding Kendall telling Frances Wharton, the woman he'd inadvertently fallen in love with at the house party, the truth about *his* identity as an earl, and to face the consequences of his lies. It had been a sensitive subject, as Kendall blamed Beau for his lying in the first place. After all, the entire pretend-to-be-servants plot *had* been his idea to begin with.

After Kendall had gone on his way and Beau suffered a nearly sleepless night, he had spent most of the day seeing to Lord Copperpot's needs. In the afternoon, he'd ended up hosting an impromptu meeting of his friends in his bedchamber, where Kendall got drunk as a wheelbarrow and had even become a bit belligerent.

Turns out Miss Wharton hadn't taken too kindly the news that Kendall was an earl—specifically, the earl whom she most disliked by reputation. To make matters worse, tonight at dinner, Miss Wharton's parents intended to announce her engagement to Sir Reginald Francis. Beau had spent no inconsiderable amount of time last night and earlier this evening trying to convince Kendall not to give up.

Beau had remained the picture of his normal calm, collected self in front of his friends all afternoon, but he had spent every spare moment contemplating what had happened between himself and Marianne in her room last night.

He'd made love to her. Well, *love* was probably a strong word. But he'd never been one to casually sleep with any willing female, and that's certainly not what this was; he wasn't Worthington, for Christ's sake. The duke was was known for his *mésalliances*, but Beau prided himself on both his discernment and his self-control.

Going for long times without bedding a woman wasn't something that bothered him overly much. Spending the night with a woman—and normally he spent the *entire* night —usually led to feelings, and feelings usually led to complications, and if there was one thing Beau steadfastly steered clear of, it was complications. Of any sort. For any reason.

They were messy, unruly things and he prided himself on a tidy, disciplined life.

Last night, however, he hadn't even thought about the feelings or the complications. Normally he was tightly in control of his baser desires, and thought through the ramifications of any choices he made when it came to carnal pleasures.

But the moment Marianne had invited him to touch her —when she'd said, "now I know your name"—every responsible thought had scattered from his brain, and all he knew was that he had to have her. Immediately.

And even in the harsh light of day, he couldn't even say he regretted it. In fact, he wanted to do it again.

Marianne was passionate. Passionate and practical. Something told him that laying with her wouldn't be like laying with anyone else. And he'd been right. The experience had been unlike any other in his life. But why? It made no sense. Why would a lady's maid, especially one with an affected accent and who was lying to him, make him feel things he'd never felt before?

Not only was she lying to him, she'd tricked him into telling her his name. Somehow, she'd known his name wasn't truly Nicholas, while she'd also known she wouldn't be giving away much by admitting that he already knew hers. He did believe that her Christian name was truly Marianne, however. He could see the veracity in her eyes when she'd said it.

Beau shook his head. He had to admit it had been clever of her to trick him into revealing his name. Quite clever. She'd outmaneuvered him. And he wasn't used to being outmaneuvered by anyone. Perhaps that was what intrigued him so much about her. He usually knew precisely who he was involving himself with. Marianne, however, was shrouded in mysteries. Mysteries that he greatly wanted to solve.

And one of the mysteries about her was what precisely had happened to her brother.

Whatever the story, it clearly wasn't one she wanted to talk about much. Why not? Because it was so painful? Something told him it was more than just that.

It was not yet midnight when a knock at the door jolted him from his thoughts. Reluctantly, he stood to answer it. No doubt it was Kendall again with more excuses about why he refused to fight for Miss Wharton.

Beau ripped open the door, saying, "You'd better get down there, no doubt dinner is mostly over."

"Dinner?" Marianne stood there in her ubiquitous blue gown *sans* apron, a confused look at her face. "In the dining room? I have it on good authority that it ended quite abruptly this evening."

Whatever she meant about dinner was quickly lost in Beau's excitement that she had come to his room. After what had happened last night, he'd half-expected her to avoid him like a bug-ridden mattress from now on.

As was their ritual, Beau glanced both ways into the corridor to ensure it was clear before tugging her softly into his bedchamber.

"You're here," he said inanely after he'd shut the door behind her.

"I am," she replied, biting her lower lip and staring at him uneasily, as if she were prepared to bolt at any moment if he made a sudden move.

She stepped toward the cot and gestured to it. "May I sit?"

"Please do," he blurted, taking a seat on the window ledge next to the bed. He wasn't about to get too close and scare her off. He wanted to hear what she had to say.

Marianne lowered herself to the cot and expelled her

breath. "I suppose you're wondering why I'm here." Her voice was calm and even.

"The thought did cross my mind," he admitted with a wry smile.

She took a deep breath. "I wanted to apologize...for running you off so quickly last night. The truth is...you frightened me."

"Frightened you?" he echoed, leaning back into the window frame and propping up one knee. He needed to hear her out, let her say whatever she needed to say.

"More than a bit," she continued, smoothing her hands down her skirts repeatedly. "I'd never..." Her cheeks turned a charming shade of pink and she dipped her head. "I'd never experienced anything like that before and I...it frightened me."

A frown marred his brow. What exactly what she saying? "You told me you weren't innocent."

"I'm not... I wasn't." Her blushed deepened, but she lifted her head to meet his gaze. "But what happened between us last night...was unlike any of the times before." She finished by expelling her breath again as if she'd just made a distressing confession.

"I feel the same," he said quietly, hoping to make her feel comfortable by admitting the truth as well.

She nodded and folded her hands together in her lap. Her blush had not completely vanished. "I don't know why I acted so strangely when you asked about my brother," she said next. "I suppose it's because I've never really spoken about it with anyone before."

He nodded too and slowly moved to sit next to her on the mattress. He tentatively reached out to lay his hand atop hers on her lap. "I understand, Marianne."

"Have you ever lost anyone close to you?" she asked.

A vision of a night many years ago flashed through his

memory, but he steadfastly shook it away. "No one close to me has ever been murdered," he answered. "Last night you said you can't talk about it."

"That's right." She nodded.

"Can't or won't?" he prompted.

She lowered her chin to her chest. "Won't...or at least I didn't want to then."

"You don't have to now if you still don't want to."

She lifted her chin and he could see tears shining in her eyes. "My brother was shot, killed in the war."

Beau nodded. "I see. I suspected as much, but when you said he was murdered, I wondered about the details."

"He was killed in the war," she repeated, staring straight ahead at the wall, unseeing.

Beau squeezed her hand. "I can see it's difficult for you to talk about. I'll walk you back to your room."

She shook her head and met his gaze. "I don't want you to walk me back to my room, Beau."

He swallowed hard. "What do you want me to do?"

Marianne stared unseeing at the wall for several moments. She looked frightened, alone. He moved closer, pulling her to his chest for a hug. He wanted to hold her, soothe her. He caressed her arms, her back. He smoothed her hair before placing a chaste kiss on her cheek. All the while, he murmured words of comfort.

She turned her face up to him. "Kiss me again."

He pulled back and searched her features. "Are you certain?"

She nodded. "Yes. When you touch me, everything else fades and there's only you. Only pleasure."

Beau went slowly at first. He lifted one hand to her neck, pulling her closer to his mouth as his lips descended to hers. But the moment their mouths met, Marianne didn't allow him to be gentle. Her tongue pushed its way between his lips, and she began ripping at his shirt.

Only moments passed before they were both naked on the cot and Marianne laid down and pulled him atop her. "Make me yours again, Beau," she breathed.

Beau's hand moved between her legs to ensure she was wet and ready for him, but unlike last night, he didn't spend time stoking the fire inside of her. They both wanted this fast and hard and he was prepared to give it to her.

He pushed her legs apart with his knee, then slid inside of her, waiting for only a second to ensure she was settled, before sliding out and pumping into her again and again. Her head moved back and forth fitfully on the pillow. The tiny groans coming from her throat were nearly his undoing.

When she grabbed his buttocks and squeezed, that was it. Beau pumped into her again and again until he was on the precipice of one of the fastest, most fulfilling orgasms of his entire life. He pulled out of her swiftly and came on the mattress beside her hip, his breathing nothing more than a series of ragged gasps.

She had a satisfied smile on her lips when he leaned up to look at her face moments later. "I apologize for that," he said with a sheepish grin. "That was rushed, and very bad form."

"Nothing to apologize for," she said, snuggling deeper into the cover, the grin still inexplicably riding her lips.

What was she grinning for? He knew he hadn't pleasured her the way he had last night.

"I don't understand," he began.

"I loved it," she replied, wrapping her arms around his neck and turning so that her lips met his ear, "because I loved making you lose control."

He had to chuckle at that. "Well, you certainly did that," he admitted, before tossing the cover over his head and descending down the length of her body. "But I fully intend to make it up to you."

As his tongue swiped between her legs, her eyes rolled back into her head and Marianne didn't have another coherent thought for several more minutes, until well after she'd come so hard, her body lifted itself from the bed.

In the aftermath, she pulled the covers up to her underarms while she considered how truly skilled the man was with his tongue. It was amazing, really.

He pulled her into his arms and held her there tightly as he had the night before, and she pretended again that whatever this was between them was real.

She waited for several silent, satisfied moments to pass before she ventured, "Why...why did you...withdraw?"

"Excuse me?" His voice held a note of confusion.

"Please don't make me repeat it," she said, her cheeks heating. "I only ask because...William never did that."

Beau pulled her close again and kissed her cheek. "Then William was a selfish ass. I did that so you wouldn't find yourself with a baby nine months from now."

Marianne nodded. Of course. And Beau was right, William *was* a selfish ass. Then again, at the time she'd thought they were going to be married, so a baby hadn't been a fear; but he hadn't ever asked her if she'd got with child. She hadn't, of course, but William hadn't known that.

She snuggled back against Beau again, pleased with the knowledge that he was taking measures to ensure their affair would not have unwanted consequences.

Several more silent moments passed before he said, "When you first arrived, you mentioned something about dinner ending early." He nuzzled at her neck.

"Yes," Marianne replied with a laugh, remembering the story she'd heard earlier. "According to Lady Wilhelmina, there was quite a commotion in the dining room tonight."

Beau leaned up on his elbow and stared down at her. He had a sinking feeling he knew something about what had happened. "A commotion?"

Marianne nodded. "Lady Wilhelmina told me one of the footmen serving the table climbed atop the sideboard, ripped off his wig, tossed it in the soup, and revealed himself to be the Earl of Kendall. Then he proceeded to ask Miss Frances Wharton to marry him—and she fled the room."

The hint of a smile tugged at Beau's lip. "Is that so?" He shook his head. Good for Kendall. The fool had apparently listened to him after all.

CHAPTER TWENTY

The next morning, Marianne was up before the sun. Not that she had slept much. In fact, she'd hardly slept a wink. After she'd sneaked back into her own bedchamber on the far end of the hall, she'd climbed into her bed and laid there, staring at the ceiling for what felt like hours. What was she doing, going to bed with a man whom she didn't even know? Beau. His name was Beau, and he was 'playacting' at being a valet. That's all she knew. She had no idea otherwise who he was.

What had he done to rid himself of Lord Copperpot's regular valet, Mr. Broughton? But more importantly, why? Why would Beau want to pretend to be a valet?

Whoever he was, she'd slept with him—not once, but twice. And she honestly had no other excuse for her actions beyond pure animal attraction. The man made her throat tight and her heart pound. Kissing him and allowing him to touch her the way he had had been bold enough, but now she'd spent the night with him *twice*. And truthfully, she wanted to do it again.

God, just the thought of his tongue on her the way it had been last night made her break out in a sweat.

Of course, she wasn't who she pretended to be either, but she had good reason for it. What reason did Beau have? The most frustrating part was now that they'd both told each other their names, neither seemed particularly inclined to say any more. The house party might well end with her not knowing who she'd had a passionate affair with. Apparently, she was willing to live with that, because it hadn't stopped her from falling into bed with him again last night, had it?

She told him the truth about her brother, but not all of it. Frederick *had* been shot and killed in the war. But there was more to the story, and that was why she was serving the Copperpots as a lady's maid at the moment. She still didn't know Beau well enough to tell him the whole truth, however, which was why she'd stopped her story where she had.

Thank heavens, Beau had seemed appeased by that, or at least he hadn't asked any more questions. God only knew if he'd ask more later. Given the fact that they were both aware they were lying to each other, she suspected he would. Just as she intended to ask him more questions about that letter he'd burned in his room several days ago. She still wanted to know what *that* had been about.

But Marianne was waiting for a letter, too—a letter she also intended to destroy. The irony wasn't lost on her. She'd accused him of being a hypocrite, but she was one too. The worst kind.

She paced around her small bedchamber. It was too early to do much of anything. Lady Copperpot and Lady Wilhelmina would not be awake at this hour. But she could steal down to the servants' hall and see about planning their picnic outing for today. Apparently, the members of the house party had picnicked earlier in the week and Lady

Copperpot and Wilhelmina had missed the planned outing. They intended to make up for it this afternoon.

Marianne wondered what sort of mood the two ladies would be in today. She knew from having listened to their conversations the last two days that Lady Wilhelmina had all but given up on the idea that Lord Kendall might arrive to meet her. And after the surprising revelation in the dining room last night, Marianne assumed Lady Copperpot would be none too pleased. Marianne had managed to help Wilhelmina change out of her clothing and had fled to the fourth floor last night before Lady Copperpot had even returned from what was no doubt a gossip-filled first floor.

There were five more days of the house party left, however. Lady Copperpot and Wilhelmina had to find some way to occupy their time, and Marianne might as well get to the business of planning their picnic.

She opened the door to her bedchamber and was about to step into the darkened hallway when voices caused her to stop. She peered out to see an older man leaving the room of one of the other lady's maids a few doors down.

The man looked as if he had absolutely no business in the hallway. In fact, judging by the quality of the clothing he'd clearly hastily put on, he appeared to be a…nobleman.

Marianne blinked, and slipped back into her room and closed the door. She wasn't entirely shocked. She'd spent enough time at house parties to have seen such things happen before. But she didn't recognize the man and she didn't know which maid's room he was leaving.

She would have to find out.

She counted to fifty, hoping to ensure the man would be gone by the time she emerged into the corridor again.

When she opened the door, she breathed a sigh of relief. He was gone and the door he'd come from was shut again. Marianne tapped her cheek, weighing her options. She finally decided a quick fib would no doubt be the best way to gain the information she sought.

Smoothing her sweaty hands down her skirts, she took quick, efficient steps toward the maid's door. When she arrived, she sucked in a deep breath, lifted her fist and rapped twice loudly enough to heard, but softly enough to hopefully keep from waking the other servants in nearby rooms.

Some shuffling ensued on the other side of the door before a young maid with long blond hair opened the door clad only in a dressing gown. The seductive sly smile on the maid's face immediately slid away the moment she saw Marianne standing there.

"Wot de ye want?" the maid demanded through narrowed, angry eyes. The sultry look on her face had been replaced with one of pure loathing.

While she hadn't expected a warm welcome, Marianne certainly hadn't expected this level of animosity. She fumbled to remember her story.

"I, uh, you're Lady Hightower's maid, Ramona, correct?" she blurted.

The maid's eyes narrowed further until they were barely slits in her face. "I'm no such thing! Now get out o' here before I call one o' me master's footmen to rid the doorstep of ye." And with that the maid shut the door in her face.

Marianne stood there for a few surprised minutes, blinking and wondering why exactly the maid had been so hostile to her. Now that she'd seen her up close, she didn't recognize her. Marianne sincerely doubted she was one of Lord Clayton's servants, who'd been nothing but friendly. No, this woman was one of the guests' servants, and she clearly wasn't employed by the Hightowers.

Marianne moved off toward the servants' staircase cursing her ill luck. She'd hoped that, if she guessed at the woman's identity, the maid would feel compelled to tell her who she truly worked for. That ploy had backfired, obviously, and Marianne was no closer to learning the girl's name than she had been when she knocked on the door.

Marianne shook her head as she made her way past Beau's door and down the staircase toward the servants' hall. Whoever the maid was, she'd certainly been rude and unhelpful. In fact, she'd been so rude and unhelpful, Marianne began to wonder if she was hiding something. Something other than a man leaving her bedroom in the wee hours of the morning—something Marianne could hardly fault her for, having just done something quite similar herself.

As she stepped into the servants' hall, a friendly voice greeted her. "G'mornin', Miss Notley. Ye're certainly up early today."

Marianne turned to see Mrs. Cotswold, the housekeeper, busily trundling around the corridor, carrying a teapot toward the kitchen.

An idea leaped to Marianne's mind. *She* might not know who all the servants were, but she guessed Mrs. Cotswold might know. "Good morning, Mrs. Cotswold," she called back, a slight smile popping to her lips. "I need yer help, please."

The housekeeper stopped and her smile widened. "I certainly will help if I can, Miss Notley."

"Excellent," Marianne replied. "I'm hoping if I describe a maid ta ye, includin' the room where she be staying upstairs, ye can tell me who she be."

CHAPTER TWENTY-ONE

I n addition to the mind-numbing sex he'd shared with Marianne last night, Beau had had a particularly busy night and morning. After Marianne had tiptoed back to her room soon after they'd laid together for the second time in as many days, Beau had sneaked downstairs to speak to Kendall again.

He couldn't help himself. He had to hear from the horse's own mouth what had happened in the dining room between Kendall and Miss Wharton last night. Turned out, Miss Wharton had run away from the earl precisely as Marianne had described. And while Kendall had chased after her and attempted to explain himself, Miss Wharton had refused to listen.

Which is precisely what Kendall had done when Beau attempted to provide the man with additional unsolicited advice telling him he had to keep trying. Kendall had finally told him to get out, and suggested that Beau go speak to Miss Wharton directly if he wanted her to change her mind. Beau had thought about it for only a few moments before deciding to do exactly that.

Of course, he'd had to wait until morning dawned and Miss Wharton had gone to Clayton's library as had become her habit. But Beau had sauntered in and had a brief talk with Miss Wharton, a talk he believed just might have served to change the lady's extremely stubborn mind.

Beau wasn't patting himself on the back quite yet, however. It still remained to be seen if Miss Wharton would, in fact, forgive poor Kendall. And the story Beau had told the young woman in an effort to convince her had come at a price.

For the second time in as many days, Beau had been forced to reminiscence about the worst mistake of his life.

"There's not a day that goes by that regret is not my constant companion," he'd told Miss Wharton. "Take it from me. The moment you make the decision you'll regret for eternity can also feel very much like being perfectly right."

Add that to the fact that there were only five more days left of the house party and he'd yet to uncover the Bidassoa traitor, and Beau was feeling entirely out of sorts. He desperately wanted to know who Marianne really was, but he knew that wasn't possible while he remained unwilling to tell her the truth about his own identity. It would be both selfish and hypocritical of him to ask her to reveal her secret when he had no intention of revealing his own.

The worst part was, there was a large part of him that *didn't* want to know the truth about who she was. What if he found out, and it meant they would be forced to end their affair? That was selfish of him too, but he couldn't stop himself from wanting the affair to continue. He wanted her whenever he saw her, whenever he smelled her, whenever she was in his presence, *and* when she was out of it. It was ludicrous, but true.

Even now, as he stood in the servants' hall waiting for a

letter that he was expecting, he couldn't help but want her. He was getting hard just thinking about her. Blast. Blast. Blast.

Marianne wasn't here in the hall. Before she'd left his bed last night, she'd told him something about needing to be up early to see to a picnic for Lady Copperpot and Wilhelmina. But even knowing she probably wouldn't be at the post call, Beau found himself searching the crowd of servants' faces for her.

The butler calling out for Nicholas Baxter finally served to distract him, and he grabbed his letter—clearly another one from the Home Office—and made his way up to his room to read it.

The letter didn't say much. Curiously, it still revealed absolutely nothing about Marianne's true identity, and all it mentioned about Mr. Broomsley was that there was nothing suspicious whatsoever in that man's past. Not exactly news to Beau. The letter asked him to concentrate on Mr. Wilson. He was their best lead at the moment, but besides noting the other night at dinner that the man had certainly appeared to be hiding something, Beau had made little progress in that quarter.

The only thing he'd done was locate Wilson's bedchamber. It was three down from his own, on the opposite side of the corridor. His next move would be to sneak into the room and search for a writing sample. He wouldn't have much more time to do it.

Beau took a deep breath. It was his sole goal for the entire day. After a morning thunderstorm, the Copperpots embarked on their picnic, and Beau had little else to do but search Mr. Wilson's room.

Beau briefly considered asking Marianne if she would serve as lookout for him. But he quickly discarded the notion. Such a request would likely prompt her to ask more questions about what he was up to. And selfish or no, he quite liked the arrangement as they had it for the moment.

No, Beau had to search Wilson's room quickly and alone.

He'd become a bloody expert at peering out into the hallway of the fourth floor to ensure the way was clear. He did so now, quickly and efficiently, pleased to discover the corridor was empty. At this time of day, he knew from experience, most of the servants were either tending to their needy masters and mistresses or down in the servants' hall chatting with one another.

After closing the door to his own room, Beau quickly made his way down to Wilson's door. Taking another glance each way, he pressed his ear against the door to ensure the man wasn't inside. He waited a full two minutes by the count of the clock in the hallway. When he'd heard neither shuffling nor snoring, he'd decided it was safe to try the door.

It opened, thank Christ, and Beau was able to see at a glance that the small room was empty.

Much like his own, the room consisted of only a small wardrobe, cot, desk, and chair. And like his own, there wasn't much lying around Mr. Wilson's room.

Beau began with the desk, reasoning that if there was any writing to be found, it might well be in the desk drawer. A search of the desk turned up a couple of odd pieces of cheap paper and a quill but otherwise nothing.

Blast.

Next, he turned his attention to the wardrobe. Swinging both doors wide, he rifled through the man's rucksack and clothing, even checking the pockets before relenting. Nothing. Not so much as a scrap of paper with a note hastily scrawled on it.

He made a cursory search beneath the bed and even inside the man's spare set of shoes before admitting defeat.

Damn. Damn. Damn. Beau stood in the center of the bedchamber for a moment thinking. He would have to get Mr. Wilson to write something. But how?

Beau didn't know how, but he knew who he would have to ask to help him.

CHAPTER TWENTY-TWO

After finding absolutely nothing of import in Mr. Wilson's room, the day had gone steadily downhill for Beau. Clayton had found him to inform him that Worth was out in the stables packing to leave, intending to forfeit their bet.

Kendall had already forfeited, of course, given the fact that the man had tossed his wig into the soup in front of the entire party. But if Worth, that competitive bastard, was forfeiting, something was seriously wrong.

Beau had marched out to the stables to see if he could talk some sense into the duke. But that had ended in nothing but frustration. Beau was completely unsuccessful at getting Worth to tell him why the bet no longer mattered to him.

Beau suspected it had something to do with Lady Julianna Montgomery, an old flame of Worth's who was attending Clayton's house party. Worth hadn't admitted a thing, but his reaction when Beau had mentioned Lady Julianna's name told him everything he needed to know. Beau had been forced to leave the stables, knowing Worth was returning to London. A damn shame.

Beau shook his head. It seemed both of his competitors had got involved in some messy dealings with ladies since this house party had begun. A good thing he wouldn't follow suit. What he had with Marianne wasn't messy in the least. It was quite tidy actually, up to and including the fact that they didn't even know each other's real full names.

He may be the winner of a substantial amount of money as of this afternoon, but the win didn't feel satisfying in the least. Both of his friends were heartbroken. How had such a simple-sounding bet become so troublesome?

He sighed. One word explained it: Women.

Well, *he* had no intention of allowing his dalliance with Marianne Notley (or whatever her name was) to bring him to *his* knees.

BEAU WAITED until he was in bed with Marianne late that night before he asked for her help. He'd decided to ask her after giving her yet another orgasm.

"If I ask for your help with something," he said after their breathing had returned to rights, "will you promise to ask no questions about it?"

A soft laugh came from the pile of bright red hair that was still splayed over Marianne's face. "No. Not at all."

He frowned. "Why not?"

"Because I'll almost certainly want to know what you're up to."

"But what if I can't tell you the details?" he countered.

"Can't, or won't?" she shot back, clearly remembering the question he'd asked her about her brother's death.

"Well-played," he replied with a smile, pulling her close to him again and kissing her delectable bare shoulder. "Marianne, sweet Marianne. I could stay here in bed with you forever."

She laughed again and swiped her hair from her eyes before sitting up against the pillows. "I somehow believe you'd get bored eventually. Besides, how do you see this ending between us?"

He wrapped an arm around her waist. "Must we talk about the end?" It was the last thing he wanted to talk about. They had four more days. Four more days in which they could pretend to be something they weren't. Strangely. He usually enjoyed pretending to be someone he wasn't; this time, it just made him feel melancholy, thinking about the end.

"You know it must end," she replied. "And I for one would like to know who you really are before it does."

"Oh, now you want to know?" He laughed.

"I've always wanted to know. But as the days go by, I want to know more."

"I want to know who you are, too," he replied. They stared at each other, both with a stubborn set to their jaws for several minutes.

"Will you be leaving before we return to Lord Copperpot's house?" she finally asked.

"Probably. Or at least soon after." He might as well tell her that much. He fully intended to find the Bidassoa traitor before this house party ended, distraction or no.

She frowned. "You don't know?"

"Not yet."

"That's a strange thing to say."

"Here we are again. Do *you* want to tell me who you are, and why you're not using your real name?"

"Does it matter?" she replied, leaning back against the pillows and pressing her forearm to the top of her head.

"Will you tell me why you're here at least?" he asked.

"Will you tell me why you're here?" she countered. She gave him a sidelong glance.

They stared at each other again, neither making a move to concede.

"I will tell you if you tell me," she finally offered.

His gaze remained skeptical as he said, "You promise?"

She nodded. "I promise."

"Very well." He lifted her hand from the blanket to his lips and kissed her knuckles. "I promise, too. I know it's hard to trust, but I will if you will. But we must also promise to ask each other no more questions."

Marianne took a deep breath. "Very well. You go first."

He chuckled at that. "Fine." He searched for the right words for a few moments before saying. "I'm here to catch a criminal."

She nodded quietly. "I am too. My brother's murderer."

It was as if all the air had been sucked out of the room for a moment. They both stared at each other as if they'd never seen each other before. Finally, Beau found his voice first. "Why would your brother's murderer be here? You said he died in the war."

"He did—and I thought *you* said we wouldn't ask any more questions."

"Yes, but damn it, now I want to know."

"Are you going to tell me which criminal you're looking for?"

"No."

"Then I'm not going to tell you what happened to my brother. I think I've said enough."

Beau's frown intensified. "How can you find your brother's murderer at a house party?"

"The same way you can find whatever criminal you're looking for here, I suppose."

He glared at her. Why was this woman so stubborn? He'd

never met anyone as stubborn as he was. Normally when he was charming, and certainly when he was seductive, he could get most women to tell him whatever he wanted them to. But Marianne was different. She wasn't about to tell him more. He could tell by the set of her jaw. She was done talking.

"Fine," he shot back, pulling his arm from her and plumping the pillow angrily behind his head. "I suppose we'll have to go to our graves not knowing each other surnames."

She laughed. "I wasn't thinking about my grave quite yet. I'm not entirely certain what will happen tomorrow at this point."

He couldn't help himself. "Do you really think your brother's killer is here? In this house?"

She glanced down at the sheets and traced her finger in a small circle. "I don't know," she allowed.

"But he might be?" Beau continued.

"He might be."

They settled back into an uneasy silence and after several minutes had passed, Marianne ventured to lay her head on his shoulder. "This is madness, you know."

"I know," Beau replied, sighing. He leaned down and kissed her head.

A few more moments of silence passed before Marianne asked, "Do you know Albina, Lady Winfield's maid?"

CHAPTER TWENTY-THREE

The next morning, sleepy as usual at least lately, Marianne was pressing one of Lady Wilhelmina's gowns for the dinner to be held in the dining room that evening. As usual, the young woman and her mother were gossiping about the house party and its guests.

"You could have knocked me over with a feather the other night when Lord Kendall climbed up on that sideboard and yanked off his powdered wig. Imagine, the man pretending to be a servant all this time. It boggles the mind," Lady Copperpot said.

"I thought it was one of the most romantic things I've ever seen," Lady Wilhelmina replied with a long, dramatic sigh. "One of the most surprising, to be certain."

"Don't be a henwit, Wilhelmina," Lady Copperpot scolded. "There was nothing romantic about it. It was shocking. Scandalous. Revolting, if you ask me."

Lady Wilhelmina snapped her mouth closed, but not before Marianne saw the hurt in her eyes at her mother's harsh rebuke.

"I'm just sick that Lord Kendall is apparently taken now.

There aren't many truly eligible bachelors left at the party, and none of them seem particularly suitable for you." Lady Copperpot frowned and shook her head.

Lady Wilhelmina nodded. "Yes. Apparently, Lord Kendall is betrothed to Miss Wharton. But I do have to wonder if Lord *Bellingham* is skulking about, pretending to be a servant."

"What? Why would you say that?" Lady Copperpot asked, her face crumpled in a scowl.

Lady Wilhelmina shrugged. "Well, someone told me there was a rumor that the Duke of Worthington had been pretending to be a groomsman in the stables. Though they say he's gone now."

"What!" Lady Copperpot's face took on a decidedly red hue.

"Yes," Wilhelmina continued with a knowing nod, "and last night at dinner, I heard Lord Clayton mention Lord Bellingham. Someone asked if he'd heard from the marquess."

Lady Copperpot's eyes widened and she leaned forward, her face bright-red and full of interest. "And what was Lord Clayton's response, Wilhelmina?"

Lady Wilhelmina waved a hand in the air as she appeared to contemplate the question for a moment. "Oh, I believe he said something terribly vague such as, 'You never know when Bell might appear.'"

Marianne gasped, and the leather walking boot she'd been holding dropped from her hand to land on the floor with a solid *thunk*.

"Well, I'm not holding my breath," Lady Copperpot replied to Wilhelmina, ignoring Marianne as usual. "Your father and I have some plans in the works for the autumn. We'll get you betrothed yet. Even before the next Season.

Now, I'm going downstairs to see if I can learn anything else about Lord Bellingham's visit. I'll see you for tea."

With that, the formidable lady stood and exited the room.

After the door closed behind her mother, Lady Wilhelmina gave an audible sigh. "I don't know why things like betrothals must be so difficult," she said out loud to the room.

Marianne stepped forward, her hands folded primly in front of her. "I'm sorry ye're having such a difficult time of it, milady."

"Oh, Marianne, be glad you're not me," Lady Wilhelmina said, a pout on her lips. "It's *such* a chore to constantly go to parties, trying to find a suitable husband. You cannot possibly know how difficult it is." The young woman shook her head pitifully.

Marianne wasn't about to miss her only chance at asking a highly inappropriate question. She cleared her throat. "Milady, if ye don't mind, do ye happen ta know wot Lord Bellingham's Christian name is?"

Lady Wilhelmina frowned and blinked. Then blinked and frowned some more. "Funny you should ask, but I do believe it's Beaumont. 'Beau' is what they call him."

Marianne gulped. She rubbed one finger behind her ear. "Did ye say *Beau?*" She'd asked again only to keep from crumpling to the floor in a heap. She tried to sound nonchalant, but her insides were quaking.

Lady Wilhelmina sighed again. "Yes. And I only know because Mama drilled his name into my head along with half a dozen others at the start of the Season. He's one of the most eligible bachelors in London, you know."

Marianne simply nodded. She didn't want to raise her mistress's suspicions, but Lady Wilhelmina seemed to be in a particularly accommodating mood at the moment, so she risked another question. "Do ye...happen ta know anythin' else about him? Lord Bellingham, I mean." So much for nonchalance, her voice clearly went up an octave.

Lady Wilhelmina frowned. "Taken a sudden interest into the affairs of the Marquess of Bellingham, have you, Marianne?"

Marianne attempted to keep her voice steady. She knew it must seem terribly strange of her to ask, but she also knew that Lady Wilhelmina was the one person she could ask such things. Marianne couldn't very well go traipsing about asking the other ladies at the party. Or even the servants, for that matter, without really arousing suspicion.

"I was just curious if I'd seen him before," Marianne finally offered. "In the servants' hall, I mean. Ye mentioned he might be playacting at being a servant."

"Why, yes, that's an excellent point." Lady Wilhelmina tapped her cheek. She was obviously warming to the topic now that she saw the benefit to herself. "Let's see. I do seem to recall some of the other young ladies saying that there's a rumor he works for the Home Office. Of course, I don't believe such rubbish. Why in the world would a *marquess* need to work for the Home Office? It makes little sense if you ask me." She rolled her eyes dramatically.

Marianne gulped again. "And…" She had to stop for a moment to ensure her voice didn't shake. "Wot does he… look like, milady?"

"Oh, he may just be the most handsome of the lot, if you ask me," Lady Wilhelmina said, a wistful look in her eye. "He's ever so tall, with close-cropped blond hair and the eyes the light blue of an angel's. He's ridiculously handsome."

With nothing more than a flare of her nostrils to betray her emotions, Marianne nodded calmly and made the last press to the gown before hanging it up in the wardrobe again. "I see," was all she said. "Well, I'll be certain ta keep an eye out fer him. If there won't be anything else right now, I believe I'll just go down ta the servant's hall ta see about arranging the afternoon tea."

"That would be fine, Marianne, thank you."

Marianne could not leave the room fast enough. She forced herself to walk slowly to the bedchamber door and open it, but once she was out in the corridor and the door was firmly shut behind her, she nearly flew down the long hallway to the servants' staircase.

Once inside the stairwell, she pressed her back against the wall and let out her pent-up breath, while a mixture of fear, shock, and undiluted amazement swirled through her body.

'Bell'? 'Playacting at being a servant'? The name *Beau*, and working for the Home Office? The exact type of position that would have him searching for a criminal. She'd begun to assume he was a Bow Street Runner, but now she had little doubt.

Nicholas Baxter, or *Beau*, was the Marquess of Bellingham, and a spy for the Home Office. And she'd been *sleeping with him* for the last three nights.

Oh, dear God. She had a very important letter to write.

CHAPTER TWENTY-FOUR

I t was two o'clock in the morning before Beau finally threw himself into his lonely cot and pulled the blanket over his head. Then he cursed. Marianne had not come. Was she waiting for him in her room?

They had a sort of an unspoken agreement that they would meet in his bedchamber. He'd spent the last two hours wondering if he should go over to hers, but now it was clear. Even if she had thought *he* was coming, why hadn't she searched him out by now, to see what was keeping him?

Blast. Probably the same thing that had kept him from going to her room. Damnable pride. Now it was far too late. If he tramped over there at this hour, he'd no doubt wake her up and embarrass himself at the same time.

They didn't have an arrangement. Not one written in stone, at any rate. So why was he so out of sorts at missing her for one blasted night?

He'd told her too much. He already knew that. He'd wanted to know more about her and while he could have lied to her about his name and about his reasons for being here, something had made him tell the truth. Their connection had made him tell the truth. And just as much as he hoped she hadn't lied to him, he hadn't been able to lie to her. It was an uncomfortable position for a spy to be in. Especially a spy in the middle of a mission. He had no business getting close to her. No business whatsoever.

Hell, he'd even had the thought for a moment to two: what if Marianne was the servant who'd helped Lord Copperpot write the letter? But he'd quickly discarded the notion. He simply refused to believe that it was her. Though he surely needed to see a sample of her writing before he could completely rule her out. Blast. Now he had two samples to gather, and very little time left to do it.

He'd spent a good part of the day trying to come up with a ploy to get Mr. Wilson to write something. But each reason he invented ended up sounding more ridiculous than the last. He'd even contemplating asking for Mrs. Cotswold's help, but she'd made it clear at the beginning of the bet that she intended to treat them all no differently than the real servants. She was committed to the end, even after Kendall and Worth had packed up and left.

What, precisely, did Marianne know? For all Beau knew, she'd made him as a spy and had been sleeping with him to ward off his suspicions. Wouldn't *that* serve him right for letting down his guard?

He'd told her he was looking for a criminal. She may well have guessed.

Beau scrubbed a hand across his face. She'd asked him about Miss Wharton's maid, Albina, last night. But when he'd told her he didn't know the woman, Marianne had dropped the subject. Surely, she didn't think Frances Wharton's *maid* had been involved in her brother's death somehow.

But that was the problem. He had more questions than answers at the moment, and he greatly disliked being in such a position.

He had managed to sneak into both Lord Hightower's and Lord Cunningham's rooms the last two days to search for any sign of their guilt. But he'd turned up exactly nothing. And listening at doors had proven useless. After the meeting between the three noblemen soon after their arrival, Beau hadn't been able to place them together again since. Clayton had also been keeping an eye on all three men, and indicated that the trio never seemed to speak at dinner or while the gentlemen drank port afterward. Frustrating.

Beau's final hope was to somehow get a sample of Mr. Wilson's writing. Or Marianne's.

Marianne. The thought of her reminded him once again that she hadn't come to his room tonight. Even if she'd guessed what he was up to, it didn't explain it. She was more the type who would arrive to confront him.

No. The fact of the matter was, it was entirely possible that Marianne simply no longer wanted him. And while he hated to contemplate that thought for longer than a moment —for reasons that he didn't want to examine—he still had to admit to himself that it was true.

His affair with Marianne had come to an untimely end, and Beau had only two days left to catch a traitor.

CHAPTER TWENTY-FIVE

Marianne woke up the next morning in a cold sweat. She'd had the dream about Frederick again. Reaching for her, asking for her help. Whenever she reached back and tried to save him, he disappeared.

She sat up and took a deep breath. She felt sick inside. The house party would be coming to an end tomorrow, and she was no closer to finding Frederick's murderer than when they'd arrived.

Marianne had told Beau the truth. She *was* searching for her brother's murderer. And she was no closer to finding the blackguard than she had been when she first began in Lord Copperpot's employ.

This house party had been a promising event. It had exposed her to additional people who might well have been suspects. But the house party would last only one more night and she'd learned almost nothing during her time here.

She'd allowed Beau to distract her. She had to admit that much. She was ashamed. If she hadn't been frolicking with him beneath the sheets, perhaps she would have had more energy to search for Frederick's killer. That's why she hadn't gone to his bedchamber last night.

But that hadn't been the *only* reason she hadn't gone. The truth was she'd considered going, considered going and allowing him to make love to her while she pretended that she didn't know who he was. But in the end, she couldn't do it. She couldn't kiss him and touch him and let him touch her, knowing that he was a *marquess*. There was just something so off-putting about it. When she'd thought he was a servant, or a Bow Street Runner, their stations in life had seemed much more equal. But now...now she couldn't touch him knowing he was the type of man who could decide the fate of her entire family. Beau was more powerful than she'd ever guessed, and something about not telling him that she knew didn't feel right.

There was one more reason she hadn't gone to him last night. And it was perhaps the most compelling reason of all. She no longer trusted her heart around him. She'd spoken nonchalantly about the end of their affair the last time they'd been together, but voicing those words had left a bitter taste in her mouth.

If she chose to end it before it ended naturally, perhaps she wouldn't feel sad. Perhaps she'd feel in control. Perhaps it would seem as if she'd actually had the power to end it all along.

They'd both agreed it could go nowhere after the house party was finished. She'd avoided his room last night to save her own heart. And no matter what other reasons she told herself, she knew deep down that that was the real reason she didn't go to him.

Yesterday, after talking to Wilhelmina, and learning Beau's identity, Marianne had rushed up to her bedchamber and written to the people who were helping her, demanding an answer from them as soon as possible.

She'd received a rush reply just this morning. The letter had come into the servants' hall along with the rest of the post, and she'd quickly grabbed her letter when Mrs. Cotswold had called her name. Then she'd hurried to a private spot beneath the staircase to read it.

Marianne's eyes scanned the page and her mouth dropped open.

She read it all once more to ensure she hadn't been confused. Then she read it one more time for good measure. She could hardly believe the words glaring back at her from the page.

She read it a fourth time. But it was clear. General Grimaldi didn't make mistakes. She needed to speak to Beau.

CHAPTER TWENTY-SIX

The blasted house party was set to end tomorrow and Beau was no closer to finding his traitor than he'd been when he arrived. The only good thing he could say for this damned party was that he'd won the blasted bet, but he'd give every farthing of his winnings and more to find the Bidassoa traitor.

He'd finally manage to contrive a reason to ask Mr. Wilson to write something. Beau had feigned a hand injury, of all inane things, and pushed a piece of paper and quill toward the man as he sat next to him in the servants' dining hall earlier this afternoon.

"Would you mind terribly, finishing this letter to my sister in London?" he'd asked, sliding the mostly written letter over to the man.

Mr. Wilson had eyed him with both distaste and suspicion, but he'd obligingly written the final two innocuous sentences that Beau had dictated to him before pushing the letter back and saying, "Here, will that do?"

Beau had thanked the man profusely and studied the handwriting extensively, but he'd known the moment

Wilson began writing that he was not the author of the traitorous Bidassoa letter.

Beau's final attempt to find the traitor was even more ludicrous than feigning a hand injury. He'd actually sneaked into Marianne's room, found her journal, and examined a few pages from it. He ensured he didn't look at any of the recent entries, if there were any. He didn't want to *completely* invade her privacy. As it was, he felt like a complete arse for suspecting her. But he'd hardly be doing his job if he didn't rule her out. And rule her out he did. Her handwriting was lovely, nothing like the scrawled scratchings of the Bidassoa traitor.

Marianne had stayed away from his room last night. He'd tried to block the thought from his mind all day, but he hadn't been able to. He hadn't even seen her since the day before yesterday. He was beginning to believe she was avoiding him. But why?

The way things stood, he knew he might not see her again before the end of the party, and that thought made him feel vaguely ill. He was waiting for a final letter from the Home Office, the one in which he would get his next set of orders. Without having made any progress on the traitor, he fully expected to be ordered to continue to investigate the matter, but he'd already ruled out Lord Copperpot. It was unlikely that he'd be asked to remain with the family. What purpose would that serve?

Beau was pacing in his small bedchamber, mentally debating. Should he go find Marianne and demand a reason for her disappearing from his life? Or would he be better off quietly leaving after the party ended tomorrow without a word to her, and cherish his memories of their nights together?

A knock at his door interrupted his thoughts.

In a foul mood, he stalked over to the door and ripped it open.

Clayton stood in the doorway, a sly smile on his face. "I swear you get more letters than I do, and I live here." The viscount stepped into the small bedchamber, holding a new letter between two fingers.

In no mood for pretense, Beau grabbed the letter from his friend and ripped it open.

His gaze scanned the page. "Christ!"

"What?" Clayton asked, excitement in his voice. The viscount leaned forward as if to glance at the letter's contents. "What is it?"

"I'm sorry. I can't tell you." Beau let both the letter and his hand drop to his side.

Beau stalked over to the window. He scanned the page again to ensure he'd read it correctly. In a hundred years, he wouldn't have guessed this. Not in a thousand years, actually. He read it for a third time. The words weren't changing. It said precisely what he'd thought it said the first two times.

"My apologies, Clayton. I must go." Beau turned and brushed past the viscount on his way out the door.

Once in the hallway, Beau glanced both ways. There was no more debate. Where was she? He had to find Marianne immediately.

CHAPTER TWENTY-SEVEN

Marianne remained scarce the rest of the day. She desperately needed to speak with Beau, but she intended to wait until they had complete privacy and the cover of darkness.

She'd spent most of the day in the antechamber of Lady Wilhelmina's room, mending some undergarments. She'd chosen the location mostly because Beau would never be able to look for her there.

It had been a success. She didn't arrive back to her bedchamber until after Lady Wilhelmina had returned from dinner. Marianne had helped the young woman change into her night rail before stealing back up to her own bedchamber on the fourth floor. Even then, she waited another hour before she moved quietly out into the corridor, down to Beau's room.

He answered the knock nearly immediately, as if he was waiting for someone.

His jaw was tight and his face was blank. Most tellingly, he didn't say a word. He merely stepped back and opened the door wide enough for her to enter. She remained silent as well as she stepped inside. She waited for him to close the door behind her before she turned to him.

"Beau, I—"

"I assume you received a letter, too?" His voice was clipped, entirely devoid of emotion.

Very well. If he was going to be this way, so would she.

"I did," she answered curtly, careful to remove emotion from her voice too.

Beau stalked over to the small desk in front of his window and grabbed his letter.

"Didn't burn yours, I see," she said.

"No. I didn't. Do you have yours?" His face remained blank. He was beginning to alarm her.

She pulled from her apron pocket the letter she'd been carrying all day. "Yes, I have it."

"Well, I suppose you won't read yours to me until I read mine to you?" His voice was harsh.

"Why don't we trade them?" she offered.

"Ah, excellent. That way we'll both know we aren't lying...for once."

She tentatively held out her letter to him and he handed her his.

They both accepted each other's letters and read them quickly.

Marianne closed her eyes. Beau's letter said the exact same thing hers had.

AGENT B,

By now you must realize that we have two operatives at the Clayton house party. You must work with Agent M to bring the Bidassoa traitor to justice. Your orders are to return with the family to Lord Copperpot's estate and await further instruction while continuing to investigate. Good luck.

G

BEAU WAS the first to speak. "You're Agent M."

Marianne nodded. "You're Agent B."

"Guilty." He scrubbed his hands through his hair and stalked toward the window. "Damn it. I don't like working with anyone else."

"Neither do I," she replied.

He turned back to face her. "What do you know about the Bidassoa traitor? You said you brother was murdered. You said you were looking for a murderer, not a traitor."

"My brother *was* murdered. By the Bidassoa traitor. My brother was Private Frederick Ellsworth."

CHAPTER TWENTY-EIGHT

Beau's eyes widened. "The devil you say! Frederick Ellsworth? Your brother was the soldier who inter-cepted the letter? The one who took it to Welling-ton?" Beau spent the next several moments trying to solidify in his mind how all of this was possible.

First, Marianne was a spy too. He'd been so enamored of her, he'd failed to see the clues that were directly beneath his nose. General Grimaldi, his commanding officer, liked to do things this way. He often put two operatives in the same location in order to test them. Then, in the end, they would be there to help one another.

Beau had simply never guessed that Grimaldi would pull this stunt on *him*, and specifically not with a female spy. Beau had never seen it coming. That was his fault. And he could bloody well kick himself for being such an obtuse fool.

Second, apparently Marianne's brother was the private who had been shot after intercepting the Bidassoa traitor's letter from the French. Having handed over the letter, Private Ellsworth had died in front of Wellington, and was posthumously awarded a medal in return for his bravery. In all of his musings, Beau had never guessed that her brother and this hero were the same man. Why would Beau have any reason to?

Marianne leaned back against the wall near the door. "Yes. The truth is that I set out to find Frederick's murderer as soon as I learned what had happened to him."

"How did you get involved with Grimaldi?" Beau asked.

She stepped toward the window, crossing her arms over her chest. "At first, I merely went to London. I was looking for the men who were in the special council, who knew about the British army's plans at Bidassoa. I soon learned there were three suspects."

"Cunningham, Hightower, and Copperpot," Beau ground out.

"Precisely. Lady Courtney, my former employer, helped me with a reference, but it was pure luck that Lady Wilhelmina was looking for a lady's maid at the same time. I found the advertisement in the paper, actually."

"That still doesn't explain how you came to work with Grimaldi," Beau pointed out.

Marianne nodded. "Grimaldi found me."

"Of course he did." Beau braced his hands on his hips and cursed under his breath. This story smacked entirely of Grimaldi.

"He'd heard rumors that I was asking a lot of questions about the special council and he came looking for me one day. I met him in the park near the Copperpots' London residence."

"And he knew who you were, didn't he?" Beau continued to shake his head.

Marianne nodded. "Yes. He knew right away that I was the sister of the murdered solider. I told him I would never stop looking for Frederick's murderer, so he asked me to join him instead of working at odds."

Beau believed every word of it. That was precisely how Grimaldi liked to operate. He showed up when he needed someone and convinced them to work for him. But why that damned puppet master hadn't seen fit to let *Beau* in on the secret, he'd no bloody idea.

"You didn't know I was working for Grimaldi until today?" Beau asked next, narrowing his eyes on Marianne's face to gauge whether she replied with the truth.

"Not until I read this letter this morning," she replied, her voice sounding tired, resigned.

She was telling the truth. The devastation in her reply told him as much. It mirrored how he felt.

Beau paced away from her and scrubbed the back of his neck. "Forgive me for asking this, but didn't you say you have an older brother, too? Why isn't *he* looking for Frederick's killer?"

She pursed her lips and arched a pale brow. "That's a nice way of you asking why *I'm* involved, being a woman—and the answer is that, regardless of my sex, the moment I learned that my *brother* had been killed, I vowed to avenge him. Men are allowed such emotions. I see no reason why women cannot be. And if you must know, my elder brother has been captured by the French."

Beau cursed under his breath again. "I'm sorry. Of course. You have every right to avenge your brother's murder. It's just that… This whole thing has taken me by surprise, and I'm not used to being taken by surprise." He put his hands on his hips again and stared at the floor.

"Likewise," Marianne replied, primly, "and speaking of being taken by surprise… Were you ever going to tell me that you're a marquess?"

Beau's head snapped up to meet her gaze. "Who told you that?" Confusion marred his brow, and he re-read her letter that he was still holding. "It doesn't say anything about that here."

"I know," Marianne replied. "I figured it out on my own."

Beau bit the inside of his cheek and let his hand holding the letter fall to his side once again. He'd been bested by another spy. A female spy. A female spy to whom he was ridiculously attracted. He refused to ask her the question that was perched on the tip of his tongue: had she been pretending when she'd slept with him? Had she merely done it to get close to him, to learn more about who he was? Because in that, he hadn't been playacting. No. He hadn't. Not for one moment.

He pinched the bridge of his nose with his free hand. "Do you mind telling me how you figured it out?" He had to ensure that no one else knew.

"Don't worry," she replied, obviously guessing his concern. "No one else knows, that I'm aware of. After you told me your name is Beau, I overheard Lady Copperpot and Wilhelmina talking about a 'Lord Bellingham.' And they mentioned that Lord Clayton had referred to him—you—as 'Bell.' After that, I put it all together when Lady Wilhelmina told me Lord Bellingham's Christian name was Beaumont."

"Damn it." Beau shook his head. "I knew I never should have told you my name."

"Well, now that it's all out in the open, I might as well tell you my full name. As I said, my Christian name is Marianne. But like my brother—as you've probably already guessed— my surname is Ellsworth, not Notley. Notley was my mother's maiden name."

Beau tossed the letter onto the desk in front of him and faced the window. "I suppose we both should have told each other more before we…slept together."

"I don't regret it," she said, lifting her chin.

"Neither do I."

"I don't regret it, but I think it's best if we don't repeat it," Marianne continued. "Especially now that we know we both work for General Grimaldi. And now that I realize you're a marquess," she added, averting her eyes.

"I agree," Beau replied, not certain he agreed at all. But he could understand why she felt that way, and he didn't want to do anything to make her feel uncomfortable.

He wanted to ask her why she hadn't come to him the last two nights, but he already suspected he knew why. She'd learned his identity and hadn't been ready to discuss it with him. "We wouldn't want it to...complicate things," he finished.

"Yes, exactly—'complicate things,'" she echoed. "I'm glad we agree on it. Especially since it appears your orders are also to return to Lord Copperpot's house after this party ends."

"Appears so," he replied stoically. "The only other clue left is whatever Cunningham, Hightower, and Copperpot were speaking about when I overheard them in the study that day. I assume Grimaldi wants us to learn more about that."

"So, you *were* listening at the keyhole that day?" Marianne asked with wry smile.

"Guilty."

"What do you think *I* was doing, walking by? I was trying to hear, too." She winked at him.

Beau shook his head, but he also had to laugh. He'd been thoroughly duped by Grimaldi and Marianne. There was no two ways about it. He'd been a damn, arrogant fool.

Marianne's countenance quickly turned serious again. "If you're going to return to Lord Copperpot's estate, you'll have to convince Mr. Broughton to stay away longer," she pointed out.

Beau shrugged. "I'm not worried about that. I have my ways."

"Which are?" Marianne put her hands on her hips and rocked back and forth on her heels.

Beau glanced at her. "They usually involve money."

"I see," Marianne replied. "It must be quite convenient to be able to use money to solve your problems."

"I assure you, it is." Beau scrubbed his hand through his hair again, still trying to reconcile today's turn of events. "Very well. For the foreseeable future, it seems we must work together to find the Bidassoa traitor."

"Seems that way," Marianne replied. "And you agree that we won't continue our, ahem, physical relationship?" She swallowed hard.

Beau gave her a sidewise stare. "Do I have a choice?"

"No."

"Then of course I agree."

She held out her hand to him. "Partners?"

"Partners," he agreed, taking her hand and giving it a firm shake. God help him. For the first time in his life, he had a partner.

CHAPTER TWENTY-NINE

Lord Copperpot's Country Estate, October 1814

I t hadn't been much of a feat to get Mr. Broughton to agree to relinquish his position as valet to Lord Copperpot for the foreseeable future.

As Beau had expected, a healthy sum of money and the promise that he would be assured a position in the future was all it took to convince the chap to take an extended holiday. Lord Copperpot, for his part, was only too ready to keep Beau on as his valet. He'd been pleased by his work and probably relished the idea of no longer having to worry about his valet's sobriety on any given night.

Weeks had passed however, and Beau was slowly going mad. It wasn't that the work of a valet was too much for him. It was quite routine, actually, once one got used to it. No. His problem with the weeks he'd spent at Lord Copperpot's estate was the proximity to Marianne. Specifically, the fact that he was in her company quite often, he wanted her as much as he ever had, and he could do nothing about it.

The monotony of his days was broken only by glimpses

of Marianne and the letters he received from Kendall. The earl, of course, did not put his address on the letters he wrote, nor did he frank them as he was entitled to do as a member of Parliament. He also didn't seal them with his crest. Any of those actions would draw too much attention to the correspondence. Instead, Kendall wrote on plain paper, not vellum, and Beau was able to get the letters in the daily post call without any of the other servants at Lord Copperpot's estate thinking anything was amiss.

Kendall's letters informed Beau that Kendall and Miss Wharton were to be married in the spring. Seems the earl had, in fact, found the love of his life while posing as a footman at the house party.

Worth, however, was in trouble. According to Kendall, the duke had left the house party after forfeiting the bet, and all he'd done since returning to London was drink too much. Apparently, his mood had further declined a few weeks ago when he'd received the invitation to Lady Julianna Montgomery's wedding to the Marquess of Murdock.

Worthington was in love with Lady Julianna. The fool always had been, but the day that Beau went out to the stables at Clayton's house party and attempted to tell the sop as much, the duke had steadfastly refused to listen. Stubborn arse. Now Beau was hours away in Guildford, completely unable to deliver one of his famous speeches to get Worth to see reason. Kendall would have to help Worth in his time of need.

Thankfully, Kendall reported that he *had* tasked himself with ensuring that Worth didn't drink himself into an early grave, while listening to story after story about the lovely Lady Julianna.

When he wasn't thinking about his lovesick friend, or obsessing over the identity of the traitor, Beau had plenty of time to think about Marianne. He saw her daily. Their paths crossed several times a day, actually, given the fact that Lord and Lady Copperpot occupied bedchambers with adjoining doors. He often saw her in the corridor as they were both exiting the rooms.

Lady Wilhelmina's bedchamber was just across the hall from her parents' rooms, and if Marianne wasn't coming out of Lady Copperpot's bedchamber, where she helped with duties since Mrs. Wimbley's health continued to be spotty, Marianne was coming or going from the younger woman's bedchamber.

Beau always nodded to Marianne in way of greeting. At times, one of them would actually say a couple of words such as, "Good afternoon." But for the most part, they acted as if they barely knew each other. They certainly didn't act as if they'd ever spent three passionate nights in each other's arms.

For her part, Marianne appeared to have no problem whatsoever with their agreement to keep their hands off of one another while they worked toward discovering the traitor. The two of them met briefly once a week to compare notes. They'd fallen into it quite casually. It was usually done on Monday mornings.

After seeing to Lady Wilhelmina's clothing before she went down to the servants' dining room, Marianne would exit the young woman's bedchamber at half past eight. Near this same time, Beau would ensure he finished laying out his lordship's clothing for whatever outing or event Lord Copperpot had planned for the late morning. He would exit his lordship's bedchamber and meet Marianne in the stairwell of the servant's staircase at the far end of the hall, much as they had done at Clayton's estate.

They spent no more than five minutes together at these meetings. And Beau would pretend the entire time that the scent of her hair didn't make him want to pull it down from its pins so that he might run his fingers through it. He pretended that the sight of the freckles along the bridge of her nose didn't make him want to kiss each one of them individually. And he further pretended that the mere proximity to her didn't make him hard. But all of these things were true, and they were slowly driving him mad.

Their time together in the staircase was brief mainly because there wasn't much to report. Beau had long ago become convinced that Lord Copperpot wasn't the culprit. During his weeks at the estate, Beau had managed to ask all of Copperpot's likely servants if they could write, and had invented excuses to see their handwriting. None of it matched the Bidassoa traitor's letter.

Beau's weekly check-ins with Marianne usually consisted of both of them saying they had nothing new to report and then nodding primly toward each other, while one of them went up the stairs and the other went down. The entire unsatisfying routine made Beau want to punch his fist through the wall each time it was over.

In fact, the only progress they'd made in the traitor investigation to date was the bland discovery of what the three noblemen had been discussing in the study at Clayton's house.

The Home Office had intercepted some correspondence between Lord Copperpot, Lord Hightower, and Lord Cunningham sent after the house party, which indicated the three men were planning...a ball. A bloody party, of all things. Nothing clandestine. Nothing suspicious. And when Beau replayed through his mind the bits and pieces of the conversation that he'd heard at Clayton's house, he realized that that's exactly what he'd been listening to. Three fathers planning a shared ball for their unbetrothed daughters.

Lord Copperpot's London residence was set to be the location of the ball, scheduled for the evening of the fourteenth of October. And the Home Office had made it quite clear to Beau and Marianne that they were expected to remain at Copperpot's estate in the meantime, then go to London for the ball with the family and investigate further.

After nearly two torturous months at Lord Copperpot's estate, they were all set to travel to London tomorrow, two days prior to the ball. Beau had already devised a way to travel in a coach with Marianne, alone.

CHAPTER THIRTY

Bright and early the next morning, Marianne settled
into the servants' coach and waited for the other
maids to join her. When nearly half an hour had
passed, and she was still alone, she began to wonder what
was keeping them.

As the coach began to roll forward, she was about to pop
her head out of the window and call to the coachman to wait
for the other maids, but then the door opened and Beau
jumped inside.

He landed on the seat opposite her with a huge grin on
his face and dusted off his jacket, easy as you please.

She blinked at him. "What are you doing? Where are Miss
Harper and Mrs. Wimbley?"

Beau leaned to the side of the seat and braced an elbow
against the squabs. "I convinced them to ride with the
footmen."

"With the footmen? That's not proper." Marianne
frowned at him.

"Perhaps not, but the money I gave them made it worth
their risk."

Marianne folded her arms over her chest. "You think you can just pay off any poor servant and get what you want, don't you?"

His face fell. "Not at all. I thought I was doing them a favor. I gave them both more money than they make in six months' time."

"You cannot buy everything," Marianne pointed out, her fist clenching in her skirts.

"I cannot help it that I have money, any more than they can help it that they don't. What would you have me do with my money, if not use it for such things?"

"I'm certain I don't know. I've never been wealthy." She felt a bit waspish after his perfectly reasonable explanation about not being able to help the fact that he had money.

Obviously deciding to change the subject, he gave her a serious look. "Are you that unhappy at the prospect of riding to London with me alone?"

Marianne glanced out the window, contemplating his words for a few moments. The ride to London from Lord Copperpot's estate would take half the day. She doubted they would stay alone in the carriage the entire time, but something about the idea of being so near him, so alone with him, did give Marianne pause.

The truth was that she didn't trust herself alone with him. She'd made certain over the last several weeks that they never spent time alone, apart from their weekly briefings in the servants' staircase. And those meetings were safe enough because they were over quickly.

However, there were nights, a score of them at least, where it had taken every bit of strength she had to keep herself from going to him, begging him to make love to her again.

She didn't go for two reasons. First, she had been the one to suggest that they keep things strictly professional between them. If she arrived in his room, ready to toss over that pronouncement, she'd look a fool. And second, there was no way a rekindled affair between them could end happily. It would only serve to break her heart. The man was a marquess, and she was a servant. It wasn't as if they could ever marry. No. The closer she was to Beau, the more difficult it would be when the time came to break things off completely. And she fully intended to have her heart intact when that time came.

"Well? I assume you wanted to speak to me alone, or you wouldn't have gone to all this trouble and expense," she said as the coach rumbled along the dirt road toward the front of the estate.

"You assumed correctly." Beau cleared his throat. "We… we need to make a plan, for what we'll do when we are in London. Lord Hightower and Lord Cunningham will both be at the ball, and some of the guests may spend the night, even if they have town houses themselves. It's not uncommon."

Marianne's foolish hope that he'd wanted to ride alone with her in order to tell her something personal—such as that he longed for her, that he couldn't stand to not kiss her again—died a quick death. She shook her head and sat up straight, taking a deep breath. Very well. If he wanted to talk about their mission, she could do that.

"I agree. In fact, I asked Wilhelmina if she knew of anyone else spending the night at the town house. She said she wasn't certain."

"No matter. We'll find out when we arrive."

"Very well," Marianne agreed. "What should we do the night of the ball?"

"It'll be important to watch for any interactions between Lords Copperpot, Hightower, and Cunningham. I'll be especially curious to watch Hightower and Cunningham."

"Yes, I agree that Lord Copperpot isn't our culprit."

Beau plucked at his lip. "Is there anywhere in Copperpot's London house where we can surreptitiously watch the proceedings in the ballroom? If either of the other two men see me, they might recognize me."

Marianne felt her cheeks heat. Indeed, there was such a place, but she didn't want to admit how she knew. She had often sneaked to the small alcove above the musician's stage in the ballroom to watch the dancing. She so enjoyed the music and the gowns and the lovely spread of refreshments and the tables full of flowers. On the handful of occasions last spring when the Copperpots had held a ball or a large party in the ballroom, Marianne had enjoyed nothing so much as quietly watching from the alcove.

"I do know of a place," she said, pressing her lips together. "I'll show you."

Beau nodded. "You watch Lord Cunningham. I'll watch Lord Hightower."

"Very well, but you'll have to point out Lord Cunningham to me. Unlike you, I've never met either of them before."

Beau nodded again. "I will point them out."

They lapsed into silence for a few minutes, each staring out the opposite coach window as the landscape moved past. Autumn was slowly arriving in the English countryside and the leaves had begun to change colors.

Finally, Beau cleared his throat. "What are the housing arrangements at Copperpot's London town home? For servants, I mean."

Marianne swallowed. "Much like the estate, the upper servants are housed in private rooms on the fourth floor. The family is on the second floor and the guests are on the third."

Beau arched a brow. "Are the upper servants separated by sex?"

"The women are on the right and the men are on the left, if that's what you mean."

"A pity," he said, shaking his head.

"Why is it a pity?" Even as she asked the question, she knew she would soon come to regret it. But she couldn't help herself all the same.

His gaze locked with hers. "Because there hasn't been a night that's gone by since the last time we were together at Clayton's house that I haven't wanted to come to your bedchamber."

CHAPTER THIRTY-ONE

Lord Copperpot's London Town House,
14 October, 1814

Perhaps Beau shouldn't have said what he'd said to her in the coach two days ago. He'd wanted to kick himself afterward. Marianne hadn't said a word. She'd just taken a deep breath and turned to stare out the window silently.

Regardless, what he'd said that morning had been nothing but the truth. An uncomfortable truth, perhaps, but one that he'd finally decided he needed to admit. If they never spent the night together again, it wouldn't be because Marianne didn't know how he felt. He wanted her. He'd always wanted her. He wanted her even now.

They'd ridden the rest of the way to the next coach stop in silence, and once they'd arrived, Beau had surreptitiously changed spots with the maids and hadn't seen much of Marianne since...until tonight.

The ball was in full effect before he met her at the servant's staircase on the fourth floor so that they could travel downstairs together. Guests had begun arriving a bit after eight o'clock, and it was nearing ten before Marianne appeared.

No longer clad in her blue maid's dress, tonight Marianne wore a simple white sarsnet gown, one entirely unlike any of her others. Small embroidered flowers graced the neck and hemlines. Her bright hair was caught up in a chignon, and her blue eyes sparkled.

Apparently, she'd forgiven him for his remarks in the coach, because tonight she gave him a warm smile.

"Good evening, Mr. Baxter," she said with a laugh as she curtsied to him.

"Miss Notley," he replied, bowing in kind. He offered her his arm. "You are breathtaking. Would you care to attend a ball with me this evening? From a distance, that is?"

Her smile was gorgeous, and when she reached out and placed her hand on his sleeve, a tingle shot up Beau's arm. He'd always thought she was lovely, but he'd never seen her like this before. Wearing a pretty gown, fresh-faced and smiling, as if she hadn't a care in the world.

Most of the other servants were down in the servants' hall, either preparing food and drink to take up to the ballroom, or—if they had no duties for the ball—talking and laughing with each other. Beau was able to escort Marianne down the staircase to the second floor at least without running into any other servants.

The moment they arrived at the door to the second-floor corridor where the families' bedchambers were, Marianne pulled her arm from his sleeve and nudged open the door a few inches. She peeked out.

Apparently, the corridor was empty, because she quickly said, "Follow me."

She led him about a quarter of the way down the hall

until they came to a small door that didn't look like the others. It appeared to be a utility door.

"What is this?" Beau whispered as Marianne wrenched the door handle to open the obviously stuck door.

"Not many people know about this place," she whispered back.

"How did you find it?" he asked.

Her tinkling laughter followed. "I'm a spy, remember? I've scoured every conceivable part of this house."

Beau smiled and shook his head. He had to stoop down to follow her through the short doorway. When the door closed behind them, they were enveloped in darkness. The strains of music from the ballroom met his ears.

"Marianne?" Beau whispered.

"Just a moment," she whispered back.

He heard the scratchy sound of a flint being struck beside him before a blaze of light brightened the space. Marianne had lit a candle in a holder on a small table near the door.

The candle illuminated a portion of the musty, cramped space. There was some old furniture against the walls, but otherwise, the small room was empty. Marianne lifted the candle and Beau had to continue to duck as she led him through the tiny room, and into an even more narrow, dark passageway. The music grew louder as they moved through the small corridor.

When they emerged at the other end, they were in a room that wasn't much larger than the one they'd left. A rickety wooden chair sat at the far end of the space and the strains of a quadrille were even clearer than before.

"Over here." Marianne made her way to the questionable-looking chair.

Beau followed her again and once he was standing next to the chair, he could see that there was a small window-like space cut into the paneling, covered with wooden slats, which afforded a view of the entire ballroom. Looking directly down, he saw that the musicians were beneath them.

"From the ballroom side, this is covered with wallpaper, you don't even notice it," Marianne explained, pointing to the slats. "But you can see nearly everything from here."

Beau nodded. "Indeed. Good work, Agent M." He turned in a circle looking for a place to sit.

"There's only one chair," Marianne said apologetically.

"One moment. I'll go back and get another one."

Taking the candle, Beau quickly made his way back through the small corridor into the bigger space, where he found an equally rickety chair that he carried back through the corridor with him.

By the time he returned, Marianne had already taken her seat and was staring out across the ballroom below. "I love this melody," she breathed, tapping her foot along with the quadrille.

Setting the candle on the ledge in front of them, Beau pulled up his chair directly next to hers and they watched as the party unfolded beneath them. Groups of four couples had taken to the dance floor, and were engaged in the boisterous dance.

Beau scanned the ballroom's occupants for a few minutes. "There is Lord Cunningham," he finally said.

Marianne leaned forward. "Where?"

"At the far end of the room on the right. He's wearing a dark-green coat. He's speaking with a woman in a pink gown."

Marianne studied the scene for a few minutes before nodding. "I see him."

"Good. Keep an eye on him." Beau paused for a few more moments, continuing his search of the crowd, before saying, "Lord Hightower is on the opposite side of the room near the refreshment table. He's wearing dark blue and speaking to two ladies who are both wearing yellow."

"Must be the color of the autumn Season," Marianne replied with a slight laugh. "I see Lord Copperpot," she added a few moments later.

"Where?" Beau asked.

Marianne leaned forward again and pointed, and the scent of her flowery soap made Beau clench his jaw.

"There, by the doorway," she said. "It looks as if he's still greeting guests."

Beau shook his head. He forced himself to find Lord Copperpot's form in the crowd. "Good. We can keep an eye on all three of them." He moved his chair a bit away from hers to restore his mental equilibrium.

They sat there, watching the crowd in the ballroom silently until Beau noticed that Marianne was swaying in time to the music. A waltz had just begun.

"Do you like to dance?" he couldn't stop himself from asking.

"I've never danced before," she replied, blinking.

"What? Are you quite serious?"

Marianne shrugged. "I've never had an occasion to dance. This might surprise you, but I've never been invited to a ball before, either."

Beau frowned. "You've never been invited to any sort of party where there was dancing?"

She tapped her cheek thoughtfully for a few moments. "I've been to country dances, if that's what you mean, but... I've never danced a waltz like this."

"Would you like to?" The words escaped his lips before he had a chance to examine them.

"Would I...?" She pressed her lips together and blinked at him again.

"I'm quite serious," he replied. "I know how to waltz, and

I'd be happy to teach you."

He could see the muscles move in her throat as she swallowed hard. "Aren't we supposed to be keeping an eye on Lords Cunningham and Hightower?"

Beau stood and pushed back his chair. "Yes. But I daresay they've been completely uninteresting so far this evening. I doubt we'll miss anything."

Marianne laughed. "You are serious, aren't you?"

"Entirely," he replied. He stood in front of her and held out his arms. "Miss Notley, if you will?"

Marianne bit her lip and glanced back and forth as if seriously debating whether dancing the waltz with him in this alcove was a good idea. But he could tell the moment she'd made up her mind, because she lifted her chin, stood, and set her own chair out of the way.

"Mr. Baxter, I'd be honored." She held her hands out to him before quickly adding. "But if I step on your foot, I cannot be held accountable."

Beau laughed at that. Then he clasped her hands in his and waited for the beat of the music to come back around. "I'm certain you've seen from watching that the waltz is done in three sets of three."

"Yes," Marianne replied, nodding. "But we don't have much room here, I'm afraid."

"We'll simply have to make do," Beau replied before taking the lead and stepping into the first trio of steps. He led the way and even managed to ensure he didn't hit his head on the ceiling beams as they waltzed in a small circle to the music drifting up from the ballroom below.

At first Marianne looked as if she were terrified that she might actually step on his boot, but after a few sets of steps, she got the pattern down brilliantly, and as her confidence grew, so did her smile.

Beau couldn't remember a dance he'd enjoyed more, and

he'd danced with some of the most popular ladies of the *Beau Monde*. But here, with Marianne in this small second floor room that smelled like dust, he actually felt for the first time in his life as if he were courting a lady. And there was no one he'd rather be with.

He was sorely tempted to pull her close, but given that she'd watched waltzes in the ballroom before, she would know that wasn't proper—not to mention that they were still pretending as if they were nothing more than colleagues, the dancing notwithstanding.

So he concentrated on his smile and his footsteps and on ensuring that Marianne continued to smile, and he tried desperately not to think about how good she smelled or how soft her hands were or how perfect she felt in his arms.

Minutes later, the music came to an end and Beau reluctantly let her go. She lifted her white skirts, curtsied deeply, and smiled. "Thank you for a lovely waltz, Mr. Baxter."

"The pleasure was entirely mine, Miss Notley," he replied.

Marianne pushed a lock of red hair behind her ear as her focus returned to the ballroom and she resumed her seat. Beau, pushing away thoughts of another dance—or something even more enticing, like a kiss—placed his own chair back in its former position and resumed his study of the ballroom.

They hadn't been watching again for more than five minutes when Marianne leaned forward in her chair and pointed. "Who is that man over there? The one standing near the potted palm, wearing a bright blue coat?"

Beau scanned the crowd until his gaze alighted upon the man in question. He narrowed his eyes. "That's Baron Winfield. The father of Kendall's intended, Miss Wharton."

Marianne shook her head. "Is it?" she said. "That's quite interesting."

Beau frowned. "Why?"

Marianne bit her lip. She stood and clasped her hands over the back of the chair. "I need to go check on something. I think I might have an idea. I'll meet you at your room at midnight."

CHAPTER THIRTY-TWO

Marianne hesitated a moment before she knocked on Beau's door at midnight. Earlier, she *had* left the alcove above the ballroom in order to follow her suspicion—but she'd also needed to leave in order to remove herself from his presence.

Beau teaching her how to waltz had nearly turned her into a puddle, and she hadn't trusted herself not to hurl herself into his arms and kiss him as she'd been longing to do since she'd met him in the servants' staircase this evening.

His strong arms, his broad shoulders, and the way he led her in the dance, teaching her so expertly. It had all been more than she could bear. That combined with the scent of his soap and the memories of their nights together flashing through her mind, and she'd been nothing but pleased to have seen something in the ballroom that had made her need to leave the room. She had to wonder if it was a good idea to be entering his bedchamber tonight.

The clock at the end of the upper servants' corridor began to chime, pulling her from her thoughts. At the far end of the hall, a door opened. Marianne sucked in her breath and pressed her back against the wall next to Beau's door.

She watched as a woman emerged from one of the bedchambers and made her way toward the staircase in the middle of the floor. Marianne expelled her pent-up breath. Thank heavens the woman hadn't come all the way down to the servant's staircase at the end where Marianne was hiding.

As soon as the maid had disappeared from sight, Marianne spun around and quickly knocked on Beau's door.

The door flew open nearly immediately and Beau pulled her inside. "Where have you been?" His voice was quiet but harsh. "I was worried about you."

Marianne eyed him carefully. She could see the apprehension in his eyes. "You were worried? About me?"

Beau paced away from her and scrubbed a hand through his blond hair. "Yes, damn it. I was. I didn't know where you'd gone or why. I thought perhaps you might need my help."

"I'm sorry I worried you," she said, somewhat taken aback by his admission. "But I had to check on something."

He turned back to face her. "Yes, you said as much. What did you find out?"

Marianne folded her hands together in front of her. "When you told me the man in the blue coat was Baron Winfield, a few things began to make sense."

Beau eyed her carefully. "What things?"

She inclined her head to one side. "Well, I'd certainly hate to have to inform Miss Wharton, but I saw the baron coming out of a maid's room at Lord Clayton's house party quite early one morning and in…ahem…a disheveled state of dress."

Beau's brows shot up. "Did you? Whose room?"

"That's what I went to check. When I asked Mrs.

Cotswold at Clayton's estate, she told me it was the room of a maid named Albina. Tonight, I went to see if the Winfields were staying overnight."

"'Albina'?" Beau echoed. "I've heard that name before — seems Kendall mentioned it was the name of Frances's lady's maid."

Marianne nodded. "Well, that would explain how Albina and Baron Winfield know each other."

Beau plucked at his lip. "It would, indeed. But why do you think Baron Winfield and Albina have anything to do with the Bidassoa traitor?"

Marianne cocked her head to the side again. "When I was watching the ballroom earlier, I wasn't only watching Lord Cunningham."

Beau narrowed his eyes on her. "Who were you watching?"

"When I noticed Baron Winfield, I began watching him," Marianne replied.

"And?"

"And he nodded his head toward Lord Cunningham three times in a row," Marianne continued. "Lord Cunningham nodded back."

Beau bit the inside of his cheek. He hadn't even *seen* Baron Winfield until Marianne had pointed him out. Beau had been too busy watching Lord Hightower and the other two men. "Did you already suspect Baron Winfield for some reason before the party?"

"No. But tonight I remembered seeing him on the fourth floor at Lord Clayton's house, and I inquired about who he was. The truth is… I've suspected Albina. I had an… encounter with her at Lord Clayton's party, and she seemed a bit…odd. I can't say exactly how."

Beau nodded slowly. "I know precisely what you mean.

I've had that same feeling about many people, time and again. In our line of work, it's important to follow such instincts."

"I agree, which is why I wanted to learn Baron Winfield's identity."

"You think Albina and Baron Winfield are involved?"

"I think it's possible. And I suppose you never suspected a woman being involved, either, did you?"

Beau arched a brow. "Why do you say that?"

"Because since I'm a woman, you never suspected me of being a spy. You seem to have a problem with women, Agent B."

Beau put his hands on his hips. "I suspected you once. I even looked for your handwriting."

She covered her mouth to keep from laughing too loud. "You didn't?"

"Of course I did."

"Well, I suspected you too, so we're even."

"Of course you did." He scrubbed his hand through his hair again. "Albina. Damn it. You're right. I never suspected her or Baron Winfield."

"Perhaps it takes a woman to watch a woman," Marianne replied, grinning at him wickedly.

"Perhaps." Beau returned her smile before he tugged at his bottom lip again. "Now that you mention it, Kendall did write and tell me that Winfield was desperate for coin. The baron has even sold his London town house. As his future son-in-law, Kendall is giving Winfield an allowance—but also mentioned that he's doling out the money carefully, which means Winfield is hardly wealthy."

"That makes sense, because I was able to confirm that both Albina and Winfield are staying here overnight. In fact, I just saw her leave her room down the hall as the clock struck midnight. Care to follow her with me?"

Beau's shrewd gaze caught hers. "You think she's going to meet up with Winfield?"

"Yes —apparently, his wife and he are not sharing a bedchamber, and I just so happen to know which room is his. I asked about that downstairs, too."

Beau arched a brow. "Lead the way, Agent M."

CHAPTER THIRTY-THREE

Marianne hurried out of Beau's door toward the end of the hall and the servants' staircase landing.

Beau followed closely behind her, while continuing to scan the space for anyone else who might see them together. Thankfully the corridor remained empty until they made it into the stairwell.

They quickly and quietly descended the stairs, careful not to speak to each other, knowing that when following someone in a crowded house at night, the fewer words spoken, the better.

When they reached the third-floor landing, Beau motioned for Marianne to stay against the wall while he nudged the door open a crack with his boot and peered out.

Marianne pressed her back against the wall and waited. Beau soon let the door quietly shut again.

"It's clear. Which room is it?" he asked.

"The fourth door on the left," Marianne replied.

Beau nodded. "Very well. I hope whoever told you that was correct. I suppose there's only one way to find out."

Pushing the stairwell door open using his hand this time, Beau silently moved it until it was wide enough for Marianne to fit through. He followed behind her. They both kept their backs to the wall and remained in the shadows. Any servant or guest might wander into the long hallway at any moment. They had to be prepared to either flee or hide.

Marianne was the first to arrive at the fourth door on the right. She pointed at it and Beau nodded. She leaned forward and placed her ear against the solid wood. Muffled voices came from inside.

Beau crept over and crouched down in front of the door. He put his ear against the keyhole and nodded to Marianne to indicate that he could hear.

"It's Baron Winfield," he whispered. "I know his voice."

"Can you tell who he's with?" Marianne asked.

"Definitely not Lady Winfield," Beau whispered back, "but a female."

"Albina," Marianne said with a nod. She crouched beside Beau so they both could hear. Being so close to him was doing funny things to her insides. But at the moment she didn't want to examine too closely the feelings that were careening inside of her.

She shook her head to clear it of the unhelpful thoughts.

"Can you hear?" Beau asked in a whisper, his mouth so close to hers that she felt his breath against her lips. She had to fight the urge to close her eyes against the pang of lust that shot through her.

"Yes," she managed with a nod.

They stayed there like that, crouching next to the door in the shadows while they listened to the exchange in the room.

"Come ta bed, me dear," Albina said.

"Not yet, darling. I need your help tonight," Baron Winfield answered.

"Help?" Albina's tone sounded both surprised and confused. "Help wit wot?"

"I need you to write another letter for me," Baron Winfield said, his tone wheedling.

Beau exchanged a loaded glance with Marianne.

Albina sighed. "Another letter? Are ye mad? I thought we was all done wit that. We about got our heads skinned the last time."

Baron Winfield chuckled. "No one ever found out, and you know it. But this *will* be the last time, I promise."

"Ye *promise*?" Albina repeated, her voice coy, clearly warming to the topic.

"Yes, and I'll give you extra coin for your help, just like last time," Baron Winfield added.

"Ye'd better," came Albina's reply.

There was some shuffling around in the room. Beau suspected that Albina was taking a seat at a writing desk.

"Now, wot do ye want me ta write, *milord*?" Albina asked with a giggle.

"Here, I've already written it. All you need to do is transcribe this. I intend to burn this one."

Another sigh from Albina. "Very well. But this don't change our plans, do it?"

"On the contrary, my dear, this letter is part of our plans. An important part."

"We're still leaving for France tomorrow, ain't we?" Albina asked next.

Beau exchanged another tense glance with Marianne.

"Of course, my darling. My idiotic future son-in-law thinks he can purchase me with a pittance of an allowance. Little does he know I have my *own* fortune waiting for me. And this time I'm taking the letter to France myself, to avoid any surprises."

Beau motioned for Marianne to go back toward the

servants' staircase. They'd already heard enough. Baron Winfield wasn't planning on dictating the letter at any rate.

Apparently, Baron Winfield and Albina were planning to leave together for France tomorrow. Beau and Marianne would somehow have to find out what was in that letter. It was certain to be far from a simple task.

CHAPTER THIRTY-FOUR

Beau and Marianne raced down the servants' staircase until they made it to the back stoop of the property. Marianne led the way around the side of the building until they reached the street. Despite the late hour, they quickly flagged down a hackney coach, and Beau directed the driver to a certain unassuming address on Shepherd Street.

Not half an hour later, they were standing in front of their commanding officer, General Mark Grimaldi. *Of course* Grim was there at that hour. The man did nothing but work.

They quickly informed him of the events of the evening, including the letter that Albina had written.

"You've no idea of the contents?" Grim asked, stroking his chin.

"No. We'll need to intercept it before they leave for France," Beau replied.

"We can't," Grimaldi shot back. "If we do that, they'll be on to us, and they won't go. We'll have no way of knowing who Winfield is working for."

"What are you saying?" Beau asked, but the excitement

that rose in his chest told him he already had an inkling.

Grim clenched his jaw. "I think you know precisely what I'm saying. We need more than the letter, Bell. We need to know who Winfield intends to meet in France."

Beau and Marianne exchanged yet another knowing look.

Grimaldi shook his head. "Damn it. It was Winfield all along, wasn't it?" The general hated to be wrong. "I was convinced it was Hightower."

"I suspect Winfield was working with Cunningham, too," Marianne replied. "Someone had to give Winfield the information from the special council."

"Yes, well, as soon as we get proof, the bastards will wish they were dead by the time I get through with them." Grim turned to face both of them. "Now, as for the two of you, your orders are to follow Winfield to France, find out who he's working with there, and secure incontrovertible evidence that he's the Bidassoa traitor, starting with that damned new letter."

"Yes, General," they both replied with sharp nods.

Grimaldi's nostrils flared. "Don't let him out of your sight."

I<small>T WAS</small> imperative for Beau to speak to Worth right away. After concluding their meeting with Grim, Beau had hired another hackney coach to rush him and Marianne over to the duke's town house.

Now, standing at Beau's side on the stoop, Marianne seemed uncertain about banging on the door of such a prestigious-looking town house in such a notable part of Mayfair at this hour of the morning.

"If you're quite certain about this," she whispered just before Beau began knocking.

"I'm entirely certain," he replied. "Worth is a good friend of mine." He cleared his throat. "Ahem, *the Duke of Worthington*, I mean."

Marianne's eyes went wide. "We're in front of a duke's door!" she cried, as her voice went up an octave.

"Yes, don't worry. Leave everything to me," Beau replied in a perfectly calm tone.

But when the sleepy-looking butler, Lawson, finally pulled open Worth's door, Beau didn't hesitate. "I need to speak to Lord Worthington," Beau thundered, "immediately."

Stolidly, the butler replied, "His Grace is asleep at the moment. What time is it?"

It might have been somewhere around three o'clock in the morning—Beau wasn't entirely certain—but he didn't give a bloody damn. This was important.

"I don't care what time it is, let me in," Beau replied, leaning forward, ready to use force against the man to gain entrance, if necessary.

"My master is asleep, my lord," Lawson repeated. "I will tell him you were here."

The fool was about to close the door—and Beau was about to push his boot against it and sock the sop in the jaw —when Worth's voice sounded from somewhere in the foyer. "It's all right, Lawson. Let him in."

Finally, Lawson stepped aside and opened the door wide enough to allow Beau entry. The butler even had the audacity to bow to him.

Beau marched inside, pulling Marianne along with him.

Worth was standing at the bottom of the balustrade. The duke blinked at them. "Care to tell me why you're here at this hour, Bell?"

Beau kept his face blank. There was little time for explanation. "We've found the Bidassoa traitor. We need to leave for France immediately, and we need your help."

CHAPTER THIRTY-FIVE

As it turned out, the Duke of Worthington owned some ships. Not just some ships—more accurately, a *fleet* of ships—and Beau hoped that, despite the blockade, the man had enough clout to get him and Marianne onto one of them that was headed to France, in the middle of the night.

Marianne waited in a large, comfortable chair in the duke's study, while Lady Julianna Montgomery, who had apparently spent the night with the duke, brought her a blanket and a cup of hot tea. Marianne wasn't about to judge either of them. She had no right to do so. And at any rate, the couple seemed to be very much in love.

Marianne had noticed Beau exchange a glance with the duke when Julianna had appeared. Worthington had merely shrugged before announcing that he and Julianna were betrothed.

The men worked out the details of the expedition while Lady Julianna was kind enough to remain quiet and not pepper Marianne with questions.

After the arrangements had been made, Beau and Marianne returned to Lord Copperpot's town house in the wee hours of the morning.

Beau drafted a letter for Lord Copperpot, informing the man that he had to leave immediately due to an unexpected illness in his family. He assured his former master that Mr. Broughton had already been sent for. Grimaldi had seen to that.

Marianne wrote a similar letter for Lady Wilhelmina. If she hadn't come to precisely *like* the young woman, at least she'd come to worry about her. Grimaldi had promised to ensure a suitable lady's maid would be found for her as well.

Marianne and Beau waited in the servants' hall beneath the staircase until they heard a footman come downstairs to indicate that Baron Winfield had ordered his coach put to. Apparently, the good baron wanted a ride to the docks.

As soon as Baron Winfield and Albina drove off, Marianne and Beau rushed across the roadway and hopped into a coach that General Grimaldi had ordered for them, waiting across the street.

The coachman gave them a letter from Grimaldi, which Beau promptly ripped open and Marianne read over his shoulder.

AGENTS M&B,

We've learned which ship they're taking. It's one of Worthington's—the same one you'll be traveling on as well. Stay in your cabin. Pretend you're a married couple.

G

THEY BOTH REMAINED silent for the remainder of the ride to the docks, while visions of all the things that could go wrong spun themselves through Marianne's brain. She'd never left

England before on a mission. She'd never left England before at all. To date, her work as a spy had involved serving as a lady's maid and listening at keyholes, but this, *this* was an entirely different type of mission. One that posed a great deal of danger.

She did her best to be brave, telling herself that obviously General Grimaldi thought she was up for the task or he wouldn't have given her orders to go. Besides, she had Beau at her side, and from what she'd learned about him, he was an experienced agent indeed.

Sailing to France would accomplish more than one of her goals, however. She'd already intended that after she had discovered the identity of the man who'd killed Frederick, she would travel to France to attempt to locate her brother, David—or die trying. This new turn of events would merely help her accomplish the second task more quickly. Did it matter that her insides were a mass of nerves and she just might cast up her accounts at any moment?

Despite her misgivings, she plastered a confident demeanor on her face for Beau's sake. He didn't need to see to her while he concentrated on such an important mission. No. She would take care of herself, and do her best to see that Baron Winfield and Albina were brought to justice.

In a matter of only a few hours, Marianne and Beau boarded the ship and were already on their way out to sea. The ride along the Thames and out into the channel was a particularly choppy one. And the October wind that sheared through the ship's wooden slats made the stateroom they'd been assigned extremely cold. The entire ordeal was made all the worse by the fact that they were confined to a cabin the approximate size of a hat box. And *not* for a big hat.

Additionally, there was only one bunk. One *tiny* bunk. Marianne took one look at it and decided not to think about it again until she had to. Instead she went about putting away the few articles of clothing she'd managed to stuff into her old, worn valise before they'd rushed off to the docks. Beau had quickly and efficiently put his things in the wardrobe before tucking his rucksack into the bottom of the cabinet.

To quell her nerves, Marianne next began looking through every drawer in the cabin. When she opened a cabinet above the small desk, she smiled. There sat a bottle of brandy and two glasses, with a note that she plucked up to read.

To MAKE *the journey more palatable,*
    Worth

"SEEMS THE DUKE LEFT US A GIFT." Marianne sat the note on the edge of the desk before pulling the bottle and the glasses from the cabinet. She set all three on the desk as well.

Beau picked up the note and read it, shaking his head. "That fool. He knows I don't drink."

"I do." The words shot from Marianne's mouth.

Beau inclined his head toward her. "By all means, please, enjoy it."

Marianne didn't need to be told twice. Brandy might be just the thing to calm her nerves at the moment. She opened the bottle and poured a healthy glass for herself. "You're certain you don't want any?"

Beau shook his head. "No, thank you." He took a seat on the edge of the bunk.

Marianne lifted the glass to her nose and sniffed its contents.

"Have you had brandy before?" Beau asked, a frown marring his brow.

"Yes," she replied. "But not often. My brothers and I were

always daring each other to do certain things. Taking a nip from Papa's brandy bottle was sometimes one of them."

Beau laughed at that. "I wish I'd had a brother."

Marianne smiled. "I loved growing up with brothers. They taught me everything they knew, but they also always made certain I was safe."

Beau braced his hands on the wooden frame of the bunk and scraped his boot along the wooden floorboards. "They sound as if they were quite good brothers. I'm sorry about Frederick."

Marianne swallowed. Tears had sprung to her eyes. She shook her head to dispel them. "I still have David at least. That is…I hope I do."

Beau turned his head to look at her. "Do you have any idea where he's being kept?"

"No. But as soon as I find out who murdered Frederick, I intend to search for him."

Beau's brows shot up. "With General Grimaldi's blessing?"

Marianne lifted her chin and swallowed. "I won't need General Grimaldi's blessing. In fact, after this is through, I intend to stay in France to look for David."

His brows inched even higher. "Really?"

"That's right." She nodded firmly. "I'm not coming back without him."

"I can understand that," Beau replied. "If I had a brother who was in trouble, I'd go to the ends of the earth to save him, too."

Marianne lifted the glass and eyed the amber liquid. "You said you don't have a brother. Do you have any sisters?"

"Yes, a younger sister, Annabelle. She's quite safe in London, however."

"How old is she?" Marianne asked, trying to picture a sister who looked and acted anything like Beau.

"Twenty-two."

"Is she married?"

"Not yet. Annabelle's a bit...spirited. At least that's the word my mother likes to use. To date, she's refused all offers —and there have been over a dozen."

"Are you close to her?"

"Not especially. She's a wonderful young lady, it's just that I've been...distracted."

"With your work?" Marianne prodded.

"Precisely." Beau sighed and scrubbed a hand across his face.

Marianne lifted the glass to her lips and finally took a tentative sip of the brandy. As soon as it touched her tongue, she frowned. "Ugh. It's just as awful as I remember it."

Beau smiled and shook his head.

Still clutching the glass, Marianne glanced around. The only other place to sit in the small room besides the bunk was the chair in front of the desk, but instead of pulling it out, she stepped over to the bed and sat a pace away from Beau. "Have you ever tried brandy before?" she asked, lifting the liquid up to the light.

"No." He shook his head. "I can honestly say the stuff has never touched my lips."

"What about port?" she asked next.

"Never," he replied.

"Really?" Marianne blinked and took another sip. Another frown followed. "That's surprising. I thought all gentlemen of the *ton* liked brandy and port."

"Not me." His voice was tight, and he was staring straight ahead at the wooden wall above the desk with a faraway but determined look in his eye.

"Why is that?" Marianne ventured.

Beau shook his head and quickly stood. "I need to go speak to the captain before we're underway."

Marianne lowered the glass to her lap and blinked at him. "What? Why? General Grimaldi said we should stay in the cabin."

"I'll be careful," Beau replied stoically before quickly opening the door and disappearing into the narrow passageway without another word.

Staring after him, Marianne took a hefty sip of her brandy. Just as she remembered, it tasted better after a few sips. Or, more precisely, her tongue was numb enough not to notice the taste after a few sips. Much better that way.

She sloshed the dark liquid around the short glass. Why was Beau still so reluctant to tell her his reasons for not drinking? He hadn't answered her when she'd asked at the servants' dinner at Clayton's house. She'd assumed it was because he'd got jug-bitten too many times. But apparently, he'd never even tasted the stuff. That was interesting. Whatever his reason, he clearly was uneasy about it; she'd never seen the man leave a room so quickly.

She stood and set her brandy glass on the desk before opening the small wardrobe that was built into the wall. Her things and Beau's were intermingled. A pang of some unexpected emotion reverberated through her chest. They were pretending to be a married couple. Something that could never truly happen. But seeing their clothes hanging in the wardrobe together, it felt real. If only for a moment.

Glancing at the door to ensure he wasn't coming back right away, Marianne leaned into the wardrobe and sniffed his shirt. Ah, it smelled like him. A mixture of soap and man and something indefinable that was unique to only Beau.

Confound it. She was sniffing shirts. She'd clearly gone mad. Sighing, she closed the wardrobe doors and turned back to stare at the tiny bunk. How in the world would they manage to sleep in that thing together without her wanting to rip off his clothing?

She giggled as she picked up the glass again and finished off the brandy. She was already feeling light-headed. Perhaps if she kept drinking, she wouldn't keep herself from ripping off his clothing. *Perhaps.*

BEAU DIDN'T RETURN until it was dark outside. Marianne had spent the day convinced he'd either been found by Baron Winfield or tossed off the ship by the captain for some reason. She was just about to go in search of him when he came barreling through the door with a tangle of rope and some books in his arms.

"Where've you been?" The question flew from her mouth. Oh, she was doing quite a fine job at sounding like a wife, wasn't she?

A hint of remorse showed on Beau's features. "I was with the captain. He's having dinner sent to us."

"That's nice of him," she replied before gesturing to the items he was carrying. "What's that for?"

First, he held up the three books. "I got these from the captain. I thought you might like them to pass the time tomorrow."

A secret thrill shot through her. She loved to read. She took the books and placed them in the cabinet. *The Taming of the Shrew*, *The History of Tom Jones*, and *Sense and Sensibility*. She had to admit, the man had made excellent choices.

"What's that?" She pointed at the tangled rope.

"This is a hammock. I thought I'd try to string it up to sleep on it."

Disappointment shot through Marianne's chest. Apparently, he'd been thinking about the size of the bunk too, and had made arrangements to avoid it.

They both looked around the tiny cabin for a few moments.

"There doesn't seem much of a place to string it," Marianne pointed out.

Beau winced. "I was afraid that might be the case."

"It's all right," Marianne replied. "The wind is picking up. If we share the bunk, we can share heat."

Beau arched a brow. "If you insist." His grin was unrepentant.

"Not for *that* reason," she said, her cheeks burning.

"Very well, but you need only say the word," he replied.

Marianne couldn't help the rush of heat that spread through her limbs at his words. She shouldn't be looking forward to sharing the tiny bunk with him, so why was she?

Beau stashed the useless hammock in the wardrobe as a knock sounded at the door. "Who is it?" he said in an accent he'd affected.

"It's dinner, Mr. Baxter, sir," a voice called back.

Beau nodded at Marianne before moving past her to open the door. A cabin boy shuffled in with a tray on his shoulder. Leaning down, he placed the tray on the desk, then turned around and doffed his cap. "The captain says if there be anything else ye need, just let me know," the boy said, pointing a thumb at his chest.

Beau flipped the lad a coin and he shuffled back out of the room as quickly as he'd come.

Marianne nearly jumped from the bed to examine the meal. "I'm starving," she announced before removing the lid from one of the platters to reveal a healthy portion of stew, a biscuit, and some peas.

"It looks delicious," she said, her stomach growling.

"Leave it to Worth to have a decent meal on a ship," Beau replied.

"Perhaps that why Baron Winfield chose it," Marianne said with a laugh.

Beau took his platter and sat on the bed to eat, leaving the desk and chair for Marianne.

AN HOUR LATER, they had consumed the meal and the dishes had been removed by the cabin boy, who'd reappeared at precisely the right time; and Marianne had imbibed a bit more brandy.

Beau blew out his breath gave her an apprehensive look. "Well." He gestured toward the bunk. "Shall we?"

Marianne tossed back the rest of her second glass of brandy. She wasn't jug-bitten, but she was certainly less anxious than she had been before she'd imbibed. "Yes," she said with a resolute nod.

"I can wait in the corridor while you—" He gestured toward the wardrobe.

"No, need," she replied. "If you'll just…turn your back."

"Of course," he said, spinning on his heel in a flash.

Marianne had to squelch her laugh. It was a bit ridiculous after all, considering the man had seen her entirely in the nude already on more than one occasion. At the moment, however, they were nothing but colleagues, and colleagues needed to turn their backs when changing clothes and sharing bedchambers.

She pulled her nightrail from the wardrobe and quickly divested herself of her gown. She was dressed and under the covers before she announced, "I'm decent."

"I'm sorry to hear that," came Beau's sardonic reply.

She pressed her lips together to keep from smiling and turned her head toward the wall so he could undress.

"I, er, normally sleep in the nude," he said.

Marianne gulped. "Well, uh, could you, perhaps, keep your breeches on tonight?"

"I can do that," he replied, humor edging his voice.

Moments later, his weight settled onto the bunk beside her. They bumped into each other and both apologized before she nearly rolled herself flat against the wall on the far side of the bunk to keep from touching him.

"That cannot be comfortable," he said with a chuckle.

"It's not," she admitted with a laugh, partially rolling back onto the mattress.

They laid like that, side-by-side, the entire lengths of their bodies touching from their shoulders to their legs.

"Comfortable?" Beau finally asked.

"Better," she admitted. She was staring at the ceiling as if the dark brown wooden slats were the most fascinating things she'd ever encountered.

Beau leaned up on one elbow and blew out the lantern that hung above them. "I suppose this is as comfortable as we're going to get."

"I suppose so." Marianne lay there in the darkness for what felt like endless moments, willing her breath to slow and her heartbeat to return to normal. Touching him, smelling him, being this close, was torture. Why hadn't she tried harder to find a place for that confounded hammock?

She was hoping against hope that he'd fall asleep quickly. But she already knew from the nights they'd spent together that he wasn't one to do so. In fact, previously they'd stayed up together for hours and talked. She again turned on her side toward the wall and tucked her hands beneath her head.

A few more endless moments ticked by before his voice sounded in the darkness. "I should have taken the hammock," he breathed.

"Why?" she breathed back.

"Because even just lying next to you like this, I'm so hard it's painful."

Marianne shuddered. She could no longer deny the overwhelming attraction she had toward this man. She wanted nothing more than to turn into his arms and kiss him. But instead she whispered, "Touch me, Beau."

His arms enveloped her from behind. His mouth came to nuzzle at her neck and his hand moved down her leg to pull up her nightrail.

His fingers moved between her legs to tease her most intimate spot and he hooked her leg over the outside of his thigh before freeing himself from his breeches. She felt him probing between her legs, hot and hard before he slowly slid inside of her, giving them both what they wanted.

Marianne closed her eyes. They both groaned.

It had been so long. Too long. And she'd wanted him every single day. She wanted this. Had wanted it for weeks. Had missed it for weeks. But until he'd touched her again, she hadn't realized how much she'd missed it.

"Oh, God, Marianne. You don't know how much I've wanted you," he breathed against her ear before he stroked inside of her again. "So much." Another stroke. "For so long." A third stroke.

Marianne was mindless. His hand hadn't stopped touching her and his finger was rubbing her in little circles that made her hips arch into his hand. His mouth continued to suck at her neck and her nipples tingled as he stroked into her again and again and again.

"Come with me," he pleaded.

Her legs shook, and when she finally fell over the precipice, she buried her face into the pillow so she wouldn't be too loud.

As always, he was careful to withdraw and spill his seed against her backside, a shuddering groan torn from his lips.

She'd wanted it. There was no question, but now that it was over, she knew what a costly mistake it had been.

She waited until he left the bunk and used a towel from the handbasin in the corner near the door to wipe up before she said, "This can't happen again."

"Why? I've wanted you for weeks, Marianne. I never stopped wanting you."

"I've wanted you every bit as much, but…" Marianne bit her lip. "We both know there's no future between a lady's maid and a marquess."

CHAPTER THIRTY-SIX

The next morning, Beau was up with the sun. He'd already decided there was no way he could spend the day with Marianne. He'd brought her the books yesterday out of guilt, and today he was happy she had them when he left to go speak to the captain again. Captain Jones was a friend of both his and Worth's, and the man was well aware that he had a potential traitor on board.

Jones and Beau had made a plan for Winfield to be followed should Beau and Marianne be separated from them somehow when the ship docked in France.

Beau told himself that he'd been working, and needed to focus on the mission. That was why he hadn't spent time in the cabin with Marianne. But the truth was that he had to reluctantly agree that she was right. He shouldn't have made love to her last night. It was unfair to her to prolong it. What was it about that woman that made him so insane that he couldn't stop touching her or wanting her?

She was right. There could be no future between a marquess and a lady's maid, and more and more of late, no matter how outlandish or impossible it might seem, Beau *wanted* a future with her. He'd considered asking her if she would be his partner on his next mission. They made a good team, the two of them. He'd never wanted to work with a partner before, but having a female partner did allow for some conveniences, such as pretending they were a married couple.

But marriage? No. That was out of the question. He didn't even know who she was. He might know her last name, but as far as he knew, she was merely the daughter of a man whose sons were in the military.

There was no way he could make her his marchioness even if he wanted to, and…God, marriage hadn't ever been anything he'd thought about truly. He supposed he'd need to marry and produce an heir someday, but he'd been so attached to his work, he hadn't had time to contemplate the sort of life that would be, or the type of changes he would be forced to make as a result.

Now, with Marianne, for the first time, he was beginning to contemplate all of it. And even though on more than one occasion, he'd looked down the barrel of a pistol just before a man shot at him, Beau had never been more frightened.

WHEN BEAU RETURNED after dark again, Marianne had finished the brandy bottle. Brandy wasn't so bad, it turned out, when one had nothing else to drink. Oh, she'd spent much of the day reading. Reading and fantasizing about Beau's hand on her thigh last night, his fingers making her cry out his name. The images of their lovemaking had flashed through her mind again and again today, making reading slow-going. But she'd still managed to put a decent dent in *Sense and Sensibility* by the time he returned. She'd enjoyed it. One of the characters had her name.

They finished dinner and it was cleared away before Marianne came over to join him on the bunk. She sat next to him, letting her feet dangle off the side. "You don't need to speak to the captain again tonight, do you?"

His brow furrowed. "No. Why?"

"Because I want to ensure you don't have anywhere to run off to before I ask you again why you don't drink."

The barest hint of a flinch crossed over his features. "You noticed I didn't want to talk about it, eh?" he said with a humorless laugh.

"It was quite noticeable," she replied, nodding.

He'd already removed his boots and he scooted back on the bunk until his back rested against the wall. Marianne scooted back to join him.

"It can't be that bad," she said. "You can tell me." Their hands rested together, their fingers touching on the mattress.

Beau expelled a deep breath and laid his forearm atop his head. "My father drank." He paused for a moment, staring forward. "To excess."

The ship swayed and Marianne had to brace herself against the roll, clutching Beau's shoulder. "I see," she said solemnly.

The ship righted itself again and Beau continued, "When I was a boy, I promised myself that I would never drink."

"I hope I didn't make you uncomfortable when I drank," she said quietly.

"Not at all. Most of my friends do. Worthington and Kendall certainly do."

Marianne paused for a moment before asking her next question. "Was your father...angry when he drank?"

Beau scrubbed a hand across his forehead. "Very. But mostly toward my mother, not me."

"Oh, Beau, no," Marianne said. Instinctively she clutched his hand and squeezed it.

Beau squeezed back. "I don't like to talk about it."

"I can understand that," she replied.

He stared at the wall above the desk again, unseeing. "When I was young, I remember bruises on my mother. Marks on her wrists. I didn't understand." He took another deep breath. "But as I grew older, I heard them argue. I would go to her room, try to stop him."

Marianne swallowed hard. "That was quite brave. How old were you?"

"Seven, eight?" He shook his head. "I came away with a bruise or two, but that wasn't what I couldn't stand. I didn't mind getting hurt myself. I couldn't stand knowing that I couldn't stop him from hurting her." His jaw clenched. Anger flashed in his sky-blue eyes like lightning on a clear day.

Marianne placed her hand on his shoulder. "It must have been awful for you."

"It was. Until I got big enough to fight back. When I was twelve, I was home from Eton, finally tall enough to fight him." He shook his head slowly, the memory clearly replaying in his mind with vivid force. "I punched that son of a bitch in the mouth and I told him if he ever laid a hand on my mother again, I would kill him."

Marianne nodded slowly. "Understandable. Did it stop him?"

Beau rubbed the back of his neck. "He never touched her again."

"That's good."

"It was good...until..." Another deep breath. "On his death bed, my father asked for me. I refused to come."

Her breathing hitched. "Oh, Beau. I don't blame you."

"I never saw him again. My mother told me that he'd wanted to apologize. He'd wanted to ask for forgiveness. I never gave him that chance."

Marianne shook her head. "You cannot blame yourself for that choice."

"It was the biggest mistake I've ever made. Everyone deserves forgiveness. My mother had forgiven him. Why couldn't I?"

Marianne nodded slowly. "I do know what you mean. The last time I saw Frederick, we argued. He didn't like the man who was courting me. He didn't think he was a good choice for me. I've wished every day since that I'd had a chance to truly say good-bye. I regret it, too."

He smiled at her wanly. "But I *knew* I'd never have another chance. I refused to take it because of my stubborn pride."

"Thank you for telling me," she whispered. "I hope you don't mind my saying that the reason you're such a good man may very well be because of the pain in your childhood."

Beau nodded. "Yes, well, my father's drinking is one reason I understand men like Mr. Broughton. They'll do anything for the chance to drink. They're slaves to the bottle."

"It's why you're a spy, too, isn't it?"

Beau bit the inside of his cheek. "I suppose I've always been preoccupied with justice being served."

She squeezed his hand again. "It's not a bad trait to have, Beau. Not bad at all."

"I suppose it's time for bed." He pushed himself off the bunk and turned around while she changed into her night rail. Then she climbed into bed, and he pulled off his shirt. They laid down together on the bunk and he blew out the lantern.

"Marianne," came his voice in the darkness, "are you truly a lady's maid? Your real accent, it would be at home in the drawing rooms of the *Beau Monde*."

"I'm not a lady's maid at the moment. I'm a spy. But I'm

215

not a marchioness. Or suitable to be one, if that's what you're asking."

~

MARIANNE SPENT the time as they neared Calais pretending to read, but all she could think about was how her relationship with Beau would end.

He'd asked if she was truly a lady's maid. Well, she hadn't been one until Lady Courtney had hired her, but then her brother had been killed and she'd met General Grimaldi and been trained to become a spy. She'd been encouraged to take the position with Lord Copperpot because of the suspicions of him being the Bidassoa traitor.

In truth, she didn't know *who* she was any more. After her father died, her mother had gone into such deep mourning she scarcely spoke, then she'd died not a year later. David and Frederick had both been gone to war. Marianne had had little choice but to find a suitable position for herself. Fortunately, her father's friend Lady Courtney had offered Marianne the position of companion while she waited for her own niece to become available.

Marianne had become so single-minded after Frederick's death that she scarcely remembered any plans before that. At one point, she'd met William. But that had been over quickly. He'd been gone before she'd barely got a chance to get her hopes up for a life with a husband and children. She'd settled back into thinking she would remain a lady's maid, when the news had come about Frederick.

Her feelings for William paled in comparison to what she'd been feeling for Beau these past weeks. And that's what made it so frightening. Beau had the ability to crush her heart. For some reason with William, she'd stupidly told herself that their love—a love that didn't even exist as far as

216

he was concerned—would be enough to overcome Society's judgement of him marrying beneath his station in life as a knight.

But she'd quickly learned that that had never been true, and never would be true. William had had no intention of marrying her; he'd only used her.

She was not worthy of a marquess and she never would be. And her time with Beau was coming to an end. As soon as they arrested Winfield and Albina, Marianne would be off to look for David, and Beau would move on to his next mission. She would have to leave him soon. It was a thought she didn't want to contemplate.

THAT NIGHT in bed Beau wrapped his arms around her. "Just let me hold you, Marianne. That's all I want to do."

She let him because she wanted him to hold her. She closed her eyes and pretended things were different.

"Marianne, what if we were partners?" came his voice in the darkness.

"No."

"But why?"

She expelled her breath. He'd shared something difficult and painful with her. She supposed it was only fair that she shared something equally difficult and painful with him. "I'm afraid of getting hurt again. I told you I wasn't innocent. The truth is that I was seduced by a man who was a member of the *ton*."

"What? Who? Who hurt you?" His voice was filled with anger.

"His name was Sir William Godfrey."

"What happened?" He pushed himself up on his elbow and looked down at her in the darkness, stroking her cheek.

"He told me he loved me," Marianne continued. "He told me he'd do anything to marry me. But it was all a lot of lies."

"I won't lie to you, Marianne. I may have used a false name with you at first. But I would never lie to you the way he did."

All she could do was nod. He was right, after all. Beau had never said he loved her.

CHAPTER THIRTY-SEVEN

When the ship docked in Calais later the next afternoon, Beau was ready. He'd removed his pistol from the wardrobe and placed it into the back of his breeches. He and Marianne had packed their bags and had departed before the rest of the ship was allowed to, having been summoned by Captain Jones.

This put them in the perfect place to follow Winfield and Albina. Beau and Marianne were waiting outside a tavern across from the dock when the other couple disembarked.

Winfield and Albina quickly hailed a coach, and Beau and Marianne soon engaged a coach of their own.

"Follow that coach," Beau instructed the driver in French.

Marianne watched out the coach's window as they rattled off through the cobblestone streets of Calais. She had changed into a soft yellow gown with a high waist. It was one of only two that she had that weren't maid gowns.

They'd traveled for less than a quarter hour when the first coach began to slow.

"Keep going," Beau told the driver. "Turn the corner and

come to a stop on the other side of that building." He gestured to a large warehouse on the corner.

Once their coach rolled to a stop, Beau flipped the driver a coin. "Wait here."

Beau jumped from the coach and turned to help Marianne down before they made their way quickly to the side of the warehouse. Beau pressed his back against the wall and turned his head, peering around the corner to see if Winfield and Albina had alighted from their coach.

"They're getting out now," he informed Marianne.

Marianne nodded and waited for Beau to motion for her to follow him before they both turned the corner and made their way to the warehouse that Winfield and Albina had entered.

Once inside, footsteps above them on the shaky staircase to their right told them that Winfield and Albina were climbing the stairs. Beau and Marianne waited until the footsteps stopped and a door opened.

"Sounds as if they went up three floors," Beau said quietly.

He and Marianne climbed the stairs after them.

At the third floor, the staircase let out in front of a row of dark brown wooden doors. When he peeked into the corridor, Beau caught a glimpse of Albina's skirts disappearing through one of the many doors.

Again, he motioned for Marianne to follow him, and they made their way silently to the door and pressed their ears against it in two different spots. Unlike the doors made of solid wood at Lord Copperpot's town house in London, this door was flimsily constructed, and Beau could hear everything without crouching down to the keyhole.

After a few pleasantries were exchanged in French, Winfield said, "Do you have the money?"

"Do you have zee letter?" came a Frenchman's voice speaking in heavily accented English.

"Yes. Here it is," Winfield replied.

There was nothing but silence for a few moments and Beau could only guess that the Frenchman was reviewing the letter Albina had written.

Several moments of silence passed before the Frenchman finally said. "Very well. Everything looks to be in order."

"Where is my money?" Winfield demanded, his voice impatient.

"I don't keep zat sort of money here," the Frenchman replied. "You'll have to come out to the camp at Coulogne tomorrow."

"Damn it. You told me you'd have my money," Winfield insisted.

"I do have eet." The Frenchman's reply was terse. "But you must wait for tomorrow. Zere is no help for eet."

"Fine," Winfield replied. "Where is the camp?"

The Frenchman cleared his throat and lowered his voice. Beau had to concentrate to understand him. "Two hundred yards northeast of zee intersection of Coulogne Road and zee Andres Highway. Come and meet us. We'll share a bottle of wine, *mon ami*. Come after dark, say, nine o'clock?"

"Do I have a choice?" came Winfield's equally terse reply. "In the meantime, you'll understand if I just *keep* the letter."

Stepping away from the door, Beau motioned for Marianne to follow him again as he returned to the staircase. They'd heard enough. No doubt Winfield and Albina would be leaving the room at any moment.

Beau and Marianne barely had time to make it back to the stairs before the Frenchman's door cracked open. Rushing into the stairwell, they flew down to the next landing. When they got there, they opened the door and hid inside the second-floor corridor until Winfield and Albina passed them heading back down to the ground floor.

"That was close," Beau said after the door to the street opened and closed behind the other couple.

"Very," Marianne agreed before arching a brow. "Are you thinking what I'm thinking?"

They exchanged a look, then Beau nodded. "Baron Winfield is being set up by the French."

CHAPTER THIRTY-EIGHT

Beau and Marianne waited for Winfield's coach to pull away before they left the warehouse, hurrying back around the corner to their own waiting coach.

"Where to?" the driver asked.

"Follow them again, please," Beau replied.

This time, Winfield's coach made its way to a small hotel near the docks. Once Beau was convinced Winfield was checking in for the evening, Beau paid the driver and helped Marianne to alight. They gathered their bags and walked around the narrow streets for a bit before finding another hotel not far away. They checked in as Mr. and Mrs. Nicholas Baxter.

When they entered the room and Marianne saw that there were two beds instead of one, she breathed a sigh—relief or regret, she didn't know. One thing was certain, no more awkwardness like their nights on the ship.

"I asked for two beds," Beau said as if he'd read her thoughts.

"Thank you," she replied.

"I also ordered a meal to be sent up."

The meal arrived soon after and they ate mostly in silence, then waited for a servant to come clear away the dishes before Marianne asked Beau to turn around so she could change into her nightrail.

By the time he turned back around, she'd already climbed into the bed nearest the window and pulled the blankets up to her chin.

"I wonder if Albina will go to the camp with Baron Winfield tomorrow night?" Marianne mused as she tried to stare out the window instead of at Beau removing his shirt. The man obviously didn't care one whit if she saw him and his chest was definitely worth sneaking a look.

"She won't if she knows what's good for her, but we'll have to wait and see," Beau replied, shucking his boots before climbing into the other bed. "They seem to enjoy each other's company."

Marianne shook her head. "I can't imagine what Baron Winfield is thinking, leaving his wife and daughters like this. I get the impression his plan is to stay here with Albina once he gets his payment."

"He's obviously controlled by money," Beau replied, expelling his breath and shaking his head too. "I've seen it before. It's a hideous affliction."

"We shouldn't take a coach tomorrow night," Marianne said next.

"I agree. It will be far too obtrusive. I'll go out tomorrow and find us a mount. We'll both ride it."

Marianne nodded. Beau blew out the candle that rested on the small table between their beds and darkness descended. Marianne turned on her side to face the window. For some reason, melancholy engulfed her. She swallowed and shut her eyes, willing sleep to come as quickly as possible. She should be pleased they were so close to finally arresting the people responsible for Frederick's death, but each moment that ticked by was one step closer to her never seeing Beau again.

At this time tomorrow night, they might be in grave danger or their mission would be over, but one way or another, her time with Beau was coming to an end.

～

"WHAT ARE YOU WEARING?" Beau asked Marianne the next evening, looking her up and down after she'd told him he could turn back around because she was finished changing her clothing.

"A shirt and breeches, of course," Marianne replied with a laugh. She was already busily arranging her thick hair into a braid, which she wrapped around her head and covered with a dark cap.

"I had no idea you had a shirt and breeches in that bag," Beau breathed, his eyes wide. "Seems you're full of surprises, Agent M."

"I can't very well go traipsing around a French camp in my skirts." She pulled the cap down to her brow. "What do you think? Do I look like a convincing boy?"

"Not at all," Beau replied. "You look as beautiful as ever."

Marianne fought a blush. "Well, I can assure you when I wear this, no one suspects I'm a woman."

"Pity," Beau replied. "What did you do to your—?" He left off, pointing, obviously not wanting to say the word 'breasts' out loud.

Marianne laughed again. "I wrapped them with linen," she replied with a shrug.

"*That's* the *real* pity," Beau said, sighing and shaking his head.

"Might I remind you we have a very important mission to

accomplish tonight?" She crossed her arms over her flattened chest and arched a brow at Beau.

"Yes, I know. Let's go. It's nearly eight o' clock." Beau pulled open the door to the room and held it wide for Marianne.

"Remember, no more treating me like I'm a lady while we're in public. I'm a boy. My name is John Smith."

"*Excellent* name," Beau replied, following her out the door. "It must have taken you *ages* to come up with it."

Once outside, they walked the few streets over to stand in front of the stores across the street from Winfield's hotel.

They blended into the crowd and took turns walking up and down the street, pretending to be casually strolling.

When Winfield appeared, Beau caught Marianne's attention with a simple whistle. She turned to look at the entrance to the hotel across the street. Apparently, Albina didn't relish the idea of being left alone, because the maid was standing at the baron's side wearing a gaudy pink gown. Moments later, a coach pulled up and Winfield helped Albina inside before climbing up after her.

Beau had tied the mount he'd secured earlier to a post across the street from the hotel. As soon as Winfield and Albina's coach took off, Beau and Marianne quickly made their way to the stallion.

Beau mounted first and then reached down to pull Marianne up behind him. They followed the coach at a leisurely pace.

Thankfully, the road out to the Andres Highway was lined with trees, and they were able to pick their way behind the coach at a safe distance without being seen.

The journey took nearly an hour, and Marianne tried to make herself concentrate on the danger they were no doubt traveling directly into, instead of the feel of Beau's washboard-like abdomen beneath her fingertips.

Baron Winfield wasn't experienced with the French, but Marianne had heard enough stories during her training with General Grimaldi to know that the French rarely kept their promises to the traitors whom they fooled into helping them.

The fact that the Frenchman at the warehouse had refused to pay Winfield upon delivery was a dangerous sign, indeed. And Winfield, if he wasn't a *complete* fool, was probably more than a bit anxious about this meeting tonight.

Marianne and Beau had spoken about it today. Beau had refreshed her memory on a variety of hand signals they were to use if they were captured, or if one of them was in danger, or saw or sensed something 'off.' In fact, after Beau had secured their mount, they'd spent the better part of the afternoon and early evening ensuring that they were prepared for any eventuality.

Their goal was to secure the letter, if at all possible. Failing that, they needed to find out as much as they were able about Winfield's dealings with the French, and anything else that might be useful to the Home Office.

Over an hour later, Winfield's coach finally rattled to a stop at the intersection of Coulogne Road and the Andres Highway. Marianne and Beau waited in a copse of trees hundreds of yards away until the baron and the maid alighted and took off toward the northeast quadrant of the intersection.

Marianne and Beau waited for the two to disappear into the forest before tying their horse to a nearby tree and quietly but quickly following along behind Winfield and Albina. The coach the two had come in was waiting at the intersection, so Marianne and Beau were forced to stay inside the treeline, out of sight of the driver, as they followed Winfield and Albina toward the French camp.

The night was silent and clear, thank heavens, and the apprehension pumping through Marianne's body kept her from being cold, though a mid-October wind rustled the autumn leaves in the trees as they picked their way through the underbrush.

Finally, they approached a break in the trees, and Beau, who was in the lead, motioned for Marianne to stay back. He crouched down and she did too.

Several yards in front of them, Winfield and Albina were hidden in the trees on the edge of the clearing. They were obviously trying to decide how best to approach the camp.

"I want ta go wit ye, me dear," Albina said in a voice that was high-pitched enough for Marianne to hear.

"That fool will bring the entire camp on our heads," Beau whispered through clenched teeth.

Marianne merely nodded, keeping her eyes trained on the couple.

Apparently, Winfield convinced his mistress to lower her voice and follow him, because soon, the two of them emerged from the treeline and crept toward the French camp.

The camp itself wasn't as large as Marianne had expected. There were perhaps a dozen large tents set up in rows of three. Several horses and a carriage were tied to trees to the right of the tents, near the forest's edge. Smoke billowing from the far side of the camp indicated that the soldiers had a fire going over there, and singing and boisterousness told her some of them must be in their cups already.

Marianne and Beau watched until Winfield and Albina disappeared into the first row of tents on the edge of the camp.

"Should we follow them?" Marianne asked, her eyes darting back and forth.

"No, let's hang back and see what happens. If I don't mistake my guess, the good baron is about to either be shot or taken prisoner."

They waited in complete silence for what had to have been at least a quarter hour before a woman's scream startled them from their rigid positions crouching in the trees.

"Albina?' Marianne whispered.

Beau cursed under his breath. "I'd stake my fortune on it. Let's go."

They took off along the treeline, but instead of going left as Winfield and Albina had, Beau went right. They stayed inside the treeline, not venturing from that cover, until they made it to the spot closest to the horses. Then Beau sprinted out to hide behind a coach, his back to the conveyance.

Marianne soon followed, mimicking his actions, and they made their way closer to the tents, crouching behind the horses until they came to the farthest tent on the right.

Motioning for Marianne to remain silent, Beau leaned his ear against the side of the tent curtain to listen.

After apparently discerning that the tent was empty, he pushed the curtain aside and Marianne held her breath until they saw that the space was indeed clear.

They did the same thing for the next two tents, Marianne's brow sweating a bit more each time.

When they came to the fourth tent one row up, Beau gave her a hand signal with one finger up to indicate that at least one person appeared to be inside. Next, he gave her the hand signal to go back. She retreated to the last empty tent and watched with bated breath while Beau listened at the curtain before parting it just barely enough to see inside without being seen himself.

He quickly let the curtain drop again and retreated to meet Marianne behind the empty tent.

"Who is it?" Marianne asked, searching Beau's face.

Beau's face was grim. "Appears to be two prisoners. They're wearing British uniforms."

Marianne sucked in her breath. "I must go see. It could be David."

"Very well. Go look, but then come back here and stay. I'm going to go a bit farther up to see if I can find out what happened to Winfield and Albina."

Marianne and Beau exchanged a glance.

"Be careful, Beau."

"You too."

He was off in a flash before Marianne took another deep breath and steeled her nerves to go look into the prisoners' tent. She knew the odds were low that one of the prisoners was David, but there was always a chance.

She quietly made her way over to the tent and pressed her lips together before pushing the curtain back little more than an inch. The smell inside the tent made her press her wrist to her nose. The soldiers sat on the ground in the middle of the tent, their backs to her, their hands tied behind them. She nearly whimpered when she realized how filthy and torn their uniforms were.

Letting the curtain drop again, she made her way around to the side of the tent where she would be able to see their faces. No use alerting them to her presence until she had to.

Holding her breath with anticipation, she nudged the curtain aside just a bit to see the dirty, bloody, gagged faces of the two soldiers. Her breath expelled in a rush. Neither was David. Her chin dropped to her chest. She hadn't realized until that moment that her entire body was shaking.

She forced herself to take another deep breath. Her first reaction had been relief, but now she realized how much she had hoped one of the men was David. Regardless, she wasn't about to wait around for Beau to return. Instead, she slipped inside the tent, putting a finger to her lips to indicate to the two men to remain silent, while she made haste pulling the gags from one soldier's mouth.

"Who are you?" he asked as soon as he was free.

"Suffice it to say I'm British," she replied. "What is your name?"

"I'm Martin Bigsley-Brown," the soldier replied.

"And what is your rank and unit?" she asked next.

"I'm a corporal with the ninth infantry."

"The ninth infantry? Were you stationed in Paris?"

"Yes."

"My brother is a captain in the ninth infantry. Captain David Ellsworth. Do you know him?"

The soldier's eyes widened. "I do indeed. He was captured with us."

Marianne was dizzy. Her chest felt tight as if it had been clamped in a vise. "Do you know if he's here then?"

"I don't know. I only know…" The man's gaze immediately dropped.

"What? You must tell me." She wanted to grab him by the shoulders and shake him.

"They were killing officers when we first arrived," he choked out.

She clenched her jaw and nodded. "If he was still alive, would he be in one of the other tents?"

The soldier shrugged. "It's possible, I suppose."

Marianne quickly moved behind the first soldier and began loosening the rope that tied his wrists together. "Thank you for your help," she said. "I'm loosening this, but I won't remove it. If we can, we'll come back for you. If not, I want you to at least have a chance to fight. But stay here and don't get in the way unless you decide to run for the treeline about twenty-five yards to the right of this tent."

The soldier nodded and Marianne moved to the other soldier's back. She loosened his wrists too before standing and dusting off her hands. "Stay quiet," she warned before moving to the curtains and peering out to ensure the way was clear. She slipped through and left the tent.

Now that she knew her brother might be here, Marianne fully intended to look for him before meeting back up with Beau.

She made her way to the next tent in the row and listened with her ear against the curtain for at least a minute before peering carefully inside. Empty.

The tent after that was even closer to where the boisterous music and laughing was coming from. After the scream earlier, the music and laughing had soon resumed and had continued since. Marianne could only hope that all of the tents' occupants were busy drinking and singing near the bonfire.

The third tent was also silent, but this time when she pressed open the curtain an inch, she saw another British soldier. Just one this time. He sat in the center of the dirt floor, his hands tied behind him, a gag in his throat. He was facing her, but his head was bent in sleep, and his shaggy dark hair fell over his face.

He was wearing an officer's uniform. Marianne's heart began to thump in her chest.

Something familiar about him made her catch her breath. Was she only fearful and desperate, or could this man really be David?

Pushing open the curtain with sweating palms, she forced herself to silently approach him. She crouched in front of him and nudged him awake as gently as possible, not wanting to startle him and cause him to make any noise.

The soldier's head flipped up nearly immediately, and a mixture of anger and surprise flashed in his eyes before she realized…it *was* David. It was her brother!

"It's all right," she quickly told him, pressing a finger to her lips. "It's me, Marianne."

The anger in his eyes quickly turned to shock, and then something that resembled pain before Marianne moved behind him to release his gag and his wrists.

As soon as he was free, he rubbed his wrists and turned to hug her.

"Mari," he said, his voice so hoarse it was nearly incoherent.

"You need water, don't you?" She struggled to keep the tears that had sprung to her eyes from falling. The last thing David needed from her right now was tears.

He continued to hug her and nodded, and she pulled out of his arms to go to a small table on the far end of the tent. She didn't bother with a glass. She pulled the entire pitcher to her chest and quickly made her way back to her brother, who was struggling to stand.

She gave him the support of her arm and he stood and grabbed the pitcher from her hands. He lifted it to his mouth, drinking in large gulps, before wiping his coat sleeve across his lips and breathing heavily.

"Thank you," he gasped before adding. "Mari, what are you doing here?"

"We don't have much time. I'm here with an agent from the Home Office. We followed the Bidassoa traitor here, and think he may have just been captured by the French also. I want you to go hide in the trees while I go look for my partner."

"The devil will I go hide in the trees," David said, a mixture of anger and resolve flashing in his bright blue eyes. "I'm coming with you."

Marianne shook her head, but there was no sense arguing with David when he had his mind made up—and he obviously had his mind made up now. Quarreling about it would only waste precious time.

"Very well," she replied. "We're looking for a tall blond man dressed like me."

David nodded. "If he's not dressed like a French soldier, he'll be easy to spot."

David insisted on leaving the tent first. Marianne rolled her eyes and allowed him to think he was doing the brave, noble thing, but once they'd exited the tent, she pointed toward the music and laughter. "My guess is that the traitor and his friend are over there. Follow me," she said, pushing ahead of her brother and giving him no other choice but to follow her.

They made their way to the tent on the far-right edge of the row near the trees and then ran across a small open space to hide behind several thick, low branches. Marianne could only hope that, in the darkness, no one had seen them.

Once they'd entered the safety of the trees, Marianne crouched down and indicated for her brother to do the same. They followed the treeline along the camp past the tents until they were able to push down some branches and view the raucous French party in progress.

Marianne's gaze scanned the crowd. It was full of French soldiers. She saw no sign of Beau. She breathed a sigh of relief, hoping that that meant he, too, was hiding in the treeline, watching the party.

A small group of the French soldiers had formed a circle around the bonfire, and they were marching around it in lock step, singing a French song that Marianne could not make out.

She watched them for a moment before one of the Frenchmen, who was obviously quite drunk, stumbled. When he fell, it broke the formation, and Marianne glimpsed the center of the ring, where Baron Winfield and Albina stood, tied to a pole.

Marianne stifled a gasp with her hand. The fire was

spread in a circle all around them, but it was obviously creeping closer and closer to them. They were being burned at the stake.

"What is it?" David whispered.

"Baron Winfield and his friend, they're in the center of the circle."

David redirected his gaze and sucked in his breath. "You're right." David narrowed his eyes. "Is that the traitor?"

"Yes." Marianne nodded. She glanced back at the two captives. Both of them were sobbing, tears running down their cheeks.

"Damn it. While I won't mind seeing him separated from his head back in England, I don't wish *this* fate on anyone," David said, shaking his head with distaste.

"Neither do I." Marianne shook her head too.

"Neither do I," came Beau's voice from behind a nearby tree.

David spun around, his fists up, clearly ready to fight.

"It's all right, David. It's only my partner from the Home Office, Beau – er, Lord Bellingham," Marianne said, placing a hand atop one of her brother's fists to lower them. She turned toward Beau and gave him a condemning glare. "You nearly frightened me witless."

Beau stepped out from behind a tree a few feet to their right, a grin on his face. "I'm pleased to learn you didn't hear me approach." He turned to face David. "I expect this is your brother."

David bowed to Beau. "Your lordship."

"None of that is necessary, Captain," Beau replied. "I thank you for your service to the Crown."

"What are we going to do about Winfield and Albina?" Marianne asked, turning back to the dire situation behind them. There would be time for explanations between her brother and Beau later. She hoped.

Beau fished in his shirt front pocket and pulled out a timepiece. He consulted the thing briefly before slipping it back inside the garment. "Don't worry. Grim wasn't about to leave us here alone. I expect the reinforcements to arrive any moment. For Winfield's sake, I do hope they are prompt."

Marianne furrowed her brow. "What? How does Grim know?"

Beau stood with his feet braced apart. "I sent a letter to Worthington's ship this morning. It's something Captain Jones and I spoke about while we were traveling here. The letter was to inform the Home Office operatives working in Calais to meet us here at half past nine."

Marianne plunked her hands on her hips. "You weren't planning to tell me?"

"Of course I was. I'm telling you now, aren't I?" Beau replied, his grin unrepentant.

David, who'd been watching the fire circle said, "I hate to point it out, but there's no time to argue at present. What's the plan?"

A far-off clicking sound met Marianne's ear just before Beau returned the sound with a click of his own tongue.

"They're here," Beau said, stepping back. "Lord Harbury, are you with us?" he asked the treeline.

A tree shook and a tall, dark-haired man stepped into the clearing. "I am."

"Excellent. Would you like to inform us of the plan?" Beau continued.

"We estimate there are no more than two dozen French soldiers out there. We suspect this camp was invented as a ruse to lure Winfield to his fate. We have over fifty men hidden in these woods. When I give the signal, we'll rush the circle. The goal is to save Baron Winfield and his companion. We need them to tell us what the letter said."

Beau nodded. He pulled his pistol from the waist of his breeches.

"I don't have a pistol," David said, frustration evident in his voice.

"Stay here," Marianne told her brother.

"You stay here, too," Beau said to Marianne. "You don't have a pistol, either."

"The devil I don't," Marianne replied, leaning down and pulling up the leg of her breeches to reveal a small pistol tucked into her boot. "You're not the only one who keeps secrets."

She gave Beau a tight smile before Lord Harbury lifted his hand and made a loud clicking sound that was different from the earlier one. The moment that happened, the trees came alive. A rush of men—pistols drawn—streamed forth, surrounding the Frenchmen, who were drunk and mostly unarmed.

A few shots were fired, and in the blur, Marianne saw Beau rush between the men in the circle to untie Albina and toss her over his shoulder. Another British spy grabbed Winfield, and the small group, including Lord Harbury, rushed back into the trees with their haul.

Shouts and shots and general loud noises continued in the clearing near the bonfire while Lord Harbury, Beau, Marianne, and David pushed aside the curtains of the nearest tent and moved inside, dragging the two traitors with them.

Two of Lord Harbury's aides soon joined them.

David fetched water for Winfield and Albina while the two wiped their wet, soot-stained faces and coughed.

"You saved us," Winfield cried, when he was finally able to speak. "We nearly died."

"Don't think we *wanted* to save you, traitor," Lord Harbury pointed out, his voice dripping with disgust. "I have my orders. And they include handing you back over to the French unless you tell us what you did for them."

Albina was nearly hysterical. David and Marianne took her aside and made her sit on a pile of blankets in the corner and drink more water while Baron Winfield eyed all of them carefully.

"You're not going to take me back to England? For trial?" the baron asked.

"We will if you tell us what we need to know. Otherwise, we may just have to report that we didn't get here in time to save you. Believe me, no one will be upset," Harbury replied.

Winfield finished coughing and rubbed his face and eyes with a towel that Beau had handed him. "Bellingham, I should have known you would be here."

"Save it," Beau replied. "Tell us what the letter said."

"What letter?" Winfield blinked at him innocently.

"The letter Albina wrote at Lord Copperpot's town house," Beau replied through clenched teeth. He was in no mood for the man's games.

Baron Winfield's face paled. "How did you know about—?"

"Let's take him back out to the bonfire, lads," Beau said, grabbing Winfield by the upper arm.

"No! No!" Winfield nearly crumpled to the ground. "I'll tell you what you want to know. I'll tell you everything."

"Good, get started," Beau replied nearly growling.

Albina sobbed silently in the corner while Winfield began his story. "They promised me money. A hefty purse. Fifty thousand pounds!" Winfield said, his eyes flaring as he spoke.

Beau shook his head. "Your first mistake was believing that. They probably don't even have fifty thousand pounds, the lying bastards."

"They gave me the money the first time," Winfield replied,

tugging at the lapels of his coat as if he took offense to essentially being told how stupid he was.

"The first time?" Beau frowned. "You mean when you had Albina write the Bidassoa letter?"

"Yes." Winfield hung his head and nodded morosely.

"Ye promised me no one would ever find out!" Albina wailed at her lover. "Ye promised me we'd be safe and happy and rich!"

"I'm sorry, darling, but it's too late," Winfield replied, tears streaming down his face once again.

"Take her out of here," Beau commanded.

David pulled Albina to her feet more gently than she deserved and he quickly exited the tent with her.

"Go on," Beau demanded of Winfield.

Winfield wiped the sooty tears from his eyes before continuing. "The second letter was a fake. They wanted it to look like the first so they could use it to throw off the British about a raid at Calais next month."

Harbury narrowed his eyes on the baron. "What do you mean?"

Winfield launched into another coughing fit. When he finally was able to speak again, his voice was low. "They were going to ensure a messenger with the letter was captured. It would make the British think that the raid would take place at Sangatte, and not Calais."

"Meanwhile they'd be gathering at Calais?" Beau finished.

"Yes." Winfield hung his head again. "They knew there were many British operatives hidden in Calais."

"Where is this letter?" Lord Harbury demanded.

"It's in General Christophe's coat pocket. I gave it to him before they tied us up to cook us."

"Your second mistake was coming here," Beau pointed out, shaking his head again. "They never intended to pay you a farthing."

Baron Winfield's only reply was a sad, sniffing noise.

Lord Harbury gave direction to one of the aides who stood near his side. "Find General Christophe out there and bring him to me."

The man hurried off and Beau, Lord Harbury, and Marianne were left with Winfield.

"You've no idea how badly I want to punch you in the bloody mouth right now, Winfield," Beau said through tightly clenched teeth. "I may just allow Mr. John Smith here, and his brother the solider who took Albina away, to do it. They deserve it more than I do. It was their brother you killed at Bidassoa."

"I didn't kill anyone!" Baron Winfield insisted, shaking his head, his voice rising with fear.

Marianne stalked over to him and stood in front of him, her arms crossed tightly over her chest, her cap pulled down to her brow. "Yes, you did, you bastard. The soldier who carried the letter to the British was shot and eventually died from his wounds. It was my brother, Frederick. He was a patriot and a better man than you'll ever be."

Baron Winfield swallowed visibly. "I suppose death in inevitable in war."

Marianne's eyes flared with rage, and in a flash, she stepped forward, put a hand on Baron Winfield's shoulder and jerked up her knee directly between his legs.

A loud *oompf* escaped his throat just before the baron crumpled to the dirt floor, wheezing in pain and clutching at his crotch.

"Frederick taught me that," Marianne announced, grinning at Beau.

The three men winced, watching Winfield writhe.

"Well done, Smith," Lord Harbury said with a smile.

A few minutes later, the aide returned with one of the French officers in tow.

"It's just as Baron Winfield said, my lord," the aid announced, handing Lord Harbury a folded piece of vellum. "This was in his front coat pocket."

Lord Harbury unfolded the paper and scanned the page. He nodded to Beau before handing the letter to him. Marianne read it too, over Beau's shoulder.

For once, Baron Winfield was apparently telling the truth. The letter indicated precisely what he'd said it did.

"Why didn't you write this yourself?" Beau asked Winfield, who was still lying on the ground. "Why make your maid do it for you?"

"I'm a highly respected member of Society," Baron Winfield whimpered, still clutching himself. "Besides, Cunningham and I didn't want our names associated with it. Who would suspect *Albina*, of all people?"

"So it *was* Lord Cunningham who fed you the information from the special council?" Marianne asked.

"Oh, dear, I thought you knew that already," Baron Winfield sniveled.

Harbury shook his head. "You make me sick, Winfield."

Beau stepped between the Frenchman and the baron to help Winfield to his feet. "You're fortunate, Baron Winfield. Your story appears to be true."

"Of course it's true," Winfield moaned, still bent slightly due to the pain in his crotch. "I only wanted money. I never actually meant for anyone to get *hurt*."

"Least of all yourself, correct?" Beau asked, still glaring at Winfield.

The French officer, who'd been standing there silently, took the opportunity to spit at Beau, who stepped out of the way just in time for the sputum to hit Winfield on the upper lip.

"Excellent aim," Beau said to the Frenchman, who glowered at him.

Another one of the spies entered the tent. "Lord Harbury, we have the area secured. All of the French are tied up and are being taken to the carriages as prisoners."

"Good work," Lord Harbury said. He motioned to Christophe and Winfield. "Take both of these men to the carriages as well. They are also prisoners of war."

The aides shuffled the two prisoners out of the tent and Lord Harbury turned back to face Beau and Marianne. "Can we offer you a ride back to Calais, Lord Bellingham?"

"No," Beau replied. "We brought a mount. We'll follow you. But please ensure Captain Ellsworth is taken with you—and there are at least two other British soldiers who were being kept here, as well."

Lord Harbury nodded. "I'll have my men search every tent before we go. I'll meet you at the crossing," he finished before sweeping back the curtain and leaving the tent.

Beau expelled a deep breath. He and Marianne were alone.

"That couldn't have gone better if it had been planned," he said.

"I agree," Marianne replied.

"Let's go back to the hotel. I'll meet Lord Harbury in the morning to discuss the plans to return to England." Beau reached a hand for her.

"I'm not leaving with you," Marianne said. She'd braced her feet apart on the solid packed earth.

Beau turned back to face her. "What?"

"I'm going back to Calais, but I'll ride in one of the carriages with David."

Beau frowned. "What? Why?"

Marianne turned to the side. She crossed her arms over her chest. "This is it. This is what we've been working toward. We found the traitor and I found my brother. I intend to return to England, but…" Her voice trailed off.

Beau's jaw was clenched. "But what?"

"But David and I can return on a different ship. As for you and I...I think it's best if we go our separate ways...as soon as possible."

Beau bit the inside of his cheek so hard he tasted blood. "Is that what you truly want?"

Marianne had turned toward the curtains. "Yes." She didn't turn around. "Good-bye, Lord Bellingham."

CHAPTER THIRTY-NINE

The Earl of Kendall's Town House,
London, Early November 1814

Beau stared at the brandy bottle that sat not an arm's length from him on the desk in Kendall's study. Kendall sat in the chair behind the desk, while Worth sat next to Beau in the other large, leather chair facing their friend. It had been more than a fortnight since Beau had returned from France, but this was the first time the three friends had been together.

"You keep glancing at the brandy, Bell. Don't tell me you want a drink." Kendall eyed him with suspicion.

Beau shook his head and returned his gaze to Kendall. "No, of course not. What was I saying?"

"We told you how the Employment Bill was voted down, even without your vote, and you were finishing the story of how you and a lady's maid named Marianne Notley took down Baron Winfield, the dirty traitor," Worth replied, settling back in his chair.

It seemed like an age ago. In the time since, Beau had

come back to England, seen to it that both Winfield and Albina were charged with their crimes, and met extensively with General Grimaldi to debrief the mission, including where they'd failed and how they'd finally succeeded. They never would have broken the case if it hadn't been for Marianne, and Beau made certain the general knew it.

In all of their talks, however, Beau had refrained from asking Grimaldi where Marianne was. He desperately wanted to know, but he didn't feel it was his right. And Grimaldi, that bastard, hadn't bothered to tell him.

"That was it," Beau continued. "The morning after the raid on the French camp, Marianne and I sailed back to England with Winfield and Albina as prisoners."

Everyone already knew that Winfield was the culprit, of course. The London papers had spread the word far and wide the moment they'd got wind of the scandalous news.

"I must admit, I never suspected Winfield, of all people," Worth said shaking his head.

"Neither did I," Kendall agreed. "I knew he was a bastard, but I had no idea how big of one. The fact that he'd intended to sneak off with his mistress thinking the *French* would reward him is nearly beyond belief. Greedy blackguard."

Beau nodded. "How is Frances taking it, Kendall?"

Kendall leaned back in his chair and steepled his fingers in front of his chest. "Better than expected. She wasn't particularly surprised. She's known for some time now that her father isn't who she thought he was."

"How is *Lady* Winfield handling the news?" Worth asked Kendall, an eyebrow arched.

"That is a different story altogether," Kendall replied with a sigh. "Lady Winfield isn't taking the news well, I'm afraid. According to Frances, she's taken to her bed, inconsolable."

"I'm sorry to hear that. I've done all I can to keep the story of the baron leaving with Albina out of the mouths of gossips, but I'm afraid his being a traitor will be his legacy," Beau replied.

Kendall nodded. "Frances was worried about *me*, actually. She wanted to know if I still wished to marry her after her family's shame."

"Of course you wouldn't reject her," Worth replied. "You're far too loyal."

"A fact of which I assured her immediately," Kendall replied with a smile. "I don't give a toss about Frances's family's reputation. I'd marry her tomorrow by special license if she would agree to it."

"Yes, Bell, that's one thing you've missed: Frances and Julianna are now planning a big wedding for us together," Worth said, laughing. "In the spring."

Beau glanced at the brandy bottle again. He was trying to pretend as if everything was normal. He'd simply finished another mission and was back to his regular life, biding time before his next mission. There was nothing new about it.

But nothing was the same. Not a moment went by when he didn't think of Marianne.

He'd left her there, with her brother at the crossroads of Coulogne Road and the Andres Highway in France. He'd traveled back to the hotel alone. David had come to the hotel to gather her belongings that night, and Beau hadn't even asked where they were staying. The next day he made his own arrangements to return to England on the ship that was taking Winfield and Albina back as prisoners. He hadn't seen Marianne since.

"By God, he *is* looking at the brandy bottle," Worth said, surprise in his voice.

"I'm not going to drink it," Beau ground out.

"Are you *considering* it?" Kendall asked.

Beau narrowed his eyes on the earl. "No. Why?"

Worth sighed and rolled his eyes. "I do think it's time, Kendall, don't you?"

"Time for what?" Beau asked, his gaze darting back and forth suspiciously between his friends.

"Time for us to give you a little speech along the lines of the ones you gave us," Kendall replied.

"What speech?" Beau replied, still side-eyeing them both.

"The one where we inform you that you're madly in love with the woman, and need to ask her to marry you," Kendall continued.

"What woman?" Beau asked, but he already felt as if a vise was being clamped around his heart.

Worth shook his head. "Seriously? 'What woman?' Don't you think we know you've fallen in love with Marianne? It's been obvious from everything you've said about her since the moment you walked in here."

"What?" Beau pushed himself back in his seat. "I was merely telling the story of—"

"Spare us," Worth replied. "We've both recently fallen in love ourselves. We know the signs. You've said her name no fewer than one hundred times."

"I have not!" Beau replied, tugging at his cravat. "And if I did, it was merely because she was an integral part of the story."

Kendall blinked calmly at Beau. "Do you want to argue with us, or do you want our help finding her?

Beau immediately sat up straight and leaned forward. "You know where she is?"

"I know where she might be," Kendall replied, "and the fact that you just asked that with such interest proves our point. Stop pretending."

Beau grouchily settled back into his chair without saying anything.

Worth's brows shot up. "You, at a loss for words, Bell? I never thought I'd see the day.

"Shut up," Beau shot back.

"Eloquent. Simply eloquent," Kendall replied with a laugh.

"Will you please admit that you're madly in love with her?" Worth said, his tone wheedling. "For me?"

"Damn you both," Beau ground out. "Fine. Unlike the two of you were, I'm willing to admit it. I love her. I've always loved her. I want to marry her, and I don't give a toss that she's a lady's maid. Are you two prepared for the scandal that will consume us all when I marry a servant?"

"See," Worth said, casually reclining in his chair once more. "That wasn't so bad, was it?"

"That was a beautiful speech," Kendall replied.

"If you have something useful to say, please say it; otherwise, do shut up," Beau replied, his fists clenched atop the arms of the leather chair. At the moment he was ready to sock both men in the jaw and leave.

"Well, I do have something useful to say as a matter of fact. Courtesy of our friend, Clayton," Kendall offered.

Beau's head snapped up to face the earl. "What?"

Kendall leaned back in his chair and steepled his fingers over his chest again. "Turns out Clayton has learned some very interesting things in Parliament of late. Including the fact that one Captain David Ellsworth is not actually *merely* a captain."

Beau frowned. "What? What are you talking about?"

"He's the son of the Earl of Elmwood," Kendall continued.

The news hit Beau like a physical blow to the chest. He fell back into his chair and expelled a deep breath. "I thought that title had no heir."

"It didn't have," Kendall replied. "The late earl's only son renounced his title and left London many years ago. That man was David's father."

"David's father?" Beau echoed.

"Yes," Kendall continued. "It turns out David Ellsworth is the eldest grandson of the last Earl of Elmwood."

"My. My. My," Worth said, in a voice dripping with sarcasm. "By my calculations, if David Ellsworth is an earl, that would make Marianne...a *lady*, wouldn't it?"

"Precisely," Kendall replied dryly.

Beau closed his eyes briefly, letting the import of the news slowly wash over him. "Where is she?" he finally asked.

His friends exchanged a knowing glance.

"Elmwood is staying at Clayton's town house at the moment. Poor man had no clue he was an earl. Clayton's agreed to sponsor him. But I have it on good authority that Marianne is staying elsewhere," Kendall said.

"What? Why?" Beau frowned.

"It was her choice," Kendall continued.

"Where is she?" Beau repeated, leaping to his feet.

"I'm afraid I don't know that," Kendall replied.

Bell slammed a palm atop the desk. "Damn it, Kendall. How am I supposed to find her then?"

Worth's crack of laughter filled the study. "You're a spy, Bell. You figure it out."

CHAPTER FORTY

"Marianne, dear, I've just come from the foyer and you have two visitors," Lady Courtney said as she entered the rose salon in her London town house.

"Visitors?" Marianne frowned. Who other than Lady Courtney and David even knew that she was staying here?

Everything had happened so quickly since they'd come back from France. First, General Grimaldi had informed them that David was an earl. Apparently, after his capture, and Marianne's stint as a spy, the Home Office had done some research on their family. Grimaldi himself had learned of the connection after tracing their last name back to the estate of the Earl of Elmwood.

Marianne still couldn't quite believe that her father, who had been so loving, kind, and humble had been born the only son of an earl.

Apparently, Papa had fallen in love with her mother, who was a commoner, when he'd been stationed in Brighton many years ago. When he informed his father of his intent to marry a woman so far beneath him, his father the earl had threatened to disown him. Rather than make Papa fall in line, that had only angered her stubborn father. He'd renounced both his father and his lineage, deciding instead to rely upon his earnings from the army and then after retiring from the military, living a simple life of a woodworker in Brighton, with no pretentions whatsoever.

David, too, had been completely unaware of their ancestry. He informed Marianne that their father had never given him the slightest hint that David was the elder son of a man who was supposed to be an earl.

David had been easily convinced to take up his place in Society, however. "Don't you see the sort of power I'd have to influence decisions if I were to take a seat in Parliament?" he'd told her the night they'd found out. "I could advocate for the rights of soldiers, and make a real difference."

Tears had come to Marianne's eyes. Her brother was noble and strong and virtuous. He would use his title and power, and the money that came with it (apparently, it was a considerable sum), to do good in the country and to help people. She could think of no better man to take up such a responsibility than her beloved brother. If only Frederick were alive to see it.

The last few weeks had been nothing but a blur. Marianne had been taken in by Lady Courtney at General Grimaldi's suggestion. The lady had taken her to the *modiste* and ensured that Marianne had a wardrobe worthy of an earl's sister.

The boxes had been delivered to Lady Courtney's town house and Marianne was now the proud owner of dozens of costly gowns, pairs of slippers, pelisses, reticules, silk stockings, fine kid gloves, night rails with lace, chemises so delicate you could see your fingers through them, and a variety of delightful bonnets. It was as if she'd awoken in a fairy tale.

She soon learned that Lady Courtney had always known

who her father was. "Your father was adamant that I not say anything, Marianne. To you or your brothers," Lady Courtney had told her by way of apology for keeping such a large secret.

"I understand," Marianne had replied. "I suppose it finally makes sense why my father had a family friend like you, Lady Courtney. I had always assumed Papa had done some woodworking for you."

Lady Courtney had given her a sympathetic smile. "I promised your mother on her death bed that I would look out for you. She would be so pleased to see you and David taking your rightful places in Society. She never wished it for herself, but she didn't like to think she was keeping her children from assuming their birthright."

That had made Marianne's eyes fill with tears. She remembered all the times she and Mama had 'pretended' that she was a fine lady, about to make her debut, as she paraded around their little cottage in Brighton. That hadn't been just a game to Mama, after all, she realized. She was trying to prepare Marianne for the possibility that she might one day live the life she was born to.

Her mother's insistence that she learn French also made sense. She'd assumed it had been so that she'd have a chance of securing a better position as a governess or maid, but now she realized that her beloved Mama had seen to it that she and her brothers had been educated according to their stations in life.

Marianne had blinked away the tears. If she had to 'take her rightful place,' she wanted to do so in a way that would honor the memories of her parents. Despite her education, she hadn't been raised to be the sister of an earl. How would she ever manage to learn all the complexities involved in being a member of the *Beau Monde*? The thought made her head spin.

The last thing Marianne wanted was to be introduced to Society. She'd heard enough stories of the snobbery and formality from Lady Wilhelmina to last a lifetime. How would the famously disapproving *ton* react to an earl's daughter with little grace, who'd been serving as a lady's maid? But Marianne had no choice. Marianne Notley was dead, and Lady Marianne Ellsworth was being reborn to take her place. In Society. The thought made her stomach lurch.

Lady Courtney had already told her she'd help sponsor her. Worse, Lady Courtney had also already begun to discuss Marianne's debut. She was already twenty-three years old. Far too old to be a debutante. The entire notion was insane.

When she wasn't worrying over her future place in 'Society,' Marianne couldn't stop herself from thinking of Beau. Not an hour went by that she didn't wonder where he was and what he was doing.

It was as if she'd lost a piece of herself the moment she'd said good-bye to him in that tent in France. It had been the most difficult decision of her life, and it had been difficult to live with every day since.

She missed him. She could admit that to herself. She missed him desperately, and she was not at all certain that she'd done the right thing in leaving him, but at the time it seemed the only choice to save her sanity.

What future had they had together? She'd had no idea that she was about to discover she was the sister of an earl. And now...now it was too late. She could hardly appear on Beau's doorstep and say, "It turns out my brother is an earl— would you be interested in marrying me?" Besides, Beau had never mentioned *marriage*. They'd merely had an affair. Why would she think he would want her as a *wife*, even now? He'd made it clear that his work was the most important thing in his life.

Marianne shook her head to dispel the distressing

thoughts that looped endlessly through her mind. She turned back to concentrate on what Lady Courtney had just said. "Two visitors? Who would want to visit me?" she asked her benefactress.

Lady Courtney replied with a kind smile just before the butler appeared at the door to the salon. "Lady Julianna Montgomery and Miss Frances Wharton to see you, Lady Marianne."

Marianne gulped. She still couldn't believe that, when someone said, 'Lady Marianne,' they were talking to her. And what were Lady Julianna—who she'd heard was the most popular debutante of the last three Seasons—and Miss Wharton doing here?

Miss Wharton no doubt would hate Marianne for her role in turning her father over for justice. But the thought that made her swallow even harder was the fact that these two ladies were betrothed to the Duke of Worthington and Lord Kendall respectively, and those two men were Beau's closest friends.

"Show them in, please, Tinsdale," Lady Courtney said for her. Marianne was grateful for the assistance. She'd never been called upon to welcome guests in a sitting room in Mayfair before. She'd scarcely any idea how to handle it.

To keep her hands from shaking, she clasped them together and placed the sweaty pair in her lap. But beneath her pretty light-blue gown, her silver-slippered foot was bouncing up and down on the rug.

Lady Julianna entered first. The tall, gorgeous, blonde was wearing the loveliest gown of celadon green. The color matched her eyes.

Miss Wharton followed behind her. When the brunette smiled, it reached her warm, dark eyes. Miss Wharton was wearing a pink gown and had a small, pink flower tucked behind her ear.

Taking her cue from Lady Courtney, Marianne rose to greet them.

"Lady Marianne," Lady Julianna said, holding out her hands to grasp Marianne's in hers. "I'm ever so pleased to make your acquaintance."

"Likewise," Miss Wharton said. The two women exchanged a private glance clearly intended as a mutual agreement that they would act as if they hadn't already met once on the middle of the night at the Duke of Worthington's town house.

Marianne managed to mumble something about the pleasure being hers and to thank both ladies for their visit, which earned her an approving nod and encouraging smile from Lady Courtney.

After all four of them had taken their seats, and Lady Courtney had requested tea be served, Marianne watched the younger women with her heart in her throat, waiting for one of them to speak.

"I suppose you're wondering why we've come," Miss Wharton began, giving Marianne another friendly smile.

Marianne nearly breathed a sigh of relief. Miss Wharton got directly to the point—she appreciated that about her. "Yes. I admit I am."

"There are two reasons, actually," Lady Julianna replied. The lady sat with her back ramrod straight, causing Marianne to self-consciously straighten her own back. She feared she'd never be as proper as Lady Julianna, no matter how long she studied under Lady Courtney's tutelage.

"The first reason is that we wanted to welcome you to Society," Lady Julianna continued.

"That's terribly kind of you," Marianne replied. "But I'd be dishonest if I didn't tell you I'm not certain I'm ready for Society. In fact, I'm not certain how you two found out where I was staying."

The two young ladies gave each other knowing looks.

"We do hope you aren't cross with us," Lady Julianna replied, "but gossip travels quickly in this town."

Miss Wharton nodded. "When we discovered that you'd once been a lady's maid to Lady Courtney, we made some discreet inquiries and learned the truth."

Lady Courtney sighed. "Leave it to the gossip mills. I told you they'd be buzzing, Marianne."

Marianne nodded. "Yes, well. I thank you both for your concern. Lady Courtney has been helping to teach me what I need to know…about Society, I mean."

Miss Wharton gave her a sympathetic smile. "It can be overwhelming, to be certain," she replied. "But we wanted to tell you that we will both do everything in our power to assist you. Though," Miss Wharton winced, "as I'm certain you're aware, as the daughter of a traitor, I'm *persona non grata* in Society at the moment. While we're on the subject, I'm terribly sorry for the things my father did, Lady Marianne. I hope you can forgive me for my relation to the man who caused your brother's death."

Marianne reached out and squeezed Miss Wharton's hand. "Oh, Miss Wharton. Please don't think I blame you. You are not your father, after all. I was worried that you'd hate *me* for having been a party to his arrest."

"My father must reap what he's sown," Frances replied solemnly. "I am only concerned about my mother now."

"Of course," Marianne replied, replacing her hand in her lap and giving both ladies an encouraging smile. "I do hope we'll be friends."

"Thank you, Lady Marianne," Miss Wharton replied. "You're quite kind. Please believe I didn't know anything about my father's schemes. Looking back, I do recall Albina asking me to teach her how to write last autumn, but I certainly had no idea what she meant to do with the knowledge. I should have asked more questions."

"You couldn't possibly have guessed," Marianne replied. "And of course I believe that you had no idea what your father was planning. Just like I had no idea my father was an earl, apparently. Fathers can be quite sneaky when they choose to be."

All four ladies laughed.

"The good news for you, Lady Marianne," Miss Wharton continued, "is that Lady Julianna here is one of the most highly regarded members of Society and engaged to a duke. With her by your side, you are certain to be readily accepted in Society."

"I don't intend to allow Society to shun you either, Frances," Lady Julianna said to her friend. "And as the *fiancée* of an earl, you have Kendall's name, Worthington's name, and my backing."

"Mine too," Lady Courtney offered. "God knows I've had a few relatives who've done things I couldn't countenance."

"Thank you so much, Lady Courtney," Miss Wharton replied. "I'm also forgetting Lord Bellingham. Lucas tells me he's offered his support as well."

At the mention of Beau's name, Marianne's back stiffened.

Lady Courtney glanced worriedly at Marianne before turning her attention back to Julianna. "You said there was a second reason you came. What was that?"

"Yes," Lady Julianna replied, turning to face Marianne once again. "Speaking of Lord Bellingham, we've come to tell you that he has been beside himself, trying to find you, and we'd like your permission to tell him where you are."

CHAPTER FORTY-ONE

Beau was sitting behind the desk in his study. He'd moved the brandy decanter—mostly there for show or for the occasional guest—to the desk in front of him, along with a glass.

He'd been staring at the liquid for the better part of an hour, but he was no closer to deciding whether to take a drink. The only thing he knew was that he'd never been more tempted to do so in his entire life.

He'd nearly torn London apart the last two days, looking for Marianne. First, he'd gone to Clayton's house to visit her brother. David had no longer been dressed as a solider, and he was considerably cleaner and less bruised than the last time Beau had seen him. The earl had cleaned up quite well, actually. He'd looked to be no more than Beau's own age. Beau was nothing but pleased to see the captain looking so hearty.

Beau was finally able to see the resemblance to Marianne as well. While the new earl had dark brown hair and no freckles to speak of, he had Marianne's bright blue eyes and dark lashes. And the smile he'd afforded Beau when he'd walked into Clayton's study was reminiscent of his sister's.

But David had been ridiculously loyal to her, refusing to tell Beau where she was, even when he explained that he was in love with her and wanted to ask her to marry him. David *had* promised to tell her that Beau wanted to see her, but Beau had left Clayton's house nearly frustrated enough to punch his fist through the bloody stone wall out front.

Next, he'd gone to see Grimaldi again. The general knew exactly where she was, Beau had no doubt. Grim, however, was even less forthcoming than David had been. At least David had appeared chagrined and apologetic when he informed Beau that he would not be able to help him. Grim seemed to enjoy his anguish.

"If one of my very best spies cannot locate one woman in London, I'm not certain I want to know about it," Grim had said with a wry smile.

Beau had left the general's office, wanting to punch his fist through the general's face.

Beau had gone to every pub, every club, and every meeting place he could think of in an attempt to hear gossip that might lead him to Marianne. The entire *ton* was ablaze with the news that the Earl of Elmwood's heir was back and that he had a sister. The entire city seemed to be talking about Marianne, but no one seemed to know where she was. It was maddening.

He'd even sent a letter to Lady Wilhelmina, but in addition to indicating her shock that her former lady's maid was an earl's sister, Wilhelmina was also at a loss as to her location.

Finally, last night, Beau had arrived at Worth's town house where Julianna, Frances, and Kendall were visiting. Beau had slumped into a chair in the salon where they all sat and declared defeat. "Why doesn't anyone know where she is? How can that be?" he groaned, burying his face in his hand.

"Someone knows," Julianna had said. "It's simply a matter of speaking to the right people."

"Well, all the people I've spoken to either don't know or aren't telling," Beau had grumbled.

Julianna and Frances had exchanged a glance, but Beau had barely noticed. He'd picked himself up and dragged himself back to his own town house, where he finally fell into an exhausted slumber.

Today, he'd done nothing more than sit in his study and stare at the bloody brandy decanter.

Slowly, he raised his hand to remove the glass stopper, when a knock at the door startled him. "My lord," came his butler's voice. "You have two visitors."

"You may open the door, Maxwell," Beau replied, hastily pushing the decanter and the glass to the side.

The door to the study opened and his butler stepped inside.

"Who are the visitors?" Beau asked, clearing his throat.

"Lady Julianna Montgomery and Miss Frances Wharton," Maxwell replied.

Beau frowned. "They're alone?"

"Their chaperones are with them, if that's what you mean," the butler replied.

"Show them in," Beau replied.

Minutes later, Julianna and Frances appeared in the doorway *sans* chaperones. They'd apparently left the two older women in one of the salons at the front of the house.

"Ah, there you are, Lord Bellingham," Frances said.

Beau glanced up at Frances, remembering the morning in Clayton's library he'd told her a story about Kendall. He liked the young woman a great deal. She was a pretty, spirited brunette, who was set on helping Kendall introduce new bills into the House of Lords for the benefit of the working classes. Beau didn't hold her father's sins against her at all.

Next, his gaze swung to Lady Julianna. She was a gorgeous blond with perfect manners and a prestigious family name. She also happened to be the only other person in the world who seemed as stubborn and competitive as his friend Worth. The two made a perfect couple.

"It's good to see both of you," Beau replied.

The two ladies took seats in front of him. "I've never been invited into a study before," Frances said, glancing around. "I quite like it. May I have some brandy, my lord?"

Beau gave her an ironic stare. "For some reason, I don't think you came here to drink brandy with me."

"Perhaps not," Julianna replied with a sigh, "but I'm not opposed to it."

Frances laughed. "Let's put the poor man out of his misery, Julianna."

Julianna sighed again. "Very well, if we must." But the wide grin on her face belied the content of her words.

Frances leaned forward, a sly smile on her face. "We've come with some news that we think you may be quite interested in hearing, Lord Bellingham."

Beau shrugged. "I'm not interested in much at the moment, but go ahead."

The two exchanged a knowing glance.

"Well," Beau prompted, narrowing his eyes on them. "What is it?"

Julianna took a deep breath. "We know where Lady Marianne is staying, and we've received her blessing to tell you."

Beau shot to his feet. "You know where Marianne is?" His heart was thumping so hard it hurt.

"Yes," Frances said with a nod and a laugh.

"She wants to see me?" Beau nearly shouted.

"We never said that. But she agreed to allow us to inform

you of where she is. If you want to take that news and pay her a visit, that is entirely *your* choice," Frances replied with a wink.

Beau nearly leaped across the desk. "Where is she?"

The ladies exchanged another glance.

"She's staying at Lady Courtney's house in Hanover Square."

"The devil she is. God, why didn't I think of that? I'm obviously a rubbish spy."

"No. You're not a rubbish spy. You're a man in love and you're not thinking clearly," Julianna replied.

"There is that, too," Beau replied with a laugh. "But I must ask, how did you find out so quickly?"

Julianna and Frances exchanged a third glance.

"If you want to learn something from gossip, you don't ask men," Julianna replied, a sweet smile on her face.

"Fair enough." Beau shook his head, but he was already making his way toward the door. "You'll excuse me if I tell you I must go now."

The two ladies laughed.

"We rather expected you'd cut our visit short," Frances replied.

He grinned at them. "Thank you for telling me, ladies. I consider you both friends."

"As we do you, Lord Bellingham," Frances said. "As we do you."

NOT HALF AN HOUR LATER, Beau was rapping steadily on the door to Lady Courtney's town house. A cold November wind had whipped up, but he barely noticed the temperature.

A confused-looking butler opened the door to see what all the commotion was about.

"I'm Lord Bellingham, here to visit Lady Marianne Ellsworth," he said in a rush.

"She's not here, my lord," the butler informed him.

"The devil she's not," Beau began, quite ready to knock down the bloody door if he had to. "I have it on good authority that she's staying here."

"No. I mean she's not here *at the moment*. She and Lady Courtney went for a ride in the park."

"Rotten Row?" Beau asked the man.

"Indeed," the butler replied.

Beau didn't waste another moment. He swiveled on his heel, ran down the steps, jumped on his horse, and took off hell-for-leather toward Hyde Park.

He made it to the park in minutes, and began racing up and down the crowded Rotten Row, that fashionable stretch of road where the *ton*'s best displayed themselves each evening.

Blast. Blast. Blast. How would he ever find her in such a throng? Coach after coach was filled with occupants bundled up in blankets and coats. He could hardly tell who anyone was.

Finally, he stopped in the middle of the roadway. "Lady Marianne!" he called in the loudest voice he could muster. "Lady Marianne Ellsworth!"

The occupants of the nearby coaches began leaning out to stare at him.

"Has Bellingham lost his mind?" he heard one coach-dweller say.

"Who is Marianne Ellsworth?" he heard another ask.

He galloped farther down the road. "Lady Marianne! Lady Marianne Ellsworth!"

"For heaven's sake," he heard a lady's voice say. "Stop that caterwauling. She and Lady Courtney are in the coach with four grays, a few back."

Heart in his throat, Beau spurred his mount forward until he found the coach in question. "Lady Marianne?" he called, hoping against hope the woman hadn't been mistaken.

Bright blue eyes blinked at him from the window of the coach, and a relief unlike any he'd felt before flooded through him. He'd found her. After all these weeks, he'd finally found her.

Lady Courtney's coach pulled out of the procession and came to a stop a few yards ahead. He jumped from his horse and tied the animal to a nearby post before running across the roadway, dodging carriages and mounts.

The door to Lady Courtney's carriage opened just as he approached.

"Was that you shouting, Bellingham?" Lady Courtney asked. "We were trying to have a civilized ride in the park. Lady Marianne here doesn't need any scandal attached to her name. Now look what you've done."

Beau glanced back momentarily to see that the entire early evening's procession along Rotten Row had stopped, and the coaches' occupants were staring at them as if they were acting out a play. He was indeed causing a scene, but at the moment he didn't give a damn.

"My apologies, Lady Courtney," Beau said, his gaze meeting Marianne's startled one. "But I couldn't wait another moment to say what I have to say to Lady Marianne."

Lady Courtney hid her smile. "Very well, lad. Go ahead and say it."

"Will you come out and meet me?" Beau asked Marianne, his heart in his throat. "Please."

Marianne nodded and he helped her to alight.

The moment she'd stepped onto the ground, Beau dropped to one knee. "I know you're the sister of an earl—I couldn't care any less. I love you, Marianne. I should have asked you to marry me the night you left me in France, but I was a bloody fool. Please, say you'll be my wife."

"Excellent decision," Lady Courtney snorted from inside the coach.

Marianne's face filled with worry. "You're truly not just asking me because of the change in my status?"

"I promise you, darling. I'd ask you if you were a washer woman in the street. I don't care about the scandal." He glanced back at the line of stopped carriages. "Does it *look* like I care about scandal?"

Marianne had to laugh at that. "David told me you came looking for me. And so did Julianna and Frances."

"Yes, and if you ask Kendall and Worth, they'll tell you I said I wanted to marry you even before Kendall informed me that your brother was an earl."

"I believe him, Marianne," Lady Courtney announced from inside the coach.

"Please, Marianne," he whispered, squeezing her hands. "Say you'll marry me. I've loved you since the moment you found me peering about Lord Copperpot's bedchamber and told me to stop."

"What about your position with the Home Office? Will you give that up?" Marianne had lowered her voice to a whisper.

"We can spy together if you like," he offered, equally quiet, before raising his voice again to say, "Or, I'll settle down and we'll have half a score of children."

"That sounds like an awful lot of children, Marianne," came Lady Courtney's muffled interjection.

Marianne laughed. "I quite agree, Lady Courtney," she replied, raising her voice.

"Fine then. Half a score. Two. Three. However many you want. I'll give you the world, Marianne, just say you'll marry me," Beau pleaded, still on his knee.

"I don't know how to be a proper marchioness, Beau. What if I embarrass you and your family?"

"We'll teach you. We'll all teach you, and you can be any type of marchioness you like. Nothing you do would ever embarrass me. Don't you see, Marianne? I adore you."

"This is quite new to me, Lady Courtney," Marianne called. "Is there anything else I should ask for before I agree?"

"Hmm," came Lady Courtney's reply. "Ask for an extended honeymoon and invite your friends."

"Not a problem whatsoever," Beau replied without skipping a beat. "With the money I won from a certain bet a while back, I'm prepared to take the whole lot of us on the best honeymoon money can buy."

"It sounds promising, Lady Courtney," Marianne replied, smiling at Beau with tears in her eyes.

"I agree, dear," Lady Courtney replied. "I quite agree. He may be a madman, but he's an eligible madman."

"Ask for some jewels!" another lady shouted from a nearby coach.

"I can't help that I'm a marquess," Beau continued, smothering his laugh about the random lady's comment, "and I cannot blame you for not relishing the role of a marchioness, but I love you madly. Please, please say yes. I'll do everything in my power to make you happy. I'll even pretend I'm a valet if it will help."

"That seems unnecessary," Lady Courtney added.

"Yes, Beau," Marianne replied. "A thousand times, yes. I'll marry you."

"Tell him you love him, girl," Lady Courtney advised.

"Oh, and yes, of course, I love you, too," Marianne added with a laugh.

Beau leaped to his feet, picked her up, and spun her in a circle as the entire line of carriages gave them a deafening round of applause.

"I love *you*, Marianne," he whispered as he set her back down and gave her a robust kiss that earned a *huzzah* from the crowd.

"I love you, Beau. I'll always have a special place in my heart for the valet who loved me."

∿

Thank you for reading *The Valet Who Loved Me*. Would you like to receive a free copy of the special Footmen's Club epilogue? All you have to do is sign-up for my newsletter at https://BookHip.com/PAWKVS.
If you're already subscribed, check my newsletter for the link.
Please page forward to see related books, my biography, and how to contact me!
Valerie

ALSO BY VALERIE BOWMAN

The Footmen's Club

The Footman and I (Book 1)

Duke Looks Like a Groomsman (Book 2)

The Valet Who Loved Me (Book 3)

Save a Horse, Ride a Viscount (Book 4)

Playful Brides

The Unexpected Duchess (Book 1)

The Accidental Countess (Book 2)

The Unlikely Lady (Book 3)

The Irresistible Rogue (Book 4)

The Unforgettable Hero (Book 4.5)

The Untamed Earl (Book 5)

The Legendary Lord (Book 6)

Never Trust a Pirate (Book 7)

The Right Kind of Rogue (Book 8)

A Duke Like No Other (Book 9)

Kiss Me At Christmas (Book 10)

Mr. Hunt, I Presume (Book 10.5)

No Other Duke But You (Book 11)

Secret Brides

Secrets of a Wedding Night (Book 1)

A Secret Proposal (Book 1.5)

Secrets of a Runaway Bride (Book 2)

A Secret Affair (Book 2.5)

Secrets of a Scandalous Marriage (Book 3)

It Happened Under the Mistletoe (Book 3.5)

Thank you for reading *The Valet Who Loved Me.* I so hope you enjoyed Beau and Marianne's story as much as I enjoyed writing it.

I'd love to keep in touch.

- Visit my website for information about upcoming books, excerpts, and to sign up for my email newsletter: www.ValerieBowmanBooks.com or at www.ValerieBowmanBooks.com/subscribe.
- Join me on Facebook: http:// Facebook.com/ValerieBowmanAuthor.
- Reviews help other readers find books. I appreciate all reviews whether positive or negative. Thank you so much for considering it!

Want to read the other Footmen's Club books?

- The Footman and I
- Duke Looks Like a Groomsman
- Save a Horse, Ride a Viscount

ABOUT THE AUTHOR

Valerie Bowman grew up in Illinois with six sisters (she's number seven) and a huge supply of historical romance novels.

After a cold and snowy stint earning a degree in English with a minor in history at Smith College, she moved to Florida the first chance she got.

Valerie now lives in Jacksonville with her family including her two rascally dogs. When she's not writing, she keeps busy reading, traveling, or vacillating between watching crazy reality TV and PBS.

Valerie loves to hear from readers. Find her on the web at www.ValerieBowmanBooks.com.

facebook.com/ValerieBowmanAuthor

twitter.com/ValerieGBowman

instagram.com/valeriegbowman

goodreads.com/Valerie_Bowman

pinterest.com/ValerieGBowman

bookbub.com/authors/valerie-bowman

amazon.com/author/valeriebowman